SPADE WORK

Jack Dillon Dublin Tale 6

Second Edition

SPADE WORK

Jack Dillon Dublin Tale 6
Second Edition

Mike Faricy

Library of Congress Control Number: 2023920384
paperback ISBN: 978-1-962080-71-2
e-Book ISBN: 978-1-962080-72-9

Published by

MJF Publishing
https://www.mikefaricybooks.com

Acknowledgments

I would like to thank the following people for their help & support: Special thanks to Nick, Roy, Julie, Mittie, and Toui for their hard work, cheerful patience and positive feedback. I would like to thank family and friends for their encouragement and unqualified support. Special thanks to Maggie, Jed, Schatz, Pat, Av, Emily and Pat, for not rolling their eyes, at least when I was there. Most of all, to my wife, Teresa, whose belief, support and inspiration has, from day one, never waned.

Ace of Spades?
You dance with the devil himself!

PROLOGUE

The taxi driver pulled to the curb and said, "Fourteen euros."

"I got it. You okay, honey?" Joey said and looked over at the blonde in the sexy black dress.

She gave him the finger.

Not that he cared. Right now, he was just thankful for the silent treatment. At least she was done bitching. He wondered how long it would be before she said anything positive. It was a mistake to have brought her over in the first place. They were on a flight back to Boston in the morning, and he planned to ditch her at the airport the moment they landed. He tossed two twenty euro notes into the front seat. "Keep the change, pal."

"Thank you, sir," the driver said and smiled into the rearview mirror.

The blonde opened the passenger door without saying a word, stepped out of the back seat, and looked at the figure hurrying toward her.

"Joey Touhy?"

Bang, bang! Bang, bang! Bang!

ONE

US Marshal Jack Dillon pulled up and over the curb, parking his car halfway on the narrow sidewalk and halfway into the street, leaving enough room for another car to pass. He climbed out from behind the wheel and clicked the lock button on his key. The lights gave a quick flash as the doors locked, and the horn beeped. He looked up at the two-story attached house. It was light-colored stucco, with the exact same floor plan as all the homes in this Dublin housing estate.

He focused on the second-floor window, the master bedroom. Candlelight flickered from behind the lace curtains, and he smiled, pulled out his phone, and reread the text message from Brianna Fallon for the umpteenth time.

"Happy birthday, baby! Front door is unlocked. Incredible wonders await.
You've got thirty minutes to get here, or I'm starting without you.'"

He opened the front gate, hurried past her car and stepped in the front door. The house was dark except for a series of small, battery-operated vigil lights flickering on every other step leading up to her bedroom. He locked the front door then hurried up the stairs, taking them two at a time. The smile on his face turned into a wide grin by the time he reached the bedroom door.

The bedroom was illuminated by a half dozen candles, at least one of which was scented, since the room had a wonderful vanilla scent.

Brianna was naked, leaning against a pile of three pillows on the black silk bed sheet, sipping from a champagne flute filled with prosecco. She kept her dark hair in a pageboy cut, and it seemed to glisten in the candlelight. A silver ice bucket with a chilled bottle sat on the end table next to her side of the bed. She wore the pearl necklace he'd given her last Christmas and a smile. She slowly ran her tongue across her full lips and, with her free hand, began to play with her navel. Dillon focused on the sunburst tattoo surrounding her navel for a moment then watched as she slowly moved her hand lower.

"I was beginning to wonder, birthday boy," Brianna said. She raised her glass of prosecco in a toast. "Yours is waiting for you, just the way you like it." She nodded at the cut crystal tumbler with a healthy inch of Jameson resting on the end table next to the door.

Dillon hurriedly undressed, tearing the button off the cuff of his shirt in an effort to quickly get the thing undone.

She giggled and said, "Relax, bad boy. We've got all night, and I intend to put it to very good use."

That only seemed to make him more frantic. He kicked his trousers off, dropped his boxers, and half jumped into bed. He rolled toward her, gave her a long kiss, then picked up the tumbler of Jameson and clinked glasses with her.

She took a small sip, set her flute next to the ice bucket, said, "Let the games begin." She pulled the silk sheet up to Dillon's chest and then proceeded to slowly slip beneath the sheet, kissing his chest along the way.

Dillon placed a hand on her shoulder and began to pull her back up.

"No, you just lie back and sip that whiskey," she said. "I've been waiting very patiently, so I get to do whatever I want, and I intend to take my time." With that, she slipped back beneath the sheet.

TWO

The opening guitar solo to George Thorogood's "Bad to the Bone" slowly dragged Dillon from his sleep. He glanced over at Brianna just as she pulled a pillow over her head. He shook his head a few times in an effort to clear the cobwebs, then tried to locate his cellphone in the dark. He'd kicked his trousers off halfway across the room, which meant he had to climb out of bed to get to his phone. The guitar solo started up again. Brianna gave a sleepy groan from beneath the pillow, and Dillon stubbed his big toe against the bedpost. He pulled the cell out of his trouser pocket, swiped his finger across the screen to stop the noise, and limped toward the door.

"What the hell," he whispered out in the hallway. His big toe was throbbing.

"Wake you?" Detective Inspector Suel asked.

"What the hell time is it?" Dillon said as he limped down the hall, turned on the bathroom light, and closed the door behind him.

"Just a little after four. There's been a shooting."

"And?"

"Two dead, a third in critical condition. He's probably in the operating room at Saint Vincent's as we speak."

"Is he American?"

"No, a Dub, the taxi driver. But the two victims are American, a couple. You'd better get over here and have a look."

"Now?" Dillon didn't mean to sound like he was whining. On the other hand, he had a momentary thought about a breakfast rematch with Brianna, and since they were already dead . . . "How long will the crime scene be—"

"Dillon, get your ass over here. Chief Inspector McCabe will be here within the hour, and it would be best for both of us, you and me if you were here."

Unfortunately, he knew Suel was right. "Oh, for Christ's sake. All right, all right, where, exactly, are you?"

"Clontarf, not far from the castle— Seafield Road, just in front of number eight as a matter of fact. At this hour, it shouldn't take you more than ten minutes to get here from your place."

Dillon saw no point in letting Paddy Suel know he wasn't home, and that, in fact, he was in Coolock. But the drive time would be about the same; ten, maybe fifteen minutes. "All right, let me get dressed, and I'll see you shortly."

"Much appreciated," Suel said and hung up.

"Great. Probably a couple of tourists," he said to his reflection in the mirror. That meant he'd have to be on the line later today, contacting some family member to ID the body. Not exactly the perfect end to a birthday. He tiptoed back into the bedroom and gathered up his clothes. He gave a longing last look at Brianna, the pillow with the black silk pillowcase still over her head and that wonderful, oh so talented body hidden beneath the duvet. He caught a glimpse of the pearl necklace she was still wearing and sighed. *Perfectly dressed*, he thought.

He quietly closed the bedroom door, dressed out in the hallway, then tiptoed down to the kitchen and wrote a quick note explaining the situation. He placed the note next to the tea kettle, where she was bound to see it. He quietly stepped outside, double-checked the front door to make sure it was locked behind him and hurried to his car.

He drove down St. Brigid's Road, which turned into Abbeyfield, from there over to Castle Avenue and down to Seafield Road. At this hour, he only passed two cars along the way, both taxis. As he turned onto Seafield, he saw the flashing lights from a couple of squad cars and an emergency vehicle up ahead. He thought the drive would take him fifteen minutes, but even after waiting for a red light, he'd made it in eight.

He parked behind Paddy Suel's car, a silver Omni. He tried to wipe the lingering image of gorgeous Brianna Fallon from his mind as he opened the glove compartment and pulled two latex gloves from the box. He sat

for a few seconds, then took a deep breath and climbed
out from behind the wheel.

THREE

White plastic tape with blue letters that read "GARDA NO ENTRY" was tied from the wrought iron fence on top of the short wall to one of the squad cars with the flashing lights.

Behind the fence rested a large, well-manicured lawn with neatly trimmed shrubs, a paved driveway, and a large, two-story white stucco home with a red tile roof. The front door to the home was positioned in the center of the structure with large, curved bay windows on either side of the door.

The house was dark, with the exception of a lamp in one of the bay windows. A man in a dark bathrobe stood in the windows, sipping tea, or maybe coffee from a white mug while he stared out at all the activity in front of his home. Dillon raised the plastic "GARDA NO EN-TRY" tape and ducked underneath. He walked toward a taxi blocking the sidewalk at an angle. The taxi rested up against the brick column that held the gate to the paved driveway. The engine wasn't running, and the lights were off.

The passenger door on the street side was open. A pair of female legs hung out of the door. The right foot, in a red stiletto heel, rested at an odd angle with the toe of the shoe wedged against the pavement. The left foot was bare. The stiletto for the left foot was maybe fifteen feet away, lying in the street. A number of brass cartridges were scattered around the stiletto. Little white plastic tent structures, six in all, numbered and maybe four inches high, had been placed next to each cartridge. A female technician in a white hazmat suit was crouched down in front of the open car door, taking photographs. Three other hazmat suits looked to be discussing something on a clipboard.

Dillon walked maybe five feet behind the technician taking pictures and peered inside the vehicle. The female wore a short black dress that rested above her thigh, revealing a black thong. Her body was positioned across the seat. Her left shoulder, left arm, and her head were hanging off the seat. What looked like a large diamond ring was on her left hand. The right wrist had a sparkling bracelet wrapped around it. More diamonds.

Her blonde hair appeared to be about shoulder-length and hung across her face, covering all but her chin. Two wounds were apparent. One, on the left side of her chest, looked like it could have hit her heart; the other had torn away a front portion of her throat. A pool of blood had collected on the floor of the taxi beneath her head. Based on the condition of her arms and hands, plus the little bit of chin he could see, she appeared fairly young; late twenties, maybe early thirties. She was large-breasted and looked to have been in fairly good shape. A stud earring, possibly another diamond, was in her right ear. A large pendant, again possibly a diamond, hung around her neck, and the one hand Dillon could see sported a fancy ring that appeared to be an emerald surrounded by more diamonds.

The second body in the back seat was that of a male dressed in a grey suit and an open-collar white shirt. It looked like he may have been neatly groomed, although what remained of the face and head after taking multiple rounds made that rather difficult to determine. He had grey hair, neatly trimmed. His right arm rested in a strange position, almost looking like someone had twisted it behind his back. The rear window and the passenger window on the far side of the interior were sprayed with blood, bits of skull, and brain matter. Dillon wondered if the couple might be a father and daughter.

"Not the best way to start our day, or for them to end their evening," a voice said from behind.

Dillon turned around, and there was Paddy Suel, sipping from a steaming paper cup. "Oh, and before I forget, happy birthday," Suel said, flashed a brief smile, then handed Dillon a paper napkin. "Jaysus, you might want to rub at least some of the lipstick off, ya gobshite."

Dillon smiled, took the napkin, and rubbed it across both cheeks.

"Back on the left side, closer to your ear. Yeah, okay, you got it. Who was he?" Suel said and grinned.

"No one who'd admit to knowing you. I'd just like to state for the record that I gave up everything I'd planned for later this morning just to come out here and join you tonight. You wouldn't happen to have another one of those teas, would you?"

"Yeah, waiting for your Lordship in the car. Come on, we might as well get comfortable until the tech team is finished," Suel said, then headed back across the street to his car.

Dillon took a moment to study the two bodies in the taxi, made some mental notes, then followed Suel.

FOUR

Dillon climbed into the passenger side of the car. Suel handed him a paper cup of tea from the console, then glanced back across the street at the taxi.

"What makes you think they're American?" Dillon asked then took a sip of tea. It was hot, and he'd been in Dublin long enough to not really mind it, the tea.

Suel continued to stare out the window at the taxi. "One of the techs told me. Apparently, there's a billfold on the floor of the backseat, a couple of hundred-dollar bills hanging out of it, and a driver's license from your state of Massachusetts."

"You get a name?"

Suel shook his head no, took another sip of tea, and turned to look at Dillon. "What do you think?"

"About the scene?"

"No, about the unfortunate woman you were sleeping with. Yes, about the scene."

"At least six shots, I'm guessing from a smaller-caliber weapon. Someone was pissed off. At first glance, given the location, the number of rounds, it certainly doesn't appear to be random."

"I wonder who in the hell they are?" Suel said and took another sip.

"Clothes look expensive. Hell of a rock on the woman's finger, plus a bracelet and a pendant. The guy's billfold is still in the taxi, so maybe robbery wasn't the primary motive. I'm guessing husband and trophy wife."

"Politicians? Business? Gangsters?" Suel said, almost to himself.

"Guess we'll find out soon enough," Dillon said, as a guy in a hazmat suit turned and began walking toward them. Suel drained his cup, Dillon took another sip, placed his cup back in the console and stepped out of the car.

"Inspector Suel, you can have at it. Need gloves?"

"No, I'm covered. Dillon?"

"No, I've got a pair," Dillon said, pulling the latex gloves from his pocket and slipping them on.

"Let's get to it," Suel said, and they headed over to the taxi.

They stopped by the red stiletto heel lying in the street. Dillon bent down and picked up one of the brass casings on the street. He reflexively smelled it, then looked at the end. The casing was small and stamped with the image of a hummingbird on the end. "Maybe a .22LR, long-range," Dillon said.

"Have a look," Dillon said, handing the casing to Suel.

Suel looked at the end of the casing, then placed it back down in the street, shaking his head. "Bollocks. Reloads?"

Dillon nodded and said, "At least that would be my educated guess." Dillon picked up the red stiletto. The name MANOLO BLAHNICK, in black letters on white, was delicately stitched on the instep of the insole. He flipped the shoe over. The beige leather outsole was stamped "Manolo Blahnick" along with the line "Handmade in Italy." The shoe size, 37, was stamped just after the name. The little bit of wear apparent on the sole suggested the shoe was barely worn, possibly new, maybe purchased within the past few days.

"These things probably go for a couple of grand a pair," Dillon said.

"For shoes? Humf, so much money they don't know what to do with it. I've gotten cars for less than that," Suel said and walked around to the far side of the taxi.

Dillon walked over to the woman's legs hanging out of the car. He lifted the toe of the shoe on the right foot and examined it. The red leather had been worn off when it scraped across the pavement, and the odd positioning of the taxi suddenly made sense. He stood, and noticed for the first time two blood-soaked twenty-euro notes on the console.

"So the driver pulls over, waits to get paid with his foot on the brake," Dillon said. "She climbs out or starts to, when someone runs up, puts two in her, three in your man next to her and one into the driver. The whole thing probably took less than five seconds. When the driver's shot, his foot comes off the brake, and the car rolls across the sidewalk and into the corner of the brick wall."

Suel didn't give a reaction. He cautiously opened the rear passenger door, ready to stop the male body from falling out of the vehicle, but the seat belt and what was left of the head, wedged in the corner of the seat, prevented it from falling out. Suel reached in, picked the wallet up off the floor, then gently closed the door.

"Half dozen credit cards, a couple of grand in euros, and—" He moved his lips, counting for a moment. "Twelve hundred in American dollars," he said, then looked up at Dillon. "I'm guessing they probably didn't fly economy-class." He turned the wallet to read the driver's license as Dillon walked around the back of the vehicle to have a look. "Yeah, Boston. Hmm-mmm, Marlborough Street, in Boston. Ever hear of it?"

"Marlborough Street? Yeah, about as pricey as it can get. One of those neighborhoods where if you have to ask, you can't afford. Couple of million easy. What's the name?"

"Touhy. Joseph Xavier Touhy. Ring any bells?"

"Jesus Christ, you gotta be kidding me, Joey Touhy? Let me see that," Dillon said, then looked at the driver's license photo. "God, it really is him. Joey Touhy. I don't believe it."

"You know the guy?"

FIVE

etective Chief Inspector McCabe arrived about fifteen minutes later. Dillon gave the heads-up. "Looks like that's McCabe pulling up now," he said and stepped back from the taxi.

The woman's body had been lying on top of her purse, a black leather thing with gold studs and a gold shoulder strap. The words "FENDI" and below that in slightly smaller letters, "ROMA," were embossed in gold. Dillon hung onto the woman's passport, set the purse down next to her feet, and walked over toward McCabe's car. Suel followed a moment later, holding the man's wallet.

McCabe lowered the driver's window and said, "How bad is it?" before either one could offer a greeting.

"There seems to be more than a little stench of the criminal element. The victims, at least based on their clothes and the money they carried, certainly weren't hurting. Robbery doesn't seem to have been the motive. It's still early in the process, but right now, it's got all the makings of a gangland hit," Suel said.

"Americans?"

Suel nodded. "Man and a woman. Possibly husband and wife, although she's a different surname and younger, a lot younger. Dillon gave an initial ID of your man," Suel said, then held out the wallet displaying the Massachusetts driver's license.

McCabe looked at Dillon. "You knew this individual?"

"Knew of him, actually. Joey Touhy, out of Boston. Not the nicest guy in town. He's got his fingers in a number of pies, has some political connections at the local and state level. Racketeering, money laundering, insurance fraud, drug distribution, heroin and cocaine mostly. He's done some federal time. I think four, maybe six years, sentenced back in two-thousand, two-thousand-one. I sent a text off to a contact; he'll send me current information." Dillon glanced at his watch. "They're five hours behind us, so it's just a little after midnight over there. I'll get the information later this afternoon."

"So this would appear to be anything but random," McCabe said. "What about the woman?"

"There's an outside chance it's random, but I'd put it at about point-zero-one percent." Dillon opened the passport. "The woman is one Geraldine Greco, age twenty-seven. A couple of questions immediately pop up. Was this a grudge or possibly some payback hit? Or does it suggest the possible start of something here, maybe a war? Then, my next question is," Dillon gave a quick look around. "This is a pretty pricey area. I have a tough time thinking they just pulled over to look at the streetlights. Were they someone's guests? Here on business? Family? Why here? We find that out. We may start to learn who pulled the trigger."

"I think whoever did this, there's a damn good chance they're at the airport right now, waiting to board a flight to Costa del Sol," Suel said.

"We'll meet in my office at ten. See if you can't put a rush on that information coming from the States," McCabe said, then raised his window, nodded, and drove off down the street.

"Charming," Dillon half laughed and shook his head.

"Oh, I don't know. Do you really want him here looking over your shoulder? Consider it a vote of confidence that he feels comfortable leaving the two of us to get on with the program. So, that being the case, we'd better get back to it," Suel said.

"You find anything that ties him to this area?" Dillon asked. "If they had the taxi stop here sometime after midnight, I'm guessing they were either staying in one of these houses or visiting someone, probably within a hundred feet of where we are. Airbnb, maybe?"

Suel looked over Dillon's shoulder. The guy standing in the bay window wearing his bathrobe was still there, watching them intently, only now he was holding a crystal tumbler in his hand, and Dillon figured it was a pretty safe guess he wasn't drinking tea.

SIX

Dillon and Suel walked up the long brick driveway toward the front door. A paved parking area, large enough for three cars, was in front of the step leading up to the door. A sporty black Porsche had been backed into the parking area at an angle, taking up two of the spaces.

The man in the bathrobe watched them approach, then rubbed a hand across his face, drained his drink glass, and hurried out of the room. He opened the front door just as Suel was about to ring the doorbell. His bathrobe was a gold and red paisley pattern with silk lapels and cuffs. A gold monogram with the letters JDR was positioned over the left breast. He wore navy-blue slippers with an identical monogram. Only the monogram on the slippers was surrounded by red laurels.

"Well, if it isn't, Mister James Dennis Ryan. Not sure if you remember me, Detective Inspector Paddy Suel, sir. Long time no see."

"Oh, umm, good—good morning, Detective," Ryan said, then sort of rubbed his face and glanced nervously over at Dillon.

"Oh, forgive me, sir. Where are my manners? Allow me to present United States Marshal, Jack Dillon. Sorry to disturb you at this early hour. Mind if we come in?" Suel said, then proceeded to more or less barge into the front entryway, elbowing Ryan off to the side.

"Believe me, Inspector, I don't have any idea what went on out there. The siren and then all the flashing lights woke me early this morning. Tragic. It looks as if the taxi ran into my wall. Did you notice any damage? Good Lord, I hope the gate isn't banged up. I just had it refinished last spring. I suppose I'll have to pay out of my own pocket, once again, to get that—"

"Ahh, yes, the gate. Your compassion is heartbreaking. Why don't you join us in the sitting room, Jimmy. I'll take a tea, no milk. Feel free to pour yourself another whiskey. Dillon?" Suel said, then proceeded to walk past Ryan and into the room where Ryan had been standing and watching them for the past couple of hours.

"Tea for me would be just fine," Dillon said and followed Suel.

They could hear the murmur of an animated conversation coming from the kitchen while they sat in two wingback chairs, taking in the thick oriental rug and the impressionist painting hanging above the fireplace. Suel held his hand up to the side of his head, indicating Ryan was on the phone, then nodded at the security camera positioned in the corner of the ceiling. After a couple of minutes, the one-sided conversation coming from the kitchen subsided, and Ryan hurried back into the room, carrying two steaming mugs of tea. He set them on the glass-topped coffee table, then stepped back and flashed a nervous smile.

"Here you are, gentlemen, just like you ordered, no milk," Ryan said, then nervously rubbed his hands together.

"Maybe pour yourself a wee dram, Jimmy. Helps to calm the nerves. Then, as you might well imagine, we've just a question or two," Suel said and flashed a quick smile.

Ryan nodded, hurried over to the far wall, and an antique buffet with burled wood panels and a white marble top. He grabbed a fresh crystal glass and poured a whiskey from a cut-glass decanter, filling the glass a little more than halfway.

"Please, Jimmy, be a good lad, take the weight off your feet and join us," Suel said, indicating the couch with his hand.

Ryan nervously sat down, took a healthy sip from his glass, and proceeded to stare at the floor.

"So, Jimmy, you were going to tell us about your guests," Suel said.

"Guests?" Ryan said, then looked over his shoulder and out the front window.

"Jimmy, please, we really don't have time to play games. And, by the way, you're in no trouble here. Well, unless you've neglected to pay your TV license," Suel said and laughed. "Now, your American friend out front, Mister Joey Touhy."

"Oh, is that who was in the taxi? I'd no idea. I don't really know him. Is he all right?"

"But he and Miss Greco were staying with you, correct?"

"Umm, actually, I'm not sure I should be talking to you, Inspector. See, I was doing a favor for a friend, and he just asked me, actually told me, he had an American acquaintance coming over just to see the sights here in Dublin. You know, the Spire, Phoenix Park, O'Connell Street, Stephen's Green, the Royal—"

"Jimmy, I really don't want to take you down to one of our interrogation rooms and question you. That's so uncomfortable for both of us. But, if that's the way the likes of you want to play this, well, okay."

At the sound of a car screeching to a stop out on the street, Dillon looked out the window. Two men in suits climbed out. The larger of the two pulled the "GARDA NO ENTRY" tape apart, and they hurried up the driveway. The older man had a bald head, pink with white fringe, and a mustache. His face seemed to grow a bit redder with every step he took, hurrying toward the front door. He carried a black leather briefcase.

The other man, the one who broke the tape, was stocky, with a thick neck wedged in an open-collar shirt. His arms looked like a pair of stuffed sausages in his dark suit coat, and they hung out from his side, suggesting he was carrying two large, invisible barrels. Neither man appeared too happy. A moment later, the doorbell rang.

"Oh, I'd better get that," Ryan said, and quickly jumped off the couch.

"Shit," Suel said and kicked the leg of the coffee table as Ryan fled the room.

A moment later, the red-faced, bald man hurried into the room. "Good morning, gentlemen. Glad I caught you before you were going to leave. Mister Ryan has no further comment to make at this time. All future conversations can be directed to me or my firm. Thank you for your time."

His speech was precise, and Dillon had the sense this maybe wasn't the first time he'd delivered that particular message. He set his briefcase on the buffet, opened it, took out two business cards, and handed them to Dillon and Suel.

"Just asking a few general questions," Suel said.

Baldy flashed a quick smile, exposing perfectly whitened teeth. "I know exactly what you were doing, and any further discussion can be directed to me, Tully McCabe. You've my number on the card you're holding, please feel free to call and schedule an appointment. I'll do my best to try and accommodate," he said, then followed with a look suggesting it would likely be a cold day in hell before their appointment was scheduled.

"Thanks for this," Suel said, waving the card. "I'm sure we'll be in touch."

"I look forward to it. Enjoy your day, gentlemen. Oh, and my kindest regards to your boss," Tully McCabe called, as Dillon and Suel walked out of the room.

The muscular guy had remained out in the entryway, standing at the door. He was even larger up close, and he held the front door open for them as they approached.

"Gee, thanks," Suel said, in a tone that suggested he meant anything but.

The guy didn't react but just closed the door behind them. Two steps later, they heard the snap of the lock clicking into place. Dillon glanced back into the sitting room window as they walked down the driveway. Jimmy Ryan appeared to be attempting to explain things to Mr. Tully McCabe and failing miserably.

"Shit. That wingey bollocks Tully McCabe, pure shite," Suel said.

"Why do I know that guy, or at least his name?"

"Tully McCabe?" Suel said as they headed down the driveway. "You were best pals with his only client, Eamon Boyle."

"Eamon Boyle? The guy whose brother was killed in that cash-in-transit van robbery at that small airport?"

"Yeah. Weston Airport. One and the same. Didn't he send you a case of whiskey or something after that?" Suel said.

"Actually, it was a mirror and a bottle of wine. The mirror was just like the one that was smashed in the room at the Sherbourne Hotel, where they grabbed Eddie Fleming, the guy who we think robbed the van."

"An American, right?"

"Fleming? Yeah, we were on him, it's just that Boyle and his gang got there first and grabbed him. Beat us by about ten minutes. We found Fleming and a woman, or what was left of them, locked in the trunk of a car. Still don't know if Boyle kept that two point five million or if he returned it to his customer, whoever that was. Probably never will know. God, so that means Joey Touhy had to be working something with Boyle. That does not sound good," Dillon said and shook his head.

SEVEN

They resumed examining the taxi along with the bodies of Geraldine Greco and Joey Touhy.

Although it wasn't particularly large, Geraldine's purse contained skin creams, three lipsticks, perfume, a nail file, a small mirror, a dollar and thirty-two cents in American coins, a two-euro coin, sunglasses, a nail clipper, dental floss, a morning after pill, tampons, mints, a set of house keys, a hairbrush, lip balm, four prophylactics, a small tube of strawberry-flavored lubricant, half a Snickers bar, a tube of hand sanitizer, a package of Kleenex, what appeared to be a small container of a powdery white substance, quite possibly cocaine, and a leather case with her driver's license and six credit cards. Dillon dutifully placed all the items in an evidence bag, labeled it and set the purse on the ground next to the rear tire.

"C'mere to me and look at this," Suel said.

Dillon walked over to the far side of the car. Suel had leaned Joey Touhy forward, holding what remained of the head with his right hand. His left hand rested on Touhy's chest as he carefully leaned the body forward.

"Look behind your man and tell me what you see," Suel said, then moved slightly to the side so Dillon could look in behind Touhy's body. As he moved to the side, a large glop of brain matter and skull bits fell onto the sleeve of his sport coat. "Oh, for feck's sake," Suel said.

Touhy's grey suit coat stuck out at a strange angle due to something beneath the coat at about the small of his back. "I'm guessing he's armed," Dillon said. "Carrying a pistol back there. It would explain the position of his right hand. He was probably trying to reach for the gun. Poor bastard sure didn't make it in time. You want me to pull it out?"

"Yeah. Just the weapon if it's holstered, unless the holster is attached."

Dillon cautiously reached behind the body and lifted the suit coat. A black pistol grip stuck out from the belt. Dillon carefully took hold of the handle between his thumb and forefinger and gently pulled. The pistol, held in a holster by a leather strap snapped around the grip, slid out of the belt.

"Okay, got it," Dillon said, pinching the grip tightly as he stood up and then stepped back. He took hold of the bottom of the black leather holster.

Suel gently pushed the body back to its original position, then pulled the sleeve of his suit coat tight and shook his arm. The glop of brain matter splattered onto Touhy's right leg. "Damn it, and this is just back from the cleaners, son of a bitch. I'll never get the damn stain out. What the hell? Now would you look at this," Suel said, bending over and staring at Touhy's face.

"Something left over from his dinner?" Dillon said as he grabbed the evidence bag Suel had set aside on the roof of the taxi, placed the pistol inside, then sealed the bag. The pistol, black handgrips exposed, rested in a shiny black leather holster that was stiff and appeared brand new. Dillon was familiar with the model, popular with some of the US Marshals Service "clientele."

Suel reached up and pulled something from Touhy's mouth. "What the . . . check this out. Ever see the likes of it?" he said, then held up what looked like an Ace of Spades playing card. A black spade was centered on the card with a human skull in the center of it.

"That was in his mouth?" Dillon said.

"I'd say it's a pretty safe guess he didn't put it there. Fecking strange," Suel said, pulling an evidence bag from his coat pocket and placing the card inside. "What's with the weapon?"

"It's a Walther, P22. Polymer frame. I can't believe he somehow got this thing through customs and over here in his luggage. He almost had to have picked it up from someone here."

"If he's carrying a pistol, he must have been expecting trouble," Suel said. He was still focused on the stain on his coat sleeve.

"Yeah, maybe. Or more likely it was just force of habit. I'm guessing the list is fairly long of people who will be happy to learn Joey Touhy is no longer with us."

"Damn it, fecking coat is ruined. Let me see that damn thing," Suel said.

Dillon handed him the evidence bag.

"Be interesting to have the lab go through this, see if it's ever been fired. It looks brand new. I'm surprised the price tag isn't on it somewhere. You find anything in your woman's purse?"

"Couple of things. It would appear young miss Greco was working while on the trip. Found about a thousand bucks' worth of makeup along with a small packet of nose candy and a bottle of strawberry-flavored lubricant."

"You see a deck of cards in there?"

"No," Dillon said.

"Then what's with the card? Were they playing a game?"

"There were stories of G.I.'s leaving the Ace of Spades on bodies in Viet Nam. Don't know if it was actually true. That would have been fifty years ago. Anything written on it?"

Suel held up the evidence bag and studied the card. "Nothing, unless they used invisible ink."

"Gambling debt?" Dillon said, more to himself.

"Classy, very classy."

EIGHT

B ack in the office, Dillon collected a plate with two paper cupcake wrappers, a McDonald's bag, the wrapper from a Cadbury's Crunchie bar, and an empty tea mug all left on his desk by persons unknown. No one looked up from their computers as he scanned the room for the perpetrators. He carried the lot into the break room, tossed the wrappers, and left the plate and mug in the sink.

Back at his desk, he placed a call to the American Embassy. The call was answered on the third ring.

"American Embassy, how may I direct your call?" a woman's voice answered politely.

"Eric Bergman, security service, please."

"Who shall I say is calling?" Sounding just a little less polite this time.

"US Marshal Jack Dillon."

"Thank you. Please remain on the line." The voice came back about forty-five seconds later. "Marshal, I'll connect you now."

Dillon heard a couple of clicks, and Bergman picked up halfway through the first ring. "Jack, great to hear from you. What's up?"

"There's been a shooting earlier this morning, over in Clontarf. Two Americans were killed."

"A shooting?"

"Yeah. No official confirmation at this point, but does the name Joey Touhy mean anything to you?"

"Touhy, Touhy . . . sorry, it rings a distant bell, but I can't place it. Who is he?"

"Boston bad guy. Drugs, extortion, convicted, did about six years, maybe ten years back, around two-thousand, two-thousand-one, for some insurance fraud scam. He was purchasing derelict buildings, then burning them down six months later for the insurance money. That's just the one they caught him on. He's gotten away with a lot more. What you might call a 'creative' individual."

"And he was shot? Here in Ireland?"

"Yeah, sometime after midnight, over in Clontarf, actually. He and a woman by the name of Geraldine Greco, also from Boston. I'd like you to check the embassy calls, notifying next of kin. It would help if you could let me know who, if anyone, is coming over, and if so, when, exactly."

"Yeah, sure, happy to help. Any idea what happened? If they were shot in Clontarf, that makes me think this might have been some sort of gang hit rather than a random thing."

"No confirmation as of yet, but that's my thought as well."

"And the woman, what'd you say the last name was?"

"Greco, Geraldine Greco," Dillon said and spelled out her last name.

"Got it," Bergman said. There was a pause for a moment, then he said, "T-O-U-H-Y?"

"Yeah. First name Joseph. Middle name Xaiver. Home address listed on the driver's license was 17 Marlborough Street in Boston. No home number available."

"And the woman, Geraldine Greco. Anything on an address?"

"Yeah, 456 Hanover Street, Unit 4, Boston. I'm guessing that's in the north end, but don't hold me to it. Official confirmation should be coming through in the next hour or two, but I wanted to give you a heads-up."

"And you just want to know the family has been notified?"

"Well, yeah, for starters. But if you found out when someone might be coming over and then if you could find out who it would be, that would be a big help."

"Okay, let me alert that department, and I'll get back to you as soon as we have something."

"Thanks, Eric. I'm buying next time we're together."

"Yes, you are. Talk to you later," he said and hung up.

Suel walked over to Dillon's desk. "Good thing you finally cleared that trash off your desk, doesn't speak well for the rest of us."

"That wasn't my trash."

"Oh, yeah, I keep forgetting."

"If I ever find the idiot who keeps doing that, they'll wish they'd never met me."

"Oh, you never know, they might just be thinking that already. You about ready to darken the door to McCabe's office?"

Dillon glanced over at the clock on the wall. "Christ, it's already ten?"

"Almost. Will be by the time we grab a couple of teas and make our way to his door."

"I suppose there's no point in putting it off. I believe it's your turn to buy the tea," Dillon said.

"Are you sure? I distinctly remember—"

"Positive. I take mine black, no milk, no sugar."

"Well, come on, if I'm buying, the least you can do is carry your own mug."

NINE

Suel knocked on DCI McCabe's open office door. McCabe was sitting at his desk on the phone, but motioned them in with a wave of his hand, then pointed to the chairs in front of his desk. "All right then. Look, my ten o'clock just walked in the door. We'll continue this later, but you know my feelings on the subject," he said, then hung up.

"So, gentlemen, progress?" McCabe said. He seemed to focus on the blood stain on Suel's coat sleeve for a moment, then looked up.

"Of a sort," Suel said and extended a hand toward Dillon, indicating he should go first.

"Based on the identification in the wallet, our male victim is Joseph Xavier Touhy, from the city of Boston in the US. The woman is Geraldine Greco, age twenty-seven, also of Boston. I should mention that Touhy was armed with a Walther 22, a weapon that appeared to be fairly new. It's down in ballistics as we speak. I have some general knowledge on Touhy. He was convicted of insurance fraud, sentenced to six years back in two-thousand-one. He's been linked to racketeering, money laundering, insurance fraud, heroin and cocaine distribution, but to my knowledge, the insurance fraud charges are the only thing that ever stuck.”

“What about the woman?”

“Geraldine Greco is, at this point, pretty much of a blank slate,” Dillon said. “I expect what information there is will begin to flow over the next couple of hours. I checked and the building she’s living in rents units for four to five grand a month, which sounds rather steep for most folks, let alone a twenty-seven-year-old. Maybe she’s on a trust fund, or she’s some movie star I’m unaware of. More probably, she was Touhy’s latest gal pal.”

“We had an ever-so-brief meeting with Jimmy Ryan,” Suel said. “Curiously, the incident took place in front of his home.”

“Jimmy Ryan? The Jimmy Ryan? Eamon Boyle’s Jimmy Ryan?”

“One and the same, sir. Unfortunately, no sooner did he hand us a mug of tea when Boyle’s solicitor, umm, Tully McCabe, arrived on the scene and before we knew it we were being ushered out the door with the instructions to contact his firm for an appointment.”

“Tully?” McCabe half-shouted and shook his head.

“Any relation, sir?” Dillon asked, and out of the corner of his eye saw Suel flinch at the question.

“Mmm-mmm, yes, unfortunately. A cousin, a very distant cousin I might add, although not distant enough. All right, anything else?”

Suel shook his head and said, “Not at the moment, sir. We’ll be back with Mr. Ryan later in the day. I’ve a call into Justice Clarke, he'll act on the paperwork, and we'll have Jimmy Ryan down here before the day is out. No doubt he'll be armed with that plonker Tully McCabe, umm, with all due respect, sir."

"Two murders and the involvement of Eamon Boyle does not bode well for a quiet future. Please keep me apprised of the situation. I'll want an update at day's end."

"Got it, sir," Suel said and stood to leave. Dillon followed suit.

"That didn't seem to go too badly," Dillon said, once they were back by Suel's desk.

"Hmmm, just wait. Like the old man hinted at, Eamon Boyle, Tully McCabe, and Jimmy Ryan are not the best recipe for things working out to our advantage."

TEN

Dillon's phone rang a little after four. He answered, hoping it was the Marshals Service with an update on Joey Touhy. It wasn't.

"Jack Dillon," was how he answered.

"Jack, Eric Bergman." Dillon's contact at the American Embassy.

"Eric, what have you got?"

"Unfortunately, not too much. Both families have been informed. The Greco family, actually a sister by the name of Jacquline, she goes by Jackie, is taking us up on the offer to meet her at the Dublin Airport. At this point, I have no information on her flight schedule. As for Mr. Touhy, his wife, Connie, has declined our offer to act as an intermediary. It's not clear if she was even going to fly over, and at least at this stage, no further information is available. I might suggest you contact the Marshals Service in the States and have them monitor flight information on both individuals."

"I'll be contacting them just as soon as I'm off the line with you."

"We hear anything else, I'll let you know," Bergman said.

"Thanks. You have anything on addresses?" Dillon said.

"Yeah. Connie Touhy is in Boston, 17 Marlborough Street. And the Greco woman, Jackie, is at . . . ." There was a pause, and Dillon could hear what sounded like a couple of pages being turned. "Yeah, here it is. Jackie Greco also lives in Boston, 531 1/2 East Third Street, number three. I'll send you a text with addresses and phone numbers."

"Thanks, Eric. Much appreciated."

Bergman's text came through just a few minutes later. Dillon copied the information then sent it on to his contact in the New York Marshals office asking for flight confirmations and passport numbers.

Suel stepped over a few minutes later. "Anything new?"

Dillon told him about the Embassy contact with the families and that Connie Touhy had declined any assistance if and when she arrived in Dublin. "Jackie Greco, the female victim's sister, sounded like she would take the Embassy up on their offer. You got anything?"

Suel smiled and waved a sheet of paper. "Warrant finally came through. I just finished up with DCI McCabe, told him we were going to give Jimmy Ryan a going-over, and we'd have something to report in the morning. Care to accompany me?"

"What are we waiting for?" Dillon said and grabbed his coat.

Traffic was already heavy due to afternoon rush hour, and what had been a ten-minute drive at four this morning was now closer to a half-hour. Suel pulled his silver Omni in front of Jimmy Ryan's home on Seafield in Clontarf and parked. The only indication there had been any sort of activity earlier in the day was a six-inch remnant of white plastic tape still hanging from the wrought iron fence in front. Just the last two letters, the R and the Y from the word "ENTRY," were on the tape.

"Damn," Suel said, as they walked up the driveway. "It doesn't look like Ryan's gate suffered any damage. Still, one can always hope."

Suel rang the doorbell, twice, before it was answered by a middle-aged, dark-haired woman wearing jeans and a sweater. "Mr. Ryan, please, An Garda Síochána," Suel said, flashing his badge and then stepping inside before the woman had a chance to close the door.

"Oh, sorry. He no here, Mr. Ryan. He called away on business this morning. He not back for very long time," she said, in what sounded like a heavy eastern European accent.

"Define 'long time,'" Suel said.

"Umm, I not sure. He travel, emergency."

"Traveled on an emergency?" Suel said and flashed a glance at Dillon.

"Yes, is emergency trip."

"Will he be back later today?"

"No, gone long time."

"Do you know where he went?"

"Think he fly to Paris. It is business."

"Oh, for feck's sake. Business my ass."

"I sorry. This is what he tell me, sir. I only house cleaner. I, I do nothing wrong. Honest. I promise."

"This is a warrant which gives us the right to inspect the premises. Are you aware there was a murder here this morning?"

"Murder? Here?" she said, then looked around frantically. "I not find mess."

"Out front, two individuals, a man and a woman in a taxi."

"I see this, the taxi. It on truck when I come this morning." She said something in a language Dillon didn't understand, then made the sign of the cross, in the orthodox manner.

"We'll have a look around," Suel said.

"I under arrest?"

"No, ma'am, you're not. Were you aware of any guests here recently?"

"Guest? Yes, two. Man and girl. They stay in one of Mr. Ryan guest room. They here last two nights. They gone now. Friend of Mr. Ryan. I think they go back America. I not see them."

"Did you talk with them?"

"No. I only see them for little minute. They sleep late. Make the—" She indicated sexual intercourse, making a circle with the thumb and index finger of her left hand, then quickly moving the index finger on her right hand in and out. "Make it lot of time," she said, raising her eyebrows and smiling. "Mr. Ryan, he call me this morning, tell me to come work. He pay me big money to work today."

"You cleaned their room?" Suel asked, sounding like he already knew the answer to that question.

"Yes. It very clean. He tell me clean it. Make it most clean. He tell me I get big money to clean it, so I do very good job."

Suel smiled, nodded, took a deep breath, and dialed it back a notch. "Could you show us the room, please?"

She seemed to think about that for a moment until Suel sort of waved the warrant in front of her. "Yes, yes, come, you follow. It right upstairs. Please, you follow me," she said and hurried toward the staircase. Dillon and Suel followed closely behind. At the top of the stairs, she took a right and headed down the hallway, then opened the first door. "This is room here," she said, opening the door, stepping inside and smiling at her handiwork.

The bed was stripped, and there was just the slightest scent, a combination of a pine-scented cleaning compound and lemon-scented furniture polish. The tiles in the attached bathroom glistened, and the chrome fixtures on the sink and tub shone like they had been scrubbed to within an inch of their life. Fresh towels hung on the heated chrome towel racks.

There were two wooden chests of drawers in the room, and Dillon pulled the top drawer open on the chest closest to him. It was empty, and he rubbed his fingers together, feeling a slight residue from the furniture polish on the wooden drawer pulls.

"You didn't happen to find any clothing left behind?"

She seemed to scoff for a moment. "She leave thong under bed. I put in trash. They pack all other things. Very good they pack. Leave no other thing." She smiled.

"Thank you, ma'am. If it's all right, we'll just take a few minutes to look things over, and then we'll see you in the kitchen. Don't let us hold you up," Suel said, and sort of motioned her toward the bedroom door.

"I not in trouble? I—I only do what Mr. Ryan say," she said, and suddenly looked like she was on the verge of tears.

"No, no, it's quite all right, not to worry," Suel said, halfway escorting her out of the room and then closing the door behind her. He waited a long moment until he was sure she was headed downstairs. "Oh, for fuck's sake. Ryan's crew took everything out of here except that stupid thong, probably burned it all, then scattered the damn ashes to the winds." He looked around the room. The smell of furniture polish seemed to be just that much stronger. "Wouldn't you know she'd be a hard worker. Christ almighty. Might as well try to see if we can get anything out of her, but I doubt she even knows their names. Damn it."

"Well, we know they were here. We can check and see when they came into the country. My guess? They planned to be here, in-country, just a couple of days, a week tops," Dillon said.

"Yeah, but why? And what in God's name were they doing with Eamon Boyle?"

ELEVEN

S uel pulled into a no-parking place alongside of the Eddie Rocket's restaurant located in Cross Guns, a franchise version of a 50s burger and soda joint. He reached over in front of Dillon, opened up the glove compartment and pulled out a sheet of paper with the An Garda Síochána logo on it in blue, and then large black letters, all capitals: "**OFFICIAL BUSINESS!**"

"Come on, you're buying," he said.

"Burgers and milkshakes?" Dillon said.

"What I need after a day like today is a lot of whiskey and a woman with absolutely no moral foundation. But then I'd still have to get up tomorrow morning and go to work, so in the long run, yeah, this is probably the better choice."

The inside of Eddie Rocket's was white walls and chrome, lots of chrome. The booths were red plastic, and they sat in one of the booths toward the back of the place. Just a half-dozen other people were scattered throughout the restaurant. Sixties music, something by Frankie Valli and the Four Seasons, was coming across the sound system. Dillon and Suel sat quietly, thinking about the day's activity and their latest update, Jimmy Ryan leaving the country. Once their meals arrived and Suel began to get some food in him, he seemed to calm down a little.

"Okay, so I'm thinking the one thing that seems to be apparent in all this is that there is something bigger, more long-term, going on here besides just the shooting of your close personal friend, Jimmy Touhy."

"Actually, it's Joey."

"Yeah, right, that's what I meant to say. If this was just simply a hit from the States, your man Ryan could plead innocent and be on completely solid ground. Instead, he's essentially been whisked away out of the country."

Dillon took another bite of his cheeseburger, chewed for a moment, then swallowed. "A couple of things come to mind. First, Ryan's got to surface at some point—Paris or somewhere—doesn't he? The other thing is, all I can come up with that Joey Touhy could offer Ryan is maybe a distribution connection, you know drug distribution, but that seems tenuous at best. If Ryan did any due diligence, I think he'd find out Joey Touhy was basically just blowing smoke. Touhy was just narcissistic enough to think of himself as a major player in distribution, but he really wasn't in Boston, and I have to believe he certainly wouldn't be over here."

"Two things," Suel said. "First, Ryan is just the conduit. Beyond having Touhy stay in his home, that's all he's providing and pretty much ends his involvement. Eamon Boyle is the man, here. For Boyle, Ryan is more like his financial savant. He makes the money untraceable, grows Boyle's legitimate investments, but any 'get your hands dirty' sort of work, that's all on Eamon Boyle, or rather his minions. It's the reason they hustled Ryan out of the country. He'd talk and not even know he was telling us anything. He's not too great in understanding personal relationships. And as far as Jimmy Ryan bobbing back up to the surface anytime soon, don't bet on it. He's likely to be unavailable for the foreseeable future, at least until any information he might have is basically of no use. Give him a computer and access to the internet, and he can work from just about anywhere."

"Sounds like he might be autistic."

"I think if you did a diagnosis, he'd be identified as having Asperger's, maybe a mild case. You notice this morning how he didn't make eye contact with us? He has a tough time reading personal or interactive relationships. Give him a financial report, numbers, and he's all over the damn thing."

"So we direct our attention to Eamon Boyle?"

"Maybe. The fact that Touhy was murdered, what does that mean? An American hit? Competition here by someone trying to position themselves in front of Eamon Boyle? Someone trying to shut Eamon Boyle down? Could be any one of those and a number of other things we haven't come up with."

"Be interesting to see if Touhy's wife ever comes over. I've a request into the Marshals Service. When her passport comes up, we'll know a flight number and arrival time."

Suel shook his head. "Don't hold your breath."

TWELVE

Dillon made it home that evening just a little after eight. He pulled into the parking area in front of his place, then climbed out of the car, closed the two iron gates behind his car and unlocked the front door.

Lucifer, his small black dog, was nowhere to be seen, but his daily deposit was in the middle of the entryway floor. Paper kitchen towels, the store package from a pound of hamburger, coffee grounds, and a half dozen cupcake wrappers, all items he'd obviously dragged out of the trash, were scattered across the entryway and back through the door leading into the kitchen.

Dillon would have normally been upset except for the fact he hadn't been home for over twenty-four hours. He heard what sounded like Lucifer jumping off the bed upstairs, and he called to him.

"Lucifer, Lucifer, come on. Outside, outside, boy."

He walked into the kitchen. The food and water dish, set next to the backdoor were both empty. He filled the water dish, then stepped back into the front entry hall and called up the stairs again.

"Lucifer. Lucifer, come on, boy, come on. Outside."

He walked back into the kitchen, set the wastebasket upright, then swept up all the trash scattered across the kitchen and entryway floor.

"Lucifer, come on, get your ass down here."

He took the bag of dog food out of the pantry cabinet and filled the metal food dish. At the sound of food filling the dish, Lucifer suddenly appeared at the top of the stairs just as Dillon was about to call him again. The dog peeked around the upstairs banister and studied Dillon for a long moment.

"Come on, Lucifer, get your ass down here. Come on, boy. Outside," Dillon said, then stepped over and opened the front door. At the sound of the door opening, Lucifer bounded down the stairs and hurried outside. He turned, squatted next to Dillon's car, and stared at Dillon while completing his task.

"Come on inside," Dillon said, once Lucifer had finished. He closed the door behind him and followed the dog back into the kitchen. Lucifer immediately became engaged with the bowl of dog food and apparently couldn't be bothered looking at Dillon.

Dillon turned on the television mounted on the kitchen wall, then pulled out a stool from beneath the kitchen counter and settled in to watch a show of no redeeming social value, followed by the late-night news. He was in bed just before eleven, set his alarm, and slept soundly through the night.

He woke about five minutes before the alarm was set to go off. He turned the alarm off, then hopped in the shower. He was dressed and had just poured his first cup of coffee when he checked his email.

"Jack. Constance Touhy, passport #580306798, issued 2013, born Boston, 11 May, 1972. Delta flight 44, NYC to DUB, arrive 9:40am Wed. Flight booked 72 hours ago. Mathews."

Pat Mathews was with the Marshals Service in New York, and the guy Dillon had asked to check flight info on Touhy's wife and Gerri Greco's sister. Dillon checked the kitchen clock, just a little before 7:00. The five-hour difference between Dublin and New York meant it was way too early to call Mathews in New York. If the flight had been booked three days ago, that was two days before Joey Touhy and Gerri Greco were murdered.

THIRTEEN

Dillon was in Terminal 2 of the Dublin Airport just after 9:00. He was waiting in the Border Management office as opposed to the actual area where passengers lined up to go through passport control and have their passports stamped. There were four individuals watching monitors in the office. Three of them were watching travelers with non-EU passports, which at this time of day, early morning, were largely flights originating in North America.

Dillon held a paper cup with lukewarm coffee that, all things considered, wasn't that bad. At least it wasn't instant.

"These folks are mostly off the Toronto flight: fairly standard most days," Poraig Sullivan explained to Dillon. "We'd a flight from Amsterdam in about an hour ago, KLM. They're run through drug-sniffing dogs in Amsterdam and then again when they land here. Our usual pinch is some stupid plonker carrying a small amount of marijuana, but every once in a while, we run into someone with a fairly large stash. Back in December of last year, just before Christmas, we had a woman who had no idea how the two bricks of cocaine ended up in her purse. Street value of something like forty-five thousand euros and she'd no idea. Imagine?" Sullivan smiled.

"She got through Amsterdam security?"

"That's the dicey part. It turns out, the bricks had been stashed in her seat pocket on the plane. Someone on the cleaning crew had placed them in there for her to pick up. She had nothing for Amsterdam security to catch so she sailed right through since the drugs were already waiting for her on the plane. They just didn't expect us to be running the same security check with drug-sniffing dogs over here. I think she'd been paid to carry the bricks with an all-expense weekend and probably a thousand euros or some damn thing for a clothes shopping spree."

"What happened to her?"

"Currently serving time," Sullivan said and smiled. "Of course, you have to wonder how many times she, or someone like her, made the trip before and got away with it."

Dillon absently watched the line move for the better part of another hour.

"Marshal Dillon," Sullivan called to him a little after ten. "Constance Touhy, your person of interest, is at station three. Jerry, raise your hand, so he gets the right monitor, increase the sound, record, and tell the customs agent to proceed."

One of the guys watching the monitors raised his hand, and Dillon stepped behind him. The guy tapped a couple of computer keys, said something into his head-set, and suddenly a woman's voice with a heavy Boston accent said, "Is there a problem?"

The Customs Agent on the screen raised the cell-phone from his ear, smiled, and said, "No ma'am. Sorry about this. Our computers seem to be slow this morning. Should be coming through in just a moment. How long will you be staying in Ireland?"

"I'll be here for just forty-eight hours. I have a return flight."

"And the purpose of your visit is business?"

"Oh, no. Just a little sightseeing, maybe attend a play. I've always heard so many good things about the Irish theatre."

The Customs and Immigration officer set his phone down, took his time paging through before stamping the passport, then smiled and handed it back to Connie Touhy. "Thank you for your patience, ma'am. Enjoy your time in Ireland," the agent said.

"Oh, I'm so looking forward to seeing the sights," she said, and smiled, then took hold of the handle on her carry-on luggage, wheeled it away from the agent and out toward the baggage area.

"We've got it on tape," Sullivan said.

"Thanks. If you could forward that to my Garda email, I'd appreciate it," Dillon said. He handed a busi-ness card to Poraig Sullivan, then hurried out the door and into the baggage area. Connie Touhy was just step-ping out of the passport control area, pulling a Louis

Vuitton bag with a matching purse behind her as she headed for carousel six, where the luggage from her New York flight was just beginning to be collected.

As he watched, Dillon pegged her appearance at fiftyish as opposed to the forty-four years shown on her passport. She appeared heavier than her passport photo, although he wouldn't have called her fat, the body type perhaps the result of hard living or just too much fun that began to catch up with everyone at her age. He stood off to the side, watching her as she waited for her luggage to arrive. Eventually, a very large Louis Vuitton suitcase came down the ramp and dropped onto the baggage carousel.

Dillon moved forward and stood next to her just as the large suitcase on the carousel approached. She reached for it, then fumbled with the handle.

"Here, let me," Dillon said, then lifted the large suitcase off the carousel and onto the floor, standing it upright for her. The bag was heavy, and he gave off a slight groan as he lifted it up.

"Oh, thanks. Wasn't sure how I was going to get the damn thing off there. I didn't know what to pack, so I just packed everything. Well, enjoy," she said, then began to wheel both suitcases toward the exit. Dillon waited until she was almost out of the baggage area before he followed. He'd just stepped out of the baggage area when he saw a large, familiar, ugly-looking man holding a sign with one word. "Connie."

Dillon knew him, or rather of him. Mousey. Your basic right-hand thug to Eamon Boyle. They'd met once for a rather unpleasant minute or two at Eamon Boyle's office maybe eighteen months back.

Mousey indicated the luggage with a nod of his chin, and two underlings immediately grabbed the Louis Vuitton suitcases from Connie Touhy and wheeled them toward the escalator. Mousey extended his large, calloused hand, and Connie proceeded to follow her luggage. Dillon waited a moment, then followed at a distance.

The group took the escalator down to the first floor and out the door to the short-term parking area. They crossed the street without bothering to look, forcing two taxis to screech to a stop. Mousey shot a glance at the first taxi. The driver immediately backed up four feet and held his hands up in an apologetic mode.

Dillon rode the escalator down to the first floor, then waited until they'd entered the short term parking lot before he ventured outside. He watched them walk toward a large, black SUV parked across two parking spaces in the back of the lot, then watched as they backed out of their parking spot, and quickly wrote down the license plate number: a Dublin register, and based on the license plate, purchased in the first six months of 2018.

He hurried over to his car. He'd parked in an employee-only spot and fortunately hadn't been ticketed, yet. He followed them out of the parking lot and waved his warrant card at the individual collecting fees at the payment booth. He followed the SUV all the way through Dublin, down to the south side, then backed off, convinced at this point that he had a pretty good idea of exactly where they were headed.

He wasn't wrong. The SUV pulled into the broad, circular drive in front of Eamon Boyle's mansion and stopped just opposite the elaborate front door. Dillon pulled over to the side of the road and watched while Mousey held the rear passenger door as Connie Touhy slid out of the SUV. Eamon Boyle suddenly appeared at the front door, offered his hand to Connie Touhy, then led her inside. Mousey growled something into the SUV and followed. The two underlings quickly gathered the Louis Vuitton bags from the rear of the vehicle, dragged them in through the front door, and closed the door behind them.

Dillon waited, thinking for a moment, then put his car in gear and headed back to the office.

FOURTEEN

Dillon had just stacked up the three small plates, two tea mugs, and the apple core that had been left on his desk when DCI McCabe stepped out of his office and said, "Suel, Dillon, a moment of your time, please." His tone suggested more of an order than a request.

Dillon hurried to the break room, dumped the lot into the sink, then hustled back over to McCabe's office, entering just behind Suel.

"Update on our double homicide," McCabe said, as he sat down behind his desk.

Suel didn't bother to take a seat. "We returned to Jimmy Ryan's home yesterday afternoon, sir. Coincidently, Ryan had an urgent business meeting. In Paris, I believe," Suel said, looking at Dillon standing next to him.

"Yeah, Paris. Barely enough time for him to get his cleaning woman in and scrub the guest room down. I'd guess some of his thugs moved everything out. Based on what we saw, you wouldn't find so much as a fingerprint in the place."

"It literally sparkled," Suel said.

"I had a text message waiting for me this morning," Dillon said. "One of my contacts in the Marshals Service. Joey Touhy's wife was on a flight arriving in Dublin this morning. She was met at the airport by Eamon Boyle's thug, Mousey, and a couple of other miscreants. Interestingly enough, she declined any assistance from the American Embassy, and, it turns out, her flight was booked three days ago."

"So she was going to join her husband?"

"Possibly," Dillon said. "Although it seems to me, things might have been crowded with the three of them in the same bed and Touhy's return flight to the States was booked for today."

"The cleaning woman seemed to indicate there was quite a bit of, ummm, activity going on between Joey Touhy and the young woman who accompanied him," Suel said.

"Not his wife?"

"Ahh, no, sir. A woman young enough to be his daughter."

"Twenty-seven years old," Dillon said.

"Mmm-mmm, interesting. And she was American?"

"Yes, sir. Arrived on the same flight with him and was also scheduled to be returning today."

McCabe pursed his lips and seemed to be thinking for a moment.

"The woman's sister has accepted the offer of Embassy assistance, and I believe is making arrangements to fly over to Dublin. I did a Google search on her address. It's an apartment in Boston, nothing fancy. I'd guess she's a working person, lives in a small apartment in what appears to be a working-class sort of neighborhood."

"Her sister was the female victim?" McCabe said.

"Yes, sir. Her sister, Gerri Greco, was the female victim. At age twenty-seven, she was living in a four or five-thousand-dollar-a-month apartment."

"Visible means of employment?"

"I don't know that," Dillon said.

"Find out as much as you can on her. Also the wife, arranging her flight two days prior—"

"Actually three days, sir," Dillon said.

"See what you can find out. I wonder, did she know about the other woman? Was it consensual? Something's not adding up."

"A number of things," Dillon said.

"This Riley individual?" McCabe said, to Suel.

"Jimmy Riley," Suel said. "Bit of a financial wizard apparently, but less than adept when it comes to the interpersonal relationship skills. I'm sure that's why they removed him from the scene for a bit. By the time he returns to Dublin, any information he may be able to impart will already be common knowledge."

McCabe's phone rang. He glanced over at it, then said, "Damn, budget meeting. What I'd give— all right, carry on, keep me in the loop."

Dillon and Suel hurried out of the office. Suel let out a deep breath as they approached Dillon's desk.

"That wasn't so bad," Dillon said.

"You can never be too sure," Suel said.

FIFTEEN

Dillon took his suit coat off and hung it over the back of his chair. He sat down, then sent Pat Mathews at the Marshals Service in New York an email requesting any and all information on Gerri Greco, the twenty-seven-year-old who'd been killed with Joey Touhy, as well as any information on her sister, Jackie, and anything on Touhy's wife, Connie. It was just a little after six in the morning on the east coast of the US, so it would be a while before he heard anything. Next, he phoned Brian McFadden at the Dublin City Morgue.

"Dublin City Mortuary," a pleasant, female voice said over the phone.

"Brian McFadden, please."

"Who shall I say is calling?"

"Is this Maura?"

"Yes, it is. Who's calling?"

"Hi, Maura. It's Jack Dillon."

"Oh, the Marshal. Howdy," she giggled. "I thought we might be hearing from you after that dreadful incident early yesterday morning."

"Yeah, hell of a way to get your name in the paper."

"So tragic. What are people thinking? Let me connect you to Brian. Nice chatting with you, Marshal. Don't be a stranger," she said, then suddenly something clicked on the line, and a phone started ringing.

"McFadden," was how the phone was answered on the third ring.

"Hi, Brian. Jack Dillon calling. Wondering if you've any information on the two Americans that arrived on your doorstep yesterday morning?"

"Ah, yes. The two gunshot victims?"

"You had other Americans dropping in?"

"Actually, yes, unfortunately we did. A traffic accident. Pedestrian stepped in front of a bus. Elderly gentleman, apparently looking the wrong way and stepped right in front of the damn thing, poor soul. But you're calling about the murdered couple. The gunshot victims."

"Right."

"Well, I can state without any doubt that the cause of death was indeed the gunshots."

"Gee, thanks, Brian. Can you copy the final reports for me?"

"I can, but it won't be for at least another hour or two. They're just finishing up, and then they'll have to write them up. If you wanted to swing by, oh, say sometime after half-past one this afternoon, I could probably have them for you."

"I can do that. Would you have time for lunch?"

"Oh, kind of you to offer. Unfortunately, I'm a bit pressed for time today, all week as a matter of fact. But swing by, and I'll let you buy me a tea."

"I'll see you then," Dillon said and hung up.

Suel walked over to Dillon's desk just as he hung up with McFadden. "Fancy going for a quick visit?"

"Where to?"

"Gardaí going door to door, yesterday, spoke to a woman across the street from Jimmy Ryan's. She apparently saw someone fleeing the scene the other night."

"She saw the shooting?"

"There seems to be some confusion on that specific point. I'm heading out now to talk with her. You're welcome to come along."

"Let's go," Dillon said. He pulled his coat off the back of his chair and followed Suel out the door.

SIXTEEN

Nora O'Malley lived across the street and one house over from Jimmy Ryan's home. Her three-story, dressed stone home, appeared to be half again as large as Ryan's. Suel pulled into the driveway and parked alongside the massive structure. The driveway was similar to Jimmy Ryan's, paved in a grey-colored stone with a granite sort of curbing along the edge. The front yard was immaculately manicured with a well-trimmed hedge behind the three-foot dressed stone wall running across the entire front of the large lot. Purple clematis ran up a large trellis on either end of the house and then across the front of the house along the second floor for another twenty or thirty feet. Rose bushes, Dillon stopped counting after twenty, ran along either side of the driveway. A dozen rose trees, in massive ceramic pots, ran along the path leading from the driveway to the front door. Elegantly arranged, trimmed holly shrubs ran all across the front of the house.

"Nice digs," Dillon said, climbing out of the car.

"Good to see how the other half is doing. One worries otherwise," Suel said and headed for the front door. He rang the doorbell, and the door opened just a moment later. The doorbell continued to chime in the background as a woman in a dark, unmemorable dress stood before them.

"Detective Inspector Suel and United States Marshal Jack Dillon to see Miss Nora O'Malley," Suel said. "We've an appointment."

"Yes, please come in. She's expecting you."

They stepped into a large foyer with three thick, massive, matching oriental rugs covering the marble floor.

"If you'll follow me, please," the woman said, then led them down the hallway, past a large sitting room and what possibly could have been a TV room. Both rooms were tastefully decorated in a traditional style. Each room had a thick oriental rug on the floor that looked to have been custom made.

"Just in here," the woman said and opened a pair of heavily carved French doors. "I'll let her know you're here," she said, then stepped aside so Suel and Dillon could enter the room. She closed the doors behind them once they'd stepped into the room.

There was a white marble fireplace with a carved mantel and a wood fire burning in the fireplace. A framed oil painting of an older, bald man holding a rolled document next to an ornate chair hung above the fireplace. An oriental rug, woven in rich reds and blues, and thick enough to almost feel spongy as Dillon walked across it, covered the wooden floor. All the walls were covered with bookshelves. The shelves were painted a creamy white that matched the marble of the fireplace. The books themselves were largely leather bound with gold embossed letters and looked to be a couple of hundred years old.

"Not your everyday flat," Suel said and sat down in a leather wingback chair, one of two next to the fire.

Dillon sat down in the matching chair opposite Suel. A paperback book sat on the end table next to his chair, and he chuckled, then held the book out toward Suel. The cover image was a shirtless muscular male holding a woman in some 18th century outfit. Dillon read the title out loud. "'Stud finder, an erotic romance.' I'm not sure it fits with the rest of the library."

"Probably a lot more interesting than the rest of this shite," Suel said, just as the doorknob clicked, and one of the doors began to swing open.

Dillon quickly placed the book back on the end table and they both rose from their chairs. A blonde-haired woman entered, flashing a smile and extending her hand. The woman who had answered the door followed her into the room, carrying a large silver tray with a silver teapot, cups, saucers, and a plate with small tea biscuits. She placed the tray on a wooden buffet that looked to be about two hundred and fifty years old, then quietly left the room, closing the door behind her.

"Gentlemen, how kind of you to come. I'm Nora O'Malley. Please, call me Nora." Her blonde hair was perfectly done. She was dressed in low heels, tan slacks, and a black silk blouse. She wore gold and diamond earrings, two diamond rings on her left hand, another one on her right, and a gold watch with a diamond-studded watchband. Dillon guessed her age to be about seventy-five.

Suel shook her hand, and half mumbled, "Pleased to meet you. Thank you for making the time."

"US Marshal Jack Dillon," Dillon said and shook her hand.

"Oh, my, a US Marshal," she said, holding onto Dillon's hand and flashing a smile at Suel. "I suppose I'd best behave myself. Now, before we get started, how about some tea." Her accent was precise, and Dillon would have thought she was English if he'd met her elsewhere.

"A tea would be grand," Suel said.

"Yes, certainly," Dillon replied.

"Wonderful. Come on then, let's dish up before we get started," she said and headed for the silver tray resting on the buffet.

She poured herself a tea, added milk, and two sugars, then took two of the biscuits, placed them on a small plate, and sat down on the couch. Suel dished up next, and then Dillon followed.

As Dillon placed a biscuit on his plate and headed for the wingback chair, she asked, "Now, Marshal, did you fly over here strictly to investigate this dreadful episode?"

"No, ma'am, I'm stationed here in Dublin. Unfortunately, there seems to be enough crime involving Americans to warrant my presence. The good news is, quite often, it consists of individuals, usually students, who have neglected to contact family and are out of touch for a week or two. As you might imagine, worried parents need to be kept informed."

"One of many lessons in life," she said, then took a sip of tea. She set her cup on the end table and clasped her hands together, almost as if in prayer. "Now, how may I help?"

"We read the notes from your interview yesterday," Suel said.

"More like a brief conversation," she said.

"Yes, which is exactly why we wanted to hear your version for ourselves. Perhaps if you could explain, in your own words."

"Well, not much to tell, actually. It was the middle of the night. I was up making one of my two or three nightly journeys to the loo," she said and rolled her eyes. "I just happened to look out the window and saw an individual standing, for the briefest of moments, at the rear door of the taxi. He appeared to have been bending down—you know, maybe glancing inside, talking to someone. I thought it was a bit strange, but I was also still half asleep and trying desperately not to wake up any further before I climbed back into bed. It was about that simple. In fact, I only viewed everything for a second or two. It just took me longer to describe it to you than the time I spent looking out the window."

"Did you hear any gunshots?"

"No, I did not. As you might imagine, this is an extremely quiet area, and something like that would have been quite apparent on any given day, let alone in the middle of the night. As I told the officers yesterday, I did not hear any gunshots. I'm quite certain."

"And did you see the taxi roll up against your neighbor's gate?"

"No. When I left the loo, I can't even recall if I glanced out the window again. There was nothing that would have suggested I take a second look."

"Did you notice if the rear door on the taxi was open?"

"No. As I just said, there was nothing that would have suggested I take a second look." She spoke a bit slower this time as if that might impart the message better.

"You're sure it was a man you saw?" Dillon asked.

She seemed to think about that for a moment. "Hmm-mmm, now that you mention it, there was nothing I saw that would suggest the individual was anything other than a male. I can state for the record that I'm ninety-nine percent positive. I've probably made an assumption or two. But I wouldn't change my assessment at this point. What sort of woman would be out and alone at that hour of the night, not to mention murdering innocent people?"

"Could you describe the individual?" Suel asked.

She lifted a biscuit from her plate, took a small bite, and seemed to think for a moment. "He was taller than the taxi. The roof of the vehicle came up to maybe his shoulder. He appeared to be white. I believe he was wearing gloves, dark gloves," she said, sounding as if this was new information. "I'm pretty sure one hand was on the top of the vehicle. And I think he had dark hair, although he was wearing a cap."

"A cap?" Suel said.

"Yes, you know, these baseball caps so popular with the young people today. No curvature in the bill of the cap, it was simply flat," she said, then motioned a horizontal line with her hand. "Looks absolutely ridiculous, in my opinion."

"Did you see the couple in the taxi, or perhaps earlier, did you happen to see them at Mr. Ryan's home, just across the street?" Dillon asked.

"No, I did not. Is that why the taxi had stopped there? Ryan? He's a bit of a strange one if you ask me. But, honestly, I had no idea that was why they were stopped there. They were staying with him?"

"We believe so," Suel said.

They talked back and forth for a few more minutes, but she had no other information to impart.

Eventually, Suel drained his teacup, thanked her for her time, and then Nora O'Malley showed them to the front door. As she opened the door, she said, "Please don't hesitate to contact me if I can be of any additional service."

Dillon and Suel smiled, thanked her, and headed back to the car.

"What did you think?" Suel said, once outside.

"I think for a glance out the window in the middle of the night, she was remarkably accurate. No reason to doubt her."

"She didn't hear any shots."

"Maybe a silencer. Maybe the shots are what woke her and she just automatically headed to the bathroom," Dillon said and shrugged.

Suel pressed the button on his car key, the vehicle chirped, the lights flashed, and they climbed in.

"You eager to get back to the office?" Dillon said, as Suel backed up then headed out of the driveway.

"Depends on what, exactly, you had in mind."

"Might be interesting just to take a short spin past Eamon Boyle's place, see if anything is happening with Touhy's wife. The flight reservation made three days in advance of his murder strikes me as a little too convenient."

"You thinking she had her husband killed?"

"Well, he was over here with a much younger woman. And Ryan's cleaning woman indicated the two of them had been going at it like a couple of dogs in heat," Dillon said, then gave the same hand movement the cleaning woman had made to them earlier.

Suel laughed. "Yeah, that was one for the books. I've got a better idea, we grab a quick lunch, then head over to Griffith Avenue and the Dublin City Mortuary, see if your man has anything on the autopsies."

"I like that idea much better," Dillon said. "You choose where we dine."

SEVENTEEN

Anderson's Food Hall & Cafe was located on The Rise in Glasnevin, an area on the north side of Dublin not too far from Dillon's house and maybe a half-mile from the Dublin City Mortuary.

Suel pulled into a parking space almost directly in front of the two-story white stucco building. Black awnings hung over the shop windows, and the two tables in the small outside eating area were occupied. The word "Anderson's" in silver letters ran across the length of the storefront.

"Have you been here before?" Suel asked.

"Sometime last spring. A friend brought me here for breakfast. We walked over from my place. Food was good, but I thought it was maybe a bit too posh for my tastes."

"The woman or the food?" Suel said, then stepped out of the car.

"Probably both," Dillon said.

They stepped in through the front door and stood reading the menu on the chalkboard attached to the wall. Suel ordered the fish pie, and Dillon ordered the toasted Parma ham sandwich. Dillon paid the tab for both of them at the cash register and then they walked into the rear room and grabbed a table in the corner of the dining area.

As they sat down, a young woman approached and said, "Can I get you something to drink? We have specials today on a Chen Blanc that is—"

"Nice as it sounds, I think just a sparkling water for me," Suel said.

"Same for me," Dillon said, then followed up with, "Sorry," when she seemed to grow a disappointed look on her face.

She was back a couple of minutes later with two plastic bottles of sparkling water and glasses. They'd just finished filling their glasses when their lunch order arrived.

"So?" Dillon asked after Suel had taken a couple of bites.

"Not bad. Quite nice, actually."

"I was actually thinking about Nora O'Malley."

Suel shoveled in another forkful of fish pie, then tore off a portion of the roll resting on a plate off to the side. "I'd say she was probably quite accurate in her description. Unfortunately, it's of almost no use to us other than to confirm at least one individual was alongside the vehicle. Based on what she described, we can't even be sure that individual was, indeed, the shooter. It could be he was simply a passer-by who peered in the car, saw what had happened, and hightailed it down the street."

He swiped the portion of bread roll through the fish pie, then placed it in his mouth.

"So if this was a hit—"

"If I was going to jump to any conclusions, that would be one of them. It was some sort of mob hit."

"So who would it be? Who are the likely individuals?" Dillon asked.

"That's two separate questions and answers. Whoever ordered it is one person. Whoever pulled the trigger is some other individual either looking to make a name for themselves, or they already have a reputation for getting the job done. Here's a question for you. Was this a getaway couple of days where Touhy was out of sight of his wife? This could be a very personal situation, Jack. You know, you start fooling around, I don't know many women who'd take too kindly to that sort of activity."

"Yeah, but would they have their husband murdered? That seems to me to be a huge leap."

"I think they'd surely consider it if they had the tools at their disposal. And Connie Touhy would have had those tools. I'm guessing she'd have a list of the sort who, for the right price, would gladly pull the trigger."

EIGHTEEN

Suel pulled up in front of the post office next door to the Dublin City Mortuary, the morgue. He drove the left side of the car up over the curb, onto the boulevard and parked. He reached into the glove compartment and pulled out the sheet of paper with the An Garda Síochána logo on it in blue and the large black letters,—"**OFFICIAL BUSINESS!**"—and handed it to Dillon.

"Put that on the dash, so some Dublin City plonker doesn't write us a ticket or get the bright idea to clamp the wheel," he said, then climbed out of the car.

Dillon placed the paper in the corner of the dash, then got out. The entrance to the morgue had recently been moved to the rear of the building. They walked up a short asphalt drive, toward the back of the building. Suel rang the buzzer next to the tall wooden door.

"Yes," a female voice answered from a speaker mounted above the door a moment later.

"Maura? Is that you?" Dillon said, recognizing the voice. "I journeyed all the way across town, and now you've locked me out."

"Who is this?"

"Dillon, Marshal Jack Dillon, and as if that isn't bad enough, I've got DI Paddy Suel tagging along with me."

"Oh, for God's sake," she said, and suddenly they heard a buzzer, and then the lock on the door snapping. Suel pulled the door open, then motioned with his hand for Dillon to go in first. They took a few short steps into the entry, then a right into a small lobby.

The lobby had a grey tile floor, white walls, and six plastic chairs arranged around a glass-topped coffee table. The outside window with frosted glass was in the middle of the wall behind them with a sickly looking palm tree drooping in front of it. The far wall had a metal rack holding pamphlets for cremation services and a half-dozen local cemeteries. The wall directly in front of them had a thick glass window with a receptionist counter and an area where paperwork could be pushed through at the base of the window.

Maura sat behind the window with a phone to her ear. She was reasonably attractive with auburn hair and large brown eyes. An open, half-empty package of Oreo cookies sat on her desk next to the phone. She waved at the two of them, then said a few more words into the phone and disconnected just as they approached. "Well, to what do we owe the pleasure? Here to see Brian?"

"Yes, if he's available."

"Yeah, he sent word up about fifteen minutes ago that everything's ready. Let me give him a call, and he'll escort the two of you's back."

"Brian," she said into the phone a moment later, then smiled and nodded at Dillon. "I've US Marshal Dillon and DI Suel to see you. No, I'm afraid not, sir," she said and laughed. "I already told them you were in. Very good," she said, then looked up at Dillon. "He'll be up in just a moment."

"Thanks, Maura. How have you been?"

"Pretty good, thanks. You know, the usual, work all day, then by the time I get home, I'm too tired to do anything, so I fall asleep and somehow manage to get up just in time to get back to work. I'm nothing if not boring."

The grey metal door next to the thick window where Maura sat suddenly buzzed, and Brian McFadden opened the door. He was dressed in blue hospital scrubs, and gold, wire-rimmed glasses. He had close-cut, thinning black hair. Dillon placed his age at a year or two on either side of forty.

"Gentlemen, come on back. Good to see yas," he said, then held the door for Dillon and Suel. They walked down an off-white hallway with framed watercolor street scenes of Dublin hanging along the wall, maybe every fifteen feet. Entrances to a series of offices were on either side of the hallway. Each office appeared to be crammed with two or three more desks than originally intended.

"You want to check them out in the viewing room, or shall we just pull the drawer out in the cooler?" McFadden asked.

"Oh, don't go through the bother of the viewing room. We can look at them back in the cooler if that works for you," Suel said.

"Works fine with me," McFadden said. "Marshal?"

"Cooler's fine. Whatever's easiest for you."

They passed the three viewing rooms, each with a brass number, 1, 2, or 3, attached to the door. Doors 2 and 3 were open, and the rooms were empty. The rooms were rather small, with grey carpeting on the floor and a viewing window in the wall. White Venetian blinds were pulled closed and covered the windows on the far side of the glass.

Door number 1 was closed, and Dillon unintentionally picked up his pace for a few steps so he wouldn't run into anyone coming out of the room.

McFadden led them through the break room and out a far door into an examination room. Three metal tables sat under bright lights. A body beneath a white cloth was laid out on the far table. An examiner in hospital scrubs was busy laying out tools of the trade. He held a small saw with a rounded blade in his hand, looked up and gave McFadden a nod, then went back to the task at hand.

McFadden led them down a hallway, past two heavy metal doors. He opened the third door, exactly the same as the first two, and they stepped into a walk-in cooler. Square industrial aluminum doors, stacked four high and ten across, covered one wall. The cold air felt damp, and although the room was small, Dillon thought their footsteps seemed to somehow echo.

McFadden stopped roughly in the middle, then punched a numeric code next to a small door. A light blinked, something seemed to snap, and he took hold of the handle and pulled. A long metal drawer rolled out, and Joey Touhy, or what was left of him, lay before them.

"I estimated his age at maybe sixty. Based on his passport information he was just fifty-three. Shot three times in the head, close range. After looking at the interior damage, I'm guessing hollow points."

Dillon and Suel just stared. McFadden pulled out a pen from the front breast pocket of his hospital scrubs and pointed at the entry wound just above Touhy's left eye. "Entrance wound here and, as you can see, the round essentially removed the occipital bone as it exited." He turned Touhy's head, ever so slightly, to expose the large hole in the lower back half of the head, where the skull used to be.

"This wound, entering the mental foramen—" he pointed to the right side of Touhy's chin, "—took out the middle nasal concha, perpendicular plate, and the orbital plate before exiting out the left side of his head, the greater wing—"

"In other words, your man had the hell shot out of him," Suel said.

"Yeah, that more or less sums it up. Need any explanation on the third round?"

"He died at the scene," Dillon said, absently.

"I'd say his death was virtually instantaneous."

"And his partner?"

"Ahh, the woman, Geraldine Greco," McFadden said. He pushed the drawer with Touhy's body closed. He input a code next to the small door just beneath Touhy's drawer. A light on the keypad blinked, something gave an audible snap and he pulled the drawer open. The woman had not been a natural blonde, and for the first time, Dillon saw Gerri Greco's face. She wasn't just pretty, she was beautiful. A small hole, smaller than a dime, entered the cleavage side of her large left breast. Her chest, from just below her neck down to her navel, had been slit open and stitched back up with a black thread that looked more like a bootlace.

"Her breasts are implants. Implants in her buttocks as well. She's had a number of botox injections in her chin, lips and around the eyes. All a bit unusual for a twenty-seven-year-old, in my opinion. Based on the damage path of the rounds, same weapon as your man. She was shot in the heart."

He pointed to the shadowed area around the entrance wound on her breast. "This is stippling, sometimes referred to as tattooing. Powder burns, actually. Your shooter would have been very close, the weapon maybe an inch or two away. Once again, death was virtually instantaneous. I'm guessing he fired a second time as he zeroed in on your man. Hit her in the neck as she went down," he said, moving the pen up toward her throat. A gash maybe two inches wide was torn across the front of her neck.

"The round basically tore out her trachea. My estimate, this entire affair, all five shots into the two of them at close range, couldn't have taken more than two, maybe three seconds at the most. Maybe another second or two to shoot the driver. How is he doing by the way?"

"Well, we haven't heard he's dead yet," Suel said.

"Whoever did this had to be right on top of them. I'm talking just inches away," McFadden said. "One other thing I should mention, and it's in the copies of the report I have for you. Your woman was pregnant, early on in her first trimester, no more than four or five weeks."

"Was Touhy the father?" Dillon asked.

"I didn't test for that. Is that a concern?"

"Not at this stage."

NINETEEN

O nce they were back in the car, Suel asked, "What do you think?"

"I think if I weren't a drinking man, I'd very quickly become one. This wasn't some young idiot with a gun. Whoever was pulling the trigger knew exactly what they were doing, from untraceable reloads, to hollow-point rounds, to the no sound of shots being fired. A professional hit. Who has the connections to pull this off?"

"Well, Eamon Boyle for one," Suel said. "But if you'd like the idea of a bit of intrigue, maybe your Russian friend, Mr. Alexei Bazanov."

"Oh God. Didn't his main man head back to Russia?"

"That plonker Yakov Gulin? A pedophile and rapist, and those were his good points. He might have returned to dear old mother Russia, but I'd say there's at least a fifty-fifty chance he could be in some dark bog hole, never to be seen or heard from again."

"No loss there," Dillon said.

"There's more to learn about this event, the murder of your man Touhy. It doesn't quite seem to be adding up."

"What about the pregnancy? Think his wife may have found out?"

"Maybe, but at four or five weeks? He'd almost have had to brag to her about it just after conception. I guess anything's possible, but I'd label it a slim possibility. He may not have even known."

"Say," Dillon said. "You want to swing past my place so I can let Lucifer out, it'll only take a minute."

"You've still got that little knacker?"

"Oh, he's okay. Part of the problem is I'm never home, between work and—"

"Between work and you begging every woman you meet to hop on, he'll be lucky if he's fed once a week."

"That seems a bit harsh," Dillon said and laughed.

Suel pulled alongside Dillon's front gate a few minutes later and parked. "I'll wait for you here."

"Shouldn't take but a minute," Dillon said, and hurried out of the car. He closed the front gate behind him, then set his house key in the lock and opened the door. He gave a quick look at Suel as he stepped inside the house. Suel already had his phone placed up against his ear. It wasn't until Dillon closed the front door behind him that he noticed the envelope on the floor.

It was large, pink, and his name, Jack, was elaborately scrawled across the front. As he picked the envelope up off the floor, he caught a whiff of perfume and felt something tangible inside, suggesting more than just a birthday card. He opened the envelope as he walked into the kitchen, and absently called, "Lucifer. Lucifer, come on down here. Let's go outside."

He stood in front of the kitchen counter, reached into the envelope, and pulled out a pair of familiar-looking pink plastic handcuffs. Fluffy pink feathers and fuzz were wrapped around the actual cuff portion, and the chain links between the two cuffs were covered in silver glitter. He recognized them as Brianna's, and when he looked at them, it suddenly dawned on him that he'd neglected to call her back.

There was a notecard still inside the envelope, and he pulled it out. Just three lines written in Brianna's gorgeous penmanship.

"Just a little reminder of all the fun you're going to miss out on.

Hope it was worth it.

Please, don't bother calling."

He pulled his phone out and quickly called her, then yelled up the stairs for Lucifer as the phone rang. After the second ring, a recording came on the line. "At the request of the subscriber, access has been denied to the number you are calling from. If you feel you have reached this number in error, please—"

He hung up, yelled up the stairs again for Lucifer, and heard him jump off the bed, then sort of stretch, and scrape his paws across the bedroom carpet. A moment later, he peeked around the corner of the banister.

"Lucifer, come on, let's go outside. Come on, boy. Come on, outside. Come on, let's go."

The dog stood and stared.

"Come on, Lucifer, come on."

Still no reaction.

"Treat? You want a treat?" Dillon said, then walked back into the kitchen and around the counter to the jar of dog biscuits sitting on the granite countertop. He picked up the jar and shook it, banging the biscuits against the metal lid on the jar. Lucifer suddenly charged down the stairway and into the kitchen.

Dillon opened the jar, took one of the biscuits out, and waved it in front of Lucifer's nose. He walked toward the door, holding the biscuit down at just about nose height. Lucifer quickly followed. Dillon opened the front door and tossed the biscuit out onto the concrete parking pad. Lucifer leaped out the door, snatched the biscuit in his mouth before it could bounce a second time, then turned to face Dillon and squatted.

Dillon closed the front door, went back into the kitchen, filled the food and water dish, and attempted to call Brianna again. The same recording came on just after the second ring, and he hung up.

He waited a moment, took another whiff of the perfume on the envelope, then opened the door and called to Lucifer. The dog bounded up the steps and inside the house to the freshly filled water dish. Dillon watched him for a brief moment, then hurried out to Suel waiting in the car.

"Everything go okay? He didn't chew a hole in your sitting room couch or scratch all the woodwork on your lower kitchen cabinets?"

"Nope, nothing like that. He's just calm and collected."

Suel looked at Dillon for a moment but didn't say anything before he eventually drove off.

As they pulled into the parking area behind their office, Suel said, "I'm still thinking about Alexei Bazanov."

"How depressing," Dillon said.

"Yeah, but try this on for size. Eamon Boyle works some supply deal through Joey Touhy. The deal will push Bazanov right out of the Irish market. So Bazanov has Touhy killed. What do you think?"

"Why wouldn't he just kill Eamon Boyle and eliminate any competition outright? It doesn't seem to make sense that Touhy would try to worm his way into the Irish market. Why go to all that trouble when he'd have more success expanding somewhere else in the US?"

"God, I just hate it the few times you begin to make sense."

TWENTY

Dillon attempted to call Brianna from his desk, but both times his calls dropped into her voicemail. He thought it best not to leave a message, maybe just let her continue to boil a little longer, and then hopefully she'd calm down.

His phone rang a little after four.

"Jack Dillon," was how he answered, trying to sound professional and hoping against hope it might be Brianna.

"Jack, Eric Bergman." Dillon's US Embassy contact.

"Yeah, Eric, what do you have?"

"Jackie Greco. She's flying out tonight from Boston to Paris, on Delta flight number one-one-eight. One-eighteen. Has an hour-and-a-half layover in Paris before she hops an Air France flight to Dublin, number seventeen-sixteen, arriving tomorrow at ten-thirty in the morning."

"And the Embassy is involved?" Dillon asked.

"Yeah, I'll be meeting her. She's staying at the Maldron Hotel."

"The Maldron. Is that the hotel right in the airport?"

"Yeah, close to terminal two. I spoke to her briefly. She gave the distinct impression she wanted to get in town and then back home just as soon as possible."

"She say anything about her sister's death, the circumstances?"

"No, just asked if I could meet her at the airport. I was planning to be right outside baggage claim waiting for her."

"Would it create any problems if I joined you?"

"I don't think so. As a matter of fact, she wants to ID the body. Maybe you could walk her through that process. I've got a full day tomorrow, a congressman, and two staffers on some scam trip flying in from the UK. It'll be an afternoon of hand-holding and telling them how great I think they are."

"I can take her down to ID the body. Not a pretty sight, I was down there viewing it earlier today."

"If you could do that, it would really help," Bergman said. "I suggested it may not be pretty, but she was insistent. She departs twenty-four hours later. Takes a hop to Paris and then back over that afternoon to Boston, gets back in the US sometime before six in the evening."

"Can you email me her flight schedule? If need be, I want someone standing by in Boston when she returns. She arrives ten-thirty tomorrow morning, and she has to clear customs, correct?"

"You got it. Like I said, I'll be right outside baggage claim, holding a sign with her name on it."

"I'll see you there, Eric. Thanks for the heads-up."

"Thanks in advance for offering to help. Although if you really wanted to help, you'd take the congressman."

"If I really wanted to help it would be best if I just stayed away from the congressman, I'm of the opinion we should vote them all out and just start over."

"If only it was that easy. See you tomorrow," Bergman said and hung up.

Dillon shoveled some paperwork off his desk, left an email for Suel and DCI McCabe explaining that he would be meeting Jackie Greco at the airport in the morning, and then grabbed his coat and headed out the door.

He stopped at the Macari's Take Out on St. Pappins Road in Glasnevin and ordered a chicken kabob tray for seven euros. He pulled into the parking area next to his front door, climbed out of the car, and stared at the brown paper grocery bag sitting on the front stoop, leaning against the door. He looked around, but didn't see anyone, then cautiously approached the bag.

He recognized the plaid boxers on top as his, and carefully moved them aside. The Guinness baseball cap and the Jameson jersey were his as well, all items left at Brianna's on one occasion or another. Farther down in the bag were his shaving razor, a can of shaving cream, a container of shower gel, a half-eaten package of sliced sandwich ham, along with the horseradish and the mustard he really liked. He noticed she didn't include the bag of Butterfinger candy bars a pal had sent over from the States, nor his Bob Seger Ultimate Hits CD.

He unlocked the door, carried the bag inside, and set everything on the kitchen counter, then called up the stairs for Lucifer. Amazingly, Lucifer was down about thirty seconds later and Dillon let him outside. He dined in front of the TV, eating his chicken kabob directly from the tray using his fingers and sipping a Galway Hooker beer directly from the bottle. He crawled into bed just after the news. Both he and Lucifer slept soundly until the alarm went off at six the following morning.

TWENTY-ONE

illon turned the coffee on, went back upstairs to grab a shower, then, once he was dressed, coaxed Lucifer off the bed and let him outside. He cooked a ham and egg omelet, poured another coffee, then phoned Eric Bergman at the Embassy.

"Bergman," was how he answered once Dillon was transferred.

"Eric, Jack Dillon."

"Are you still going to make it this morning?" Bergman asked, the concern apparent in his voice.

"Yeah, I'll be there. Listen, just thinking that if you'd like, I could call the Border Management office at the airport, we can watch Jackie Greco on the monitor going through customs."

"You expecting a problem?" Bergman asked.

"No, not at all. But it might be nice just to have a look when she arrives."

"I see what you mean. Yeah, sure, I'd be willing to do that."

"Let me get it lined up, and I'll be back to you," Dillon said, then hung up and dialed the Border Management office.

"Border Management, Dublin," was how the male voice answered the phone.

"US Marshal Jack Dillon. I'm trying to reach Poraig Sullivan," Dillon said.

"One moment and I'll connect you." The phone rang four times before Sullivan answered.

"Poraig Sullivan."

"Poraig, Marshal Jack Dillon. I've got someone coming through on Air France flight seventeen-sixteen out of Paris, arriving ten-thirty this morning. I'd like to watch her on the monitor going through customs."

"Not a problem on this end," Sullivan said. "Anything we need to be concerned about?"

"No, she's coming in to ID her sister's body, the woman shot the other morning out in Clontarf. I'm not expecting any difficulty, I just don't know much about her. At this stage, all indications are she's an employed individual dealing with a stressful family situation. I'll have Eric Bergman with me from the US Embassy, and I'll be shepherding Miss Greco to and from Dublin City Mortuary later in the day. She's scheduled on a return flight back to the States tomorrow."

"Let me write down her name, and do you have a passport number?"

"I do," Dillon said, and read them off to Sullivan, then said goodbye and hung up.

He next sent a text to Bergman instructing him to meet at ten o'clock at O'Brien's Sandwich Bar at the airport. He received a three-word response just a moment later. "See you there."

Bergman arrived at O'Brien's Sandwich Bar a little before ten. Dillon was already waiting. They both ordered coffee, then made their way into the Border Management office. Poraig Sullivan put the two of them in his office, then stuck his head back in a few minutes before ten-thirty.

"Lads, Air France flight seventeen-sixteen just touched down. It'll be a bit before they dock and begin to unload, but it has arrived. Feel free to join us whenever you've a mind to."

Dillon drained his cup and stood. Bergman followed suit, and they wandered out to the monitors.

"All our officers have her name and passport number. Whichever station she steps up to, we'll be alerted. Everyone in here has a printout of her passport image, so if, or rather when, she's spotted in line we can focus on her. You've seen her before?"

"Only a passport image," Dillon said. "Initial indications are she's just a regular sort who finds herself in an unfortunate circumstance."

"I think I've found your woman," a voice called about twenty minutes later, then turned around and raised his hand.

Dillon recognized him as the same man who had helped ID Joey Touhy's wife, Connie, the other day, but he had difficulty coming up with the guy's name.

"Thanks, Jerry," Sullivan said, reading the situation correctly. "Check it out, lads," he said, then gave a nod toward the monitors.

Jerry had a sheet of paper on the counter in front of him with a blurry copy of Jackie Greco's passport photo. He looked back and forth from the blurry image to that of the figure on the monitor screen. There seemed to be no difference other than the woman on the monitor screen appeared to be a lot more tired-looking.

Her dark hair was neatly trimmed just above her shoulders. She had a black carry-on suitcase which she pulled behind her. She was attractive, very attractive, despite looking tired. She seemed to yawn every other minute while waiting in line. She appeared to be traveling alone. They watched her while she waited in line, slowly moving toward the front until she was waved forward by one of the officers. She presented her passport to him, and a moment later, a red light went on, indicating the individual they were waiting for was now in front of an agent.

Jerry adjusted the volume on his monitor so they could all listen.

The agent took his time paging through the passport.

Jackie Greco yawned.

Then the agent said, "Your first trip to Ireland?"

"Yes."

"And how long do you plan to stay?"

"Just overnight, then back to Boston. I'm flying back out tomorrow morning. Some brief business concerning a death in the family."

"I'm sorry your trip isn't under a more pleasant circumstance."

"Yeah, me too."

He studied her photo for another moment, then stamped her passport and handed it back. "Safe journey home."

"Thank you," she said, then took her passport and exited the customs area.

"There you go. Need anything else?" Sullivan asked.

"No, that should do it. We better catch up to her, it looks like that might be all the luggage she's got," Dillon said.

TWENTY-TWO

Dillon and Bergman hurried out to the baggage claim area and Jackie Greco. She had stopped alongside one of the baggage carousels, but only to get her bearings. The baggage from her flight was being unloaded on carousel three, and she made no effort to head in that direction. Instead, she began to pull her carry-on suitcase toward the exit. Bergman called out to her before she reached the exit.

"Miss Greco, hold on, please."

She turned and stared, then waited for Dillon and Bergman to catch up. She had a questioning look on her face, maybe suggesting, "Just who in the hell is this?"

"Eric Bergman, with the US Embassy. We messaged back and forth yesterday."

"Oh, yes, I thought I'd probably see you outside." She held out her hand and shook Bergman's, then looked at Dillon.

"US Marshal Jack Dillon. Miss Greco, my condolences on your loss."

She nodded but didn't say anything for a moment, then took Dillon's hand and said, "Thank you. Please, call me Jackie."

A guy in a Red Sox windbreaker with dark, curly hair and about a four-day growth of beard suddenly passed, looked at Jackie Greco, and said, "Oh, too bad, honey. I would have shown you a good time." He kept on moving toward carousel three.

Dillon made a mental note of the teardrop tattoo at the corner of his right eye. "Friend of yours?" he asked, then watched the guy until he stopped at carousel three.

"Not really. More like a pain in the ass creep from the Boston flight. Couldn't seem to get away from him in Logan Airport. Then he kept coming back to my seat, trying to buy me drinks on the flight over to Paris. He walked all the way back from first class four or five times. Just wouldn't take no for an answer. I finally had to pretend I was asleep. Wouldn't you know, he was coming here too. God, I just can't seem to catch a break lately."

Dillon watched him standing at carousel three. There was something about him, a cockiness, maybe. He wasn't big, wasn't imposing in any real way, yet there was something besides the teardrop tattoo. Maybe just a rich prick.

They headed out of the baggage area and through the crowd of people waiting for arrivals.

Dillon saw him before he saw Dillon. Mousey, Eamon Boyle's thug, all two hundred and eighty pounds of muscle and bad attitude. Next to Mousey and looking bored stood one of the hoodlums he'd been in the airport with yesterday when they had picked up Connie Touhy. Today he was holding a sign that simply read, "Richie."

"Anyone else meeting you?" Dillon asked Jackie.

"Me? No, I don't know anyone here."

"Eric, maybe take Jackie to her hotel, get her checked in. I'll follow up in just a minute. I forgot to check on something."

Bergman looked like he was about to say something, then thought better of it. "We'll see you at the hotel. Come on, Jackie, it's just a two-minute drive," he said, then led her down the escalator to the short-term parking lot.

Dillon was pretty sure Mousey hadn't spotted him. He stepped off to the side, into the bookstore area, and waited behind a counter of discounted bestsellers. Mousey seemed focused on the crowd, looking for someone exiting the baggage claim area. Eventually, the guy in the Red Sox windbreaker came out, pulling a suitcase behind him. He gave a short wave toward Mousey. They shook hands, and Dillon had the distinct impression it was an introduction as opposed to old friends meeting. At Mousey's direction, the underling took the guy's suitcase, and Mousey led the way out of the terminal.

Dillon got on his phone and called Poraig Sullivan.

"Poraig Sullivan," he eventually answered.

"Poraig, Jack Dillon."

"What'd you forget?"

"Can you check on an individual getting off that Air France flight? He flew first-class from Boston, and I'm guessing first class from Paris. First name Richie, probably short for Richard. He was wearing a blue, Red Sox windbreaker. It's got a red collar, cuffs, and waistband with a red 'B' for Boston over the left breast. He had about a four-day growth of beard, and I'd peg his height at maybe five foot ten or eleven, average weight. Has a teardrop tattoo just beneath the corner of his right eye."

"Problem?"

"I hope not," Dillon said.

TWENTY-THREE

illon lingered behind Mousey and company, watching as they climbed into the same black SUV they'd transported Connie Touhy in yesterday. Today the SUV was parked in an area designed for dropping off passengers so they could hurry into the airport. The SUV was parked against the curb in such a way that it took up two spaces. More than one driver forced to go around the vehicle gave it a dirty look.

As Mousey stepped out of the airport terminal, the SUV pulled forward and stopped, blocking the crosswalk. As people were forced to hurry around the vehicle before the light changed, Mousey and company climbed in with Mousey taking the front passenger seat.

Dillon ran into the short-term parking lot, screeched out of his parking place, flashed his warrant card at the same guy who was manning the payment booth yesterday, and headed out of the airport. He spotted the SUV leaving the airport after a minute or two and followed. As they pulled onto the M50, it was clear they weren't heading to Eamon Boyle's home. They eventually pulled off the M50, taking the Finglas exit, turned onto a side street two traffic lights later, and pulled up in front of a nondescript pub named This Little Piggy. Dillon had never heard of the place.

Mousey began to climb out of the front passenger seat just as Dillon drove past. Fortunately, he didn't so much as glance at Dillon's car. He reached into the passenger seat and pulled out what looked like a computer bag.

Dillon took a left at the next corner, pulled to the curb, then hurried out of his car and cautiously peeked around the trimmed hedge on the corner just as Mousey and Richie entered the pub. One of the underlings dragged Richie's suitcase behind him. A few minutes later, Mousey and the underling walked back out of the pub and climbed into the SUV. The computer bag, along with Richie and Richie's suitcase, were nowhere to be seen. As the SUV pulled away from the curb, Dillon hurried back across the street and quickly climbed into his car. He caught the SUV in his rearview mirror as it drove past the street where he was parked.

He pulled out his phone and called Bergman, who answered on the second ring.

"Bergman."

"Eric, sorry for the delay. I'll be at the hotel in about fifteen minutes."

"Everything okay?"

"Yeah, I'll fill you in when we have a second. How's Jackie?"

"In the bathroom at the moment. I'm actually standing out in the hallway. She said she was really beat.

She's going to take a quick shower and then hit the sack for a bit. What'd you see that got your attention at the airport?"

As long as Bergman was standing in the hallway, Dillon went on to tell him about Mousey meeting the guy named Richie in the Red Sox windbreaker and how they'd dropped him off at the pub named This Little Piggy.

"You ever hear of the place? It's in Finglas," Dillon said.

"Amazingly, no, but it doesn't sound all that charming."

"Yeah, I'd guess not a lot of five-star reviews. I put a call into Poraig Sullivan. Hopefully, he can get me a name and passport number on this Richie character. I'm not liking the looks of him, but that's just a gut reaction. At this stage, no facts to base anything on, well, other than he's met by a crowd of psychopathic degenerates, and they dropped him in one of the shittier-looking pubs in Dublin."

"We both had the same reaction," Bergman said. "You said you're heading over here to the hotel?"

"Yeah, I should be there shortly."

"We're up on the fourth floor. I'm in the hall outside room four-eleven. I don't expect to see Jackie. I'm guessing she'll just hit the sack, try and catch up on some sleep."

"I'll plan to just cool my heels out in the hallway once I get there and let you get on with your day," Dillon said. "What did you say you got going? A congressman?"

"Yeah. Bound to be a long day. Want to trade places?"

"No, thanks. Dublin City Morgue or dealing with a congressman? I'll take the morgue every time. See you shortly," Dillon said, then hung up.

TWENTY-FOUR

Dillon chatted with Bergman in the fourth-floor hotel hallway for a moment, then commandeered a chair from the area just opposite the elevator. Two reasonably comfortable chairs had been positioned on either side of a table with a china vase and silk flowers, pink silk roses to be exact. He dragged one of the chairs down the hall and set it just outside the door to room four-eleven.

The housekeeping staff, two heavyset women, conversing in a language other than English, gave him an odd look. He had the distinct feeling they were discussing him for a moment, but beyond that, they didn't say anything. They started at the far end of the hall and slowly worked their way toward him. When they approached room four-eleven, Dillon waved them off with a shake of his head. He pointed toward the door and said, "Sleeping." They seemed only too pleased to move on.

He'd been sitting out in the hall for the better part of two hours when his phone rang.

"Dillon," was how he answered.

"Marshal, Poraig Sullivan. Sorry for the delay. Just getting back to you on your request. The individual you requested information on is one Richard Joseph Nolan. A US Citizen, Boston resident, passport number . . . ." Sullivan read off the passport number.

"Can you send me that information in an email, please."

"I'm in the process of sending it to you now."

"Thank you, Poraig, much appreciated."

"Anything we should be aware of here?"

"Umm-mmm, just speculation on my part. He was met at the airport by some less than stellar Irish citizens. They dropped him off at some dive named This Little Piggy and—"

"This Little Piggy? That wretched place in Finglas?"

"Sounds like an accurate description. What can you tell me about it?"

"Good lord, why it hasn't been closed down is beyond me. There seems to be a shooting or some kind of assault there on a fairly regular basis. At least one person has ridden a horse through there within the past month. Not exactly what you'd describe as the nicest clientele, more a collection point for undesirables. They ought to put a net over the place, gather up everyone inside, then haul them about twenty miles out to sea and dump them."

"But other than that, it's okay?" Dillon joked.

"And they dropped your man off there?"

"Yeah, this Richie Nolan character."

"That guy, he'll probably fit right in. I believe they've had a couple, maybe three or four rooms unofficially for rent over the years. Not that they've ever advertised them. They're more or less available on an hourly basis if that translates."

"I get it."

"Email just went out now. You should see it in just a moment," Sullivan said.

"Thanks. I appreciate it, Poraig. I'll be escorting Jackie Greco back to the airport tomorrow morning, so if it's okay, I'll pop in and say hello."

"I look forward to your visit," Sullivan said, then laughed and hung up. His email came through a moment later.

Dillon quickly read the email, then forwarded the information to Pat Mathews in New York, adding a quick line asking for anything Mathews could find on Richie Nolan.

TWENTY-FIVE

Dillon's stomach growled loudly, not for the first time, just as the door to room four-eleven opened. He looked up just as Jackie Greco peeked out the door.

"Oh, God, I'm so sorry. You must think I'm dreadful. And you've been waiting out there this whole time? I really am dreadful."

"Not a problem. Believe me, I'm familiar with trying to deal with jet lag."

"Your friend is gone?" she said, peeking out a little further and looking up and down the hallway.

"Yeah, he had other business he had to take care of. If you'd like, I could escort you to the Dublin City Mortuary. I believe you said you wanted to view your sister."

"Yeah. Not looking forward to that, so if you wouldn't mind, I'd really appreciate it. I'd like to just get it over with."

"Whenever you're ready. It's after three now, so we should probably get going, they're open till four-thirty or five and we're maybe fifteen minutes away."

"If you'll just give me a couple of minutes, I'll be out."

"I'll call them and let them know we're on our way," Dillon said.

She closed the door to her room, and Dillon called Brian McFadden about twenty minutes later. He answered on the third ring.

"Brian McFadden."

"Hi Brian, Jack Dillon. Hey, I'm bringing Jackie Greco down to view her sister's body. She came in on a flight this morning and will be heading back out tomorrow morning."

"Thanks for the call. Think she'll be able to sign off on the paperwork?"

"Yeah, it's just the standard form, right?"

"Yeah, a signature and date. We got the birth date off the passport. If she knows the current address that will help, but it's not necessary. She can work out shipment back to the States through the Embassy later."

"I'll brief her on the way over." The door to four-eleven suddenly opened, and Jackie Greco stepped out. She was dressed in grey slacks and a black sweater. Her hair was brushed, and apparently, fresh makeup had been applied. She flashed a sparkling white smile at Dillon. "We're just leaving now. See you shortly," Dillon said to McFadden and disconnected.

"I really appreciate you taking the time," Jackie said. Dillon extended his hand toward the elevators, then picked up the chair he'd been sitting in and followed her down the hall.

"Not a problem. Glad to be of service. I was just on the line with our contact. He'll have everything ready for us so you can get in and out of there just as fast as possible. They have a very short form to fill out. You can deal with things like transport of your sister back to the States through the American Embassy at a later date."

"It's all happened so fast. I feel like I just got the phone call about an hour ago and here I am. I really can't believe any of this."

"Well, my limited experience is you're in the midst of dealing with the shock, not to mention the circumstances, and then the distance adds to the complexity of your particular situation. You'll be focused on making arrangements, getting things lined up, and suddenly you're going to put your head up and a week has gone by, and it's behind you in sort of a big blur. In a way, that turns out to be kind of nice."

He set the chair down next to the table with the china vase and the silk roses, then pushed the button for the elevator.

Jackie stepped onto the elevator, and Dillon followed. Once the elevator door closed behind them, he became aware of a wonderful perfume scent.

"Right now, I think I'm just in that blur part of the situation you described," she said, then stepped off the elevator and followed Dillon out the door of the hotel.

Dillon took the back road out of the airport, past the runways, then waited at the roundabout for the light to change. He took the Ballymun Road exit off the roundabout.

"We'll take a left onto Griffith Ave at the next light," he said a few minutes later, breaking the silence. "We're just a couple minutes away."

"Lovely area," she said, as they passed Albert Park on the left just next to Dublin City University and proceeded down Ballymun Road. "Can you tell me anything about the incident? I haven't been able to get much information from anyone. I tried to call the police over here, but I think I was calling the wrong number. They didn't know what I was talking about, and I had a hard time understanding what they were trying to say."

"I might be able to give you a little information," Dillon said. "What do you want to know?"

"Well, I'd like to know where this happened. What the circumstances were, for starters."

Dillon clicked on his left blinker, then turned off Ballymun and onto Griffith Avenue. The homes were large, attached in groups of two or four. All the front gardens were well-tended. Broad sidewalks ran along the street. A grassy boulevard was on either side of the street and lined with nicely trimmed trees that grew out and over to the center of the street, the branches and leaves giving the effect of a long, shaded tunnel.

"God, this is gorgeous," Jackie said.

"Yeah, it's a lovely street. I don't live too far from here and have the chance to walk along here on occasion. It's always nice."

"You were going to tell me about Gerri's . . . situation."

"It occurred in an area of Dublin called Contarf. It's another very nice area. She was on a nice street in the back of a taxicab."

"With that asshole Joey Touhy, right?"

"Yeah, he was in the taxi too. I think it's a pretty safe assumption that he was the intended target, and your sister ended up in that situation only because she was next to him."

"God, the times I've warned her about that worthless bastard. And the driver was killed too?"

"He was shot. He survived, at least thus far, but he's in critical condition. We haven't been able to talk with him if that's what you're wondering."

"I told her time and again, Touhy was no good for her. I wasn't the only one, all her friends told her the same thing, but she just wouldn't listen. She's always been a little too fast and loose." She glanced over at Dillon, maybe looking for a response to that last comment.

"Even in high school, she had the reputation of being easy. Knew just what the guys were looking for. God, she was sleeping with college guys when she was fifteen. When our folks grounded her, she would just sneak out the window at night. There was no controlling her.

"She ended up with Touhy, fucked his brains out on a regular basis, and he put her up in that fancy condo he owned. The bastard was married, for God's sake, and my stupid sister Gerri would ride him three or four nights a week. No surprise it ended up this way. God love her, but she's been heading down this path for the last ten years, ever since she got out of high school. In a way, I'm sort of glad, at least we can all stop worrying about her, wondering what in the hell was going to happen next, or when the worst thing was going to happen. God, now it finally did."

TWENTY-SIX

Dillon pulled up onto the boulevard and parked in front of the post office next to the morgue. He led them up the short asphalt drive to the door at the rear of the Dublin City Mortuary.

"Oh, sneaking us in through the back door?" Jackie said and gave a nervous sort of laugh.

"Actually, no. This is the main entrance now. I know it looks kind of strange, there's the fancy gate out there at the front of the building, the granite stone with the facility name and the fancy front door, but this is the main entrance, back here. Welcome to Ireland," he said, and gave his own nervous sort of laugh, then pressed the buzzer next to the door.

"How may I help you?" the familiar voice said.

"Good afternoon, Maura. US Marshal Jack Dillon with Miss Jackie Greco." He tried to sound somewhat formal, so Maura didn't give a jokey response.

"Please come in," she said, then the buzzer sounded, the door lock gave an audible snap, and Dillon pulled the door open.

They stepped into the lobby, and Dillon approached Maura sitting behind the receptionist window. "We're here to see Brian McFadden. I spoke with him earlier, he's expecting us."

"I just paged him. He should be up shortly," Maura said, then gave Jackie Greco the once-over and smiled.

Brian McFadden opened the door leading back to the viewing rooms before they'd had a chance to settle into the uncomfortable plastic chairs. He was dressed in his blue hospital scrubs. Dillon noticed he'd removed his glasses, and his hair appeared a bit neater than usual.

"Hello, Marshal. Miss Greco?" McFadden said and extended his hand.

"Yes. Please, call me Jackie," she said, shaking his hand.

"My condolences to you and your family. Thank you for taking the time and making the effort to journey over. If you'd care to follow me, we'll get this over with just as quickly as possible. Marshal," McFadden said, as he headed down the hallway. "We'll be in viewing room two."

They followed McFadden down the hallway, past the cramped offices and the framed watercolors of Dublin street scenes hanging on the walls. They passed the open door with the brass number one hanging on it. McFadden stopped at the second viewing room and indicated they should enter.

Jackie took a deep breath as she entered the room. Dillon followed her into the room.

McFadden gave a nod to Dillon and said, "I'll only be a moment. I've got everything set up on the other side." Then he closed the door behind Dillon and left the two of them standing in the small room.

It felt about fifteen degrees warmer in the room than the hallway, and the walls seemed to suddenly crowd in just that much more. Jackie stopped after a couple of steps into the room, not quite sure what to do next. Dillon walked past her and up to the viewing window with the closed Venetian blinds.

"We can view your sister through here, Jackie. Just take as much or as little time as you want."

She moved forward, taking up a position next to Dillon. She took a deep breath, then looked at Dillon. "You have to do this very often?"

"On occasion. I'm happy to be here with you. No one should have to go through this alone."

The Venetian blinds suddenly rose, and Jackie let out a short gasp, then seemed to hold her breath as she looked through the window at her sister.

Gerri Greco was laid out on a gurney. She was covered from her feet all the way up to her chin with a crisp white shroud that was folded and neatly tucked just beneath her chin. Fortunately, McFadden had arranged the shroud so that it was tucked tightly beneath her chin, completely covering the open bullet wound running across her throat. None of the stitching closing her chest cavity was visible. Her implants remained erect, presenting two large, distinct mounds beneath the shroud. It appeared obvious that McFadden, or someone, had taken the time to apply some makeup, minimizing the facial discoloration. Her hair had been carefully adjusted, but still somehow didn't look quite right. Her eyelids were at half-mast, and you could still make out the glassy look to nowhere coming from her brown eyes.

Jackie stared for a long moment, then slowly shook her head and mumbled, "Oh, Gerri. God, how many times did I tell you? Look at you, damn it. You stupid, stupid little cow." She sniffled a couple of times, then looked up at Dillon with watery eyes. A single teardrop ran down her right cheek, and she said, "Okay, I've seen enough. Wherever in the hell she is, it's gotta be a better place."

Dillon nodded at McFadden, who reached over and closed the Venetian blinds. Dillon reached into his pocket, pulled out a pocket-sized package of Kleenex, and handed it to Jackie.

"Umm, thanks," she said, then pulled a couple of pieces out of the package, carefully wiped both eyes, then blew her nose. There was a small metal wastebasket in the corner of the room sitting just beneath a little table. A white, 5x7 card and a pen lay on the table. She took three steps over and dropped the Kleenex into the wastebasket then gave a quarter turn to the card with her finger and sort of moved her head back an inch to focus.

"They'll need you to fill that card out, attesting to your sister's ID. I think basically, all they need right now is today's date, the nineteenth, her name, and your signature. You can deal with the rest of it when you want to. You can even do it online if you want," Dillon said.

She picked up the pen, quickly filled out the card, listing not only her sister's name but Gerri's address, their relationship, Jackie's own address, and lastly, her signature. She set the pen down on the table just as McFadden stepped into the room.

"All right then, may I get you a tea or a coffee, Miss Greco?"

"No, thanks. That's very kind, but it's not necessary."

"We, umm, have some personal items, jewelry actually. Rings, a pair of earrings, a large diamond pendant. They appear to be of value. If you'd like, I could—"

"Keep them. I don't want anything to do with them. It's not the Gerri I knew, or at least the Gerri I want to remember."

McFadden nodded as if that may not have been the first time he'd heard something along those lines.

She looked over at Dillon and said, "If you wouldn't mind, I could sure use a drink about now."

Dillon nodded, said, "Thanks, Brian. I'll be in touch," and then led the way out the door.

TWENTY-SEVEN

Dillon knew of a little Italian restaurant called Il Corvo, just a couple of blocks away down Drumcondra Road. They handed the 5x7 card Jackie had filled out through the receptionist window, gave a polite nod to Maura behind the glass, then hurried out the door. Two minutes later, Dillon pulled to a stop almost in front of Il Corvo.

They were led to a table by the front window. Jackie quickly perused the wine menu and ordered a bottle of Montepulciano d'Abruzzo. "Don't worry," she said, once the hostess stepped away. "I'm getting this."

"Not necessary. I'm sure it's been a tough afternoon, make that a tough trip. Under different circumstances, you'd probably find the country a pretty nice place."

"Thanks, but I'm still getting this, and dinner too if you have the time. I really appreciate all you've done." She shook her head. "Gerri. She's been on this path since we were teenagers. She was working as an escort," she said and rolled her eyes. "It's how she met that asshole Touhy. Unfortunately, this is one of the more logical

conclusions. God, those bolt-on boobs, the dermal fill-
ers, her botox, she wasn't thirty, and he had her doing all
that shit. She thought she was the queen, had it all laid
out how she was going to be the princess of Boston, and
look where it finally got her. Bastard."

At this hour, they were only the second couple in the
place. The other table was occupied by an older couple,
sitting just close enough to hear that last comment and
shoot a quick look in Dillon's direction.

A moment later, a server arrived and displayed the
wine bottle to Dillon. He nodded toward Jackie, and the
server held the bottle out toward her. She smiled, said
something in Italian, and the server replied. They ex-
changed comments while he opened the bottle and
poured a small amount into her glass.

Jackie swirled the wine around in her glass, examined the side of the glass, then tasted the wine and nodded a moment later, judging it satisfactory. He filled
their glasses, set the bottle on the table, then said a final
something in Italian and stepped away.

"You speak Italian," Dillon said, not so much asking
a question, but simply making a comment.

"Yeah, my grandparents came from Italy, Calabria.
You know it?"

"Not really." Dillon shook his head.

"It's the toe of the boot. They came over just after
the war. My folks spoke Italian at home when they didn't
want us to know what they were saying, well, or they
were just mad at us. My grandma taught me. God, I'm

so glad she's not around to have to deal with this. Anyway, I know enough to maybe chat up that server, but if he started a serious discussion, say, about politics or a soccer team, he'd lose me in a minute."

"Well, it sounded pretty good to me," he said and raised his glass. They clinked glasses, and each took a sip. "You going to order something to eat?" Dillon asked.

"You kidding? I wait much longer, I'm liable to waste away to nothing," she laughed, then took another sip and picked up a menu. They ordered, chatted all around the reason for her trip, and emptied their wine glasses.

Jackie reached out, refilled the glasses, flashed a quick smile then said, "So what do you think the chances are they'll ever nail the bastard that killed Gerri?"

"I don't know, to be honest. I can promise you they'll do the very best they can to get whoever was responsible. Unfortunately, your sister was essentially an innocent bystander in what looks like some version of a mob hit. It would appear the intended target was Joey Touhy, and whoever did this had little or no idea who your sister was any more than he knew the name of the taxi driver. The two of them, your sister and the driver, were just in the wrong place at the wrong time."

She shook her head and said, "God, I've lost count of the times I told her, warned her, but she was all about the expensive condo he'd put her in, the trips, the jewelry, the dinners out. A lot of damn good it all does now."

Dillon debated his next move for a long moment, and she seemed to pick up on it.

"I'm guessing there's something you're not telling me," she said.

"What makes you say that?"

"Let's just say I've been around the block a few times. Go ahead, what is it? Gerri was having sex in the back seat when she was shot?"

"No. Ummm, actually she was pregnant, maybe just four or five weeks along."

"Oh, Jesus. The hits just keep on coming, don't they?" she said, then drained her wine glass, reached for the bottle and refilled her glass. "God, Gerri, you can't make it up. What in the hell were you thinking?"

"I'm sorry. Maybe I shouldn't—"

"No, you should have. As a matter of fact, I'm glad you did. I'd probably find out anyway when I start clearing out her place. Better to learn this way, but God," she said, then took another healthy swallow.

Dillon's phone signaled a text message coming across. He reflexively pulled out his phone and checked the message. It was from Pat Matthews, his New York contact with the Marshals Service.

"Hmm-mmm, interesting," he said, then focused on his phone screen. An image stared back at him, unsmiling and cold. There was a Boston address below the image and then the name. Nolan, Richard Joseph.

"This guy look familiar?" Dillon said and turned the phone around so Jackie could see the image. She sort of frowned for a moment, then said, "Is that the jerk from the plane? The one who wouldn't leave me alone?"

"Yeah, your pal."

"Believe me, he was no friend of mine."

"His name is Richie Nolan. He—"

"How come Gerri's address is there, beneath his picture?"

"What?" Dillon glanced at the screen, "456 Hanover Street, #1, Boston" was just beneath the image of Richie Nolan.

"Yeah, that's Gerri's address, well, the unit number's wrong, she's in number four. It's the fancy place that son of a bitch Touhy put her up in. Bastard owns the building. Made her think she was some sort of princess, conveniently forgetting where she came from, or what she had to do to get there."

"That's the building your sister lived in, and Touhy owns it?"

"Yeah. You mean to tell me that creep lives in the same building? The few times I was there, I never saw him."

"Well, you're right, apparently he lives there. In fact, he was met at the airport this morning by a couple of local bad guys," Dillon said, not bothering to mention that the same people had met Joey Touhy's wife the day before and that she appeared to actually be staying at Eamon Boyle's home. "There was something about him that rubbed me the wrong way," he said, not going into detail on the teardrop tattoo. "So, I got his name and passport number then asked the Marshals Service back in the States to run a check on him."

"What's he doing over here?"

"That's one of the questions we have. Probably just coincidence he was on the same flight as you. Good thing you gave him the brush-off."

"What a creep. I see that type coming I turn around and run in the opposite direction. Life is too short," she said, then took a sip of wine and just shook her head.

They ate a leisurely meal. Jackie seemed to lighten up a bit after her second glass of wine. Despite her protestations, Dillon picked up the check, then drove her back to the Maldron Hotel. He pulled up in front of the hotel and said, "Let me walk you to your room."

"Oh, thanks, but no, you already got stuck with the dinner bill. You are *so* not walking me to my room."

"It's no big deal, honest."

"Which is exactly why you're not doing it. Listen, thanks for letting me mess up your work schedule. Very nice to meet you. I wish it had been under different circumstances."

"Well, I'll be by in the morning and take you to the airport."

"You don't have to do that. I can see the terminal from here. It'll take me about four minutes to walk there."

"I'm still going to pick you up. Besides, I have to check in with the Custom Agents anyway. You've got an eleven-fifteen flight on Air France to Paris. I'll meet you in the hotel lobby at nine. Okay?"

She paused for a moment, swallowed and gave a little sniffle, then leaned over, gave Dillon a peck on the cheek and hurried out of the car.

He watched her enter the hotel and kept watching her through the glass door until she disappeared from sight. He waited a moment longer before he put the car in drive and headed home.

TWENTY-EIGHT

Lucifer actually seemed pleased to see him at home. Dillon let him out, then coaxed Lucifer back in with a dog biscuit. He read in the sitting room until close to eleven, then climbed into bed and was sound asleep in just under thirty seconds. His phone ringing woke him sometime after four.

"Dillon," he half growled into the phone, then pulled it away from his ear to read the caller ID.

"Sorry to be calling so early. God only knows you can use the beauty sleep," Suel chuckled.

At the sound of Suel's voice, Dillon was wide awake. "What's up?" he asked. He immediately began running through a mental list of all the things that might have happened to Jackie Greco.

"Not really sure, but thought you might be interested. A shooting in the city center, just outside the Odessa Club, on Dame Court. Two individuals, both known to us. Russians. Apparently they were just sitting in the car. Bullet in the back of the head to the driver and two in the face to his passenger."

"So what does that have to do with me?"

"Not really sure. Just taking a long shot here, but it's similar, sort of, to the Touhy murder, and whoever did this left us a calling card."

"A calling card?"

"Ace of Spades, the playing card, left in the driver's mouth."

"Like Touhy?"

"Exactly. Isn't that sort of an American thing?"

"Supposedly, although the little I know about it, it's more fiction than fact. You down there now?" Dillon asked as he climbed out of bed.

"Yeah, I'm standing in Dame Court literally next to the Odessa Club. The tech team is in the process of wrapping up. They're thinking this happened about four hours ago, right around midnight."

"I'll be down there in about thirty minutes."

"I'll be here," Suel said and hung up.

Dillon pulled on a sweater and a pair of black jeans. He glanced over at Lucifer, already curled up on Dillon's pillow and halfway tucked under the blanket, sleeping soundly.

"You've got way more sense than me," Dillon said, then pulled the blanket up over Lucifer's shoulder and headed into the bathroom.

There was a light rain on the way into the city center and Dame Court. With little to no traffic at this early hour, it was a quick drive. Dillon pulled up behind a squad car, just a few feet from the blue and white plastic tape with letters that read "GARDA NO ENTRY." The tape was stretched across the entrance to the area, more a narrow alley or pedestrian walkway than a street. He could see Suel up ahead, talking to a familiar face in a hazmat suit, although Dillon couldn't seem to come up with the individual's name.

Dillon ducked under the plastic tape, and two steps later an officer suddenly stepped out of a darkened doorway. He was wearing a high visibility vest, although Dillon hadn't seen him in the dark and the officer was just pulling his hat on. "Hey, you got trouble reading? You can't be walking through here."

Dillon half jumped with surprise, then pulled out his warrant card along with his badge. "DI Suel's expecting me," he said. He gave a nod in Suel's direction and kept moving.

The officer didn't say anything and stepped back into the darkened doorway.

Suel nodded as Dillon approached and said, "Perfect timing. They just concluded their examination. Ready to take a look?"

Dillon nodded and followed Suel over to a dark blue Mercedes, an S-class 500 coupe. He thought they went for about a hundred and fifty thousand euros, just a little out of his price range. He leaned down and looked in the driver's window. The window was open, and he wondered if it had been raining when the shooting occurred.

The driver's body, with pale skin and blonde hair, long on the top and shaved along the sides, was slumped, leaning over the console. Two things stood out; the bullet hole alongside the victim's right eye and the playing card, the Ace of Spades, inserted in his mouth.

The passenger was held in place by his seatbelt, not that he was going anywhere soon. He wore an expensive-looking black leather jacket. His dark hair appeared to be cut at the same length all over his head, maybe just a quarter of an inch long, with a widow's peak precisely in the middle of his forehead. Two bullet holes, about an inch apart and maybe a half-inch above his right eye, kept him in the seat. His head hung down with his chin resting on his chest. The roof on the inside of the car had blood and bits of skull splattered across it, as did the area behind the passenger seat.

Suel held out two plastic ID cards and read the names off. "Vlad and Marat Volkov, brothers, apparently."

"You know anything about them?"

"I believe they're known to us, associated with Alexei Bazanov and his contingent of ne'er-do-well bollocks."

"How long has it been raining?" Dillon said.

"How long?"

"Yeah, the driver's window is down. I'm wondering if they were sitting out here like this or did someone maybe knock on the window, possibly someone they knew. They lower the window and boom."

"Mmm-mmm. We had an anonymous call come in a little after midnight saying something didn't look right and then hung up. My understanding is a woman, Dublin accent, but can't be sure about that last part. The call is on tape, we can listen later on. It's that damn card in your man's mouth that has me wondering."

"At first glance, it certainly seems similar," Dillon said. "Two people shot in a vehicle. Smaller caliber weapon. And that damn Ace of Spades. But two Russians this time. Could it all be just gangland bullshit? Maybe a slight or some sort of presumed disrespect?"

"So you don't mind my calling you?" Suel said.

"Oh, it was worth it. Plus, you offering to buy me breakfast and all, that's worth it right there."

"I didn't— just where in hell are you expecting to get a breakfast at this hour?"

Dillon glanced over Suel's shoulder. "Looks like the lights are on in the Odessa Club. I think it might be wise to ask some questions and maybe suggest we're hungry at the same time."

Suel laughed, but then headed for the kitchen lights.

TWENTY-NINE

They were seated at a heavy wooden table in the Odessa Club's kitchen. The table looked like it could seat eight comfortably and had a thick butcher block sort of top. A slight dusting of flour was scattered across the table, and there were maybe a dozen loaves of bread baking in a nearby oven.

"They come here, never any trouble. Never any trouble. We a good place. Tourist come from all over. China, France, Japan, Germany, even many Americans come. They all like our food and drinks. You like it, the breakfast? Is good, no?"

Dillon swallowed the mouthful of smoked salmon eggs Benedict, nodded and said, "Mmm-mmm, yes, it's delicious."

Suel nodded in agreement and continued chewing.

The Russian woman they'd been talking with for the past half hour, Yana Litvin, smiled and took another sip from her coffee mug. Dillon guessed her age at around fifty. She was slight, with thin, pale lips and dark brown eyes. Her hair had been dyed a sort of auburn some time back based on the half-inch worth of dark roots showing. As they spoke, she extinguished a cigarette, her second, in a glass ashtray. She'd insisted on serving them break-fast. From the size of the platters they'd been working through, Dillon guessed they might be eating a double order, not that he was about to complain.

"Mmm-mmm, but you did know them, the Volkov brothers, correct?" Suel said, then shoved another fork-ful of garlic roast potatoes into his mouth.

"I know them only as the customer. They always seem very nice. Never a problem. Always behave," she said.

"Alexei Bazanov. You know him, too?" Dillon asked.

"I know him only through the newspaper. What it is I read or hear on news. If he come in here, I not know who he is. He here, I never know."

He might have been a criminal, but Alexei Bazanov was well known, very well known in the Russian com-munity. Dillon had his doubts about Yana Litvin not be-ing able to recognize Bazanov if he should walk in the front door, but there wasn't much he could do about it. As long as she was going to lie to them, it was nice to be able to listen to it over a meal of smoked salmon eggs Benedict. He believed her when she said she knew noth-ing about the double murder outside her place, obviously not the best advertisement for future business. And it seemed to make perfect sense that she was unaware of anything having happened until the Garda arrived in re-sponse to the anonymous phone call.

"Yana, thank you so much for taking the time to chat with us," Suel said. He dabbed across his mouth with a linen napkin, then picked up the last crumb of English muffin with his fork and placed it in his mouth. "Should you hear anything," he said, then handed her his business card.

"But of course," she said, taking Suel's card then rising from her chair, suggesting by her movement that it was time for them to leave.

Dillon and Suel both stood, said thanks once again, then headed out the kitchen door. Two gurneys were alongside the Mercedes with their passengers resting in black body bags zipped closed and tightly strapped onto the gurneys. A tow truck was in the process of backing down the lane toward the Mercedes. It would haul the vehicle back to the Serious Crime Investigation garage, where a more thorough investigation would be undertaken.

"What do you think?" Dillon asked as they walked back toward the Mercedes.

"I'm thinking that had to be some of the best eggs Benedict I've ever had," Suel said.

"I meant about this nonsense," Dillon said and indicated the Mercedes.

"Not quite sure what to make of it. The playing card doesn't bother you?"

"The Ace of Spades? Something's not right, that seems to put a whole new element into the investigation. Some kind of connection to the Touhy murder, unless it was just there to throw us off track. Which reminds me, I'd better head over to the Maldron. I told Jackie Greco I'd escort her over to the terminal."

"Oh?" Suel said and smiled.

"Hey, give me some credit here. She's a nice lady and all, but she's got a lot on her plate at the moment. Besides, I want to check the tapes on our friend Richie Nolan going through customs."

"You got a line on him?"

"Not the sort of individual you want visiting for any length of time. Let me look at those tapes, put some other information together, and I'll touch base with you when I'm leaving the airport."

Dillon left Suel ready to chat with the tow truck driver and headed out to the airport and the Maldron Hotel.

THIRTY

Yana Litvin smoked her cigarette just outside the kitchen door and watched as Dillon walked back to his vehicle. Suel appeared to be engaged in a friendly conversation with the tow truck driver, the two of them laughing and exchanging jibes, unaware she was even out there. She took a long drag from her cigarette, exhaled a moment later, blowing the smoke up into the air. She pulled out her cellphone, hit her contact list, then the number and put the phone to her ear. She stood there in the dark, listening to the phone ring, her left arm wrapped across her chest, the phone pressed against her ear in her right hand.

A groggy voice answered just before her call dropped into voicemail.

"Yes," he said in Russian.

"Alexei. It's Yana, at Odessa. Two Gardaí were just here, asking about a shooting."

"Who was shooting?" Alexei Bazanov asked, still sounding groggy. He followed up by clearing his throat a couple of times.

"I don't know who was shooting, and I don't think they knew either. But the dead, it's the Volkov brothers."

Bazanov was suddenly wide awake. He sat up in bed, and half-shouted, "The Volkov brothers? Vlad and Marat?" The young woman next to him rolled over on her side and pulled the bed covers up over her shoulder

"Yes, the twins."

"How are they?"

"Were you listening? I just told you. They're both dead. They were shot just outside my club, both of them sitting in their car."

"Dead?"

"Yes, both of them."

"Tell me they arrested someone. Tell me they have the shooter."

"No, nothing, at least as far as I know. All they have is the car and the two bodies. The Gardaí were here for at least an hour, asking me all sorts of questions." She neglected to mention she bought them breakfast.

"And what did you tell them?"

"I told them the truth, Alexei. I know nothing. The brothers were here. I buy them a vodka like always, they leave, end of story. I didn't know they were killed. I didn't know there was a shooting. No one here knew."

"Where are they now?"

"The Gardaí One is still here, he's—"

"I don't care about them, stupid bitch. The boys, Vlad and Marat. Where are they now?"

"Outside in body bags strapped to gurneys. It looks like they'll be taking them away shortly. A tow truck is in the process of loading their Mercedes. I would guess in thirty minutes there will be nothing to see here."

"Do you know the names of the Gardaí?"

"One of them gave me his business card."

"Keep it. I'll have someone get it from you later this morning. Keep your ear to the ground, and see what you can learn. Someone must know something down there."

"I'll call you if I hear anything."

"Thank you, Yana. I'm sorry for my outburst a moment ago. This is just such a shock. They were loyal, good men, and to lose them like this—"

"You will make this right, Alexei. We all have faith in you."

"Call if you hear anything. I'd better go, there is suddenly a lot on my plate," he said and hung up.

Yana watched as the Mercedes was pulled up onto the bed of the tow truck, then stepped back into the kitchen.

Alexei Bazanov sat in bed for a long moment, thinking. He looked over at the woman lying next to him. She had the bed covers pulled up over her shoulders, covering half her face as she snored softly. He searched his brain for a moment, trying to remember her name, but couldn't, then decided it didn't matter anyway. He slipped down beneath the covers and hoped he could get back to sleep.

THIRTY-ONE

It was rush hour now, or the beginning of rush hour, and it took Dillon nearly twenty-five minutes before he pulled up in front of the Maldron. He opened the glove compartment and pulled his piece of paper with the An Garda Síochána logo in blue and the large black letters, all capitals, **"OFFICIAL BUSINESS!"** and placed it on the dashboard. He climbed out, pushed the button on his key to lock the doors, then headed into the hotel lobby.

He looked around the lobby, didn't see Jackie Greco, and sent her a text message.

"In the hotel lobby. No rush."

She replied almost immediately.

"On my way."

She was down in the lobby three minutes later wearing jeans, tennis shoes, and a loose-fitting sweater.

"Were you waiting long? I got your text just as I was heading for the elevator," Jackie said.

"No, I literally just arrived. Do you have to check out?"

"Already did. Amazingly, as tired as I was, I woke up just a little after four this morning. Wide awake, if you can believe it."

"Yeah, welcome to jet lag."

"Hoping I'll be able to dial into some boring movie and fall asleep on the flight back to Boston."

"Well, let's get you checked in. Come on. I'm parked right out front," Dillon said, then picked up her suitcase and headed for the door. He drove over to terminal two, no more than a four-minute drive even after waiting for a stoplight. He pulled up at the far end of the terminal building, left his An Garda Síochána with **"OFFICIAL BUSINESS!"** on the dashboard, and climbed out of the car.

"You don't have to walk me in. I can make it from here. You've been more than kind," Jackie said.

"It's my pleasure. You have a safe flight back, and I wish we'd met under better circumstances," Dillon said, then pulled her suitcase out of the car.

"You know, I was thinking about it after you dropped me off last night. God, I'm going to miss her, but to tell you the truth, Gerri and I, we have just been growing apart more and more over the last twenty-four months. She knew how I felt about what she was doing, and in the end, as much as I love her, she didn't care what I thought. It didn't matter. And, this, this whole fiasco has just been the unfortunate logical conclusion. That poor baby she was carrying wasn't going to have a snowball's chance in hell. God, but it didn't have to happen this way," she said, then shook her head, took her suitcase from Dillon, and headed into the terminal.

He stood in line with her while she waited to check-in and print her boarding pass, then rode the escalator with her up to the second floor and walked her to the security gate. She turned to face him, held out her hand, and he shook it.

"Thanks again," she said.

"Yeah, my pleasure. You take care of yourself, and here," he said, pulling a business card out of his pocket. "Any problems give me a call, I'd be happy to help."

She looked at the card for a moment, shoved it into a back pocket, then went up on her tiptoes, gave him a quick peck on the cheek, and hurried off toward the first of a number of security stations.

THIRTY-TWO

Dillon watched Jackie Greco begin to make her way through airport security before he headed to the Border Management office. There was a security desk at the entrance to the office with a woman in a blue Gardaí uniform sitting behind the desk. She was furiously tapping keys on her computer keyboard as Dillon approached.

"Hi, sorry to bother you," Dillon said, then watched as she half-jumped out of her chair.

"Oh, lord," she laughed. "You scared the bejaysus out of me."

"I'm here to see Poraig Sullivan. He's expecting me."

"Certainly. Your name, sir?"

"Dillon, Marshal Jack Dillon."

"One moment, please," she said, then picked up the phone and punched three different keys. She flashed another smile in Dillon's direction, then focused on her computer screen for a moment, hitting a couple of keys on the keyboard. "Oh, hi, Sonja, it's Michelle. I've got a Mr. Marshal Jack Dillon out here to see Poraig, said he's expecting him. Yes. Yes, okay, I'll let him know.

Thanks," she said and hung up. "They'll send someone out in just a minute," she said and returned to attacking her keyboard.

A moment later, the door behind her opened up, and a guy in a short-sleeve white shirt with a loosened tie stepped out. "Marshal Dillon?"

Dillon nodded and said, "Thanks, Michelle," as he walked around the desk toward the open door. He recognized the fellow holding the door as one of the guys who was viewing the monitors yesterday when Jackie Greco had arrived, but they'd never been introduced.

"Thanks for coming to get me, Jack Dillon," Dillon said extending his hand.

The guy gave him a weak handshake, nodded, and said, "Yeah, I remember you from yesterday." He turned and led the way down a hall to the room with the monitors without ever giving Dillon his name. As they entered the room, he said, "He's right in there," and sort of indicated Sullivan's office with a flick of his wrist before he headed toward an empty chair in front of the monitors. Dillon stepped over to Sullivan's office and knocked on the door frame.

Sullivan was seated behind his desk with his back facing the door. As Dillon knocked, he turned around and said, "Oh, I've got someone coming in the office, honey. I'll call you later. Yeah, you too, love you."

"Poraig, hope I wasn't interrupting," Dillon said.

"Not at all. Thanks for saving me. The wife is lobbying for new kitchen cabinets, and I'm slowly but surely losing the battle. What can I do for you?"

"I'd like to view the tape from yesterday morning, Richard Nolan. You were going to set it aside for me."

"Yeah, we've got it sitting in the cloud. You can view it on one of the screens out there. Come on, let me get you set up." With that, Sullivan stepped out from behind his desk and led Dillon back out to the monitor room. There were two empty desks against a far wall. Sullivan pulled a chair out from one of the desks and sat down, clicked a couple of keys on a keyboard, and the screen sprang to life. "You said the surname was Nolan, right?"

"Yeah, Richard Nolan."

Sullivan clicked the mouse a couple of times and said, "Yeah, here's the file. You should be all set. Take this seat," he said, standing up and indicating the chair he'd just been sitting in.

The image on the screen was Nolan in his Boston Red Sox jacket standing in front of the officer checking his passport. Dillon clicked on the image, and the tape, a mere minute and twelve seconds long, began to roll.

"Hi," Nolan said and handed his passport across the counter to the officer.

The officer seemed to nod, then took the passport and began to quickly page through the document.

"The speed he's turning pages is an indication they're blank," Sullivan said.

"Are you here on business?" the officer said.

"No, just here to see the sights. I'm Irish," Nolan said.

"Irish?" the officer said, looking up at him.

"Yeah. You read that thing?" the guy said, pointing to his passport. "My last name's Nolan. That's Irish, ain't it?"

"You were born in the States?"

"Yeah, Boston. I'm a southie."

"And how long do you plan on staying in Ireland?"

"I got a flight back in five days. I got me tickets to a Celtics game. I ain't gonna miss that."

The officer smiled and nodded. Dillon guessed he had no real frame of reference regarding American basketball. He stamped the passport and handed it back to Nolan. "Enjoy your stay."

"I will," Nolan said and hurried away.

Dillon replayed the tape a half dozen times then clicked the mouse on a box off to the side that was labeled "image." It immediately brought up a frontal and two side shots of Nolan's face. The teardrop tattoo was apparent in two of the three images. He studied the images for a few minutes, then closed down the computer and walked back to Sullivan's office.

"Learn anything?" Sullivan asked.

"Maybe a little, nothing that really stands out. You might want to keep that file close at hand. I just have a feeling."

"No offense, but hopefully you're wrong," Sullivan said.

"Yeah, I hope so too."

THIRTY-THREE

Back in the office, Dillon dutifully cleared the two tea mugs, a plate with pastry crumbs, and four plastic half-ounce cream containers from his desk. He sent an email to Pat Matthews back in New York looking for confirmation on Richie Nolan's return flight, four days from now, as well as a heads up on Jackie Greco's return flight to Boston. He also asked Matthews to confirm who owned the building Gerri Greco lived in, and finally, he asked again for any and all information on Richie Nolan and followed up with, *"I owe you big time on this Pat. Thanks."*

He phoned Brian McFadden at the Dublin City Mortuary and ended up leaving a message. "Brian, Jack Dillon here. I'd like you to do a paternity test on the fetus Gerri Greco was carrying. It would appear Joey Touhy may be the father, but I'd like to confirm that. Call me with any problems," he said, then hung up.

He saw Suel walk in the office and waved him over.

"Please tell me you got something on our victims," Suel said.

"Not really, although it's come to light that Richie Nolan, that jerk from the airport yesterday . . . ."

"The plonker with the teardrop tattoo?"

"Yeah, that's the guy. Turns out, he lives in the same building as the female victim, Gerri Greco. And get this, Joey Touhy supposedly owns the building."

"Small world, isn't it? I'm not much of a fan of co-incidences," Suel said.

"Me either. I just sent off a request to get that infor-mation confirmed. I keep thinking, what if Nolan is over here to even the score on Touhy's murder?"

"Even the score with who?" Suel said. "Eamon Boyle? Alexei Bazanov? Why would Bazanov care or even know about Touhy being over here? And, maybe the more logical question would be, what could Touhy's murder possibly get Bazanov? Well, other than a major headache."

Dillon's cellphone rang. He glanced at the caller ID, then looked at Suel and said, "Pat Matthews calling from New York. Maybe we're about to find out." He swiped his finger across the phone screen, then said, "Pat, thanks for calling."

"Yeah, Jack, great to hear your voice. I just wanted to see how things are going on your vacation."

"Vacation? Believe me, right now, it's anything but a vacation. Say, we had a murder over here two days ago, a couple of Americans."

"Yeah, Joey Touhy out of Boston, and forgive me, but I'm having a senior moment, and I'm blanking on the woman's name."

"Greco, Gerri Greco, also from Boston."

"Yeah, right."

"Greco's sister flew in here yesterday morning. She's on a flight heading back to Boston this morning. Another guy from Boston, name of Richard 'Richie' Nolan, arrived on the same flight. At present, I believe that to be a coincidence. But he's apparently living in the same upscale building as the female victim, Gerri Greco, and now it appears Joey Touhy owned the building. I'd like to get that information confirmed and then get anything you can find on this Nolan character."

"Nolan. I sent you his picture, didn't I?"

"Yeah, along with his address. Greco's sister actually pointed it out that it was the same address as the murder victim. We had another homicide over here last night, this time two Russians. It just all seems a little too coincidental. Anything you can get would be a help."

"I should be able to have that coming your way in the next thirty minutes. I just sent off a request to confirm Nolan's return flight. Soon as that comes across, I'll send it to you. In the meantime, let me go through a couple of databases and get information coming your way."

"Thanks Pat. Much appreciated."

"Not a problem. Thanks in advance for that bottle of Red Breast you're sending me."

Dillon laughed, then said, "Let me see what I can do on that."

THIRTY-FOUR

I nformation on Richie Nolan began to come in about forty minutes later. His career began early. As a ten-year-old juvenile delinquent, he was arrested for shoplifting an autographed baseball, signed by the Red Sox, naturally. From there, things grew a little more complicated, assaults in eighth, ninth, and tenth grade. At the age of sixteen, he was sent to Plymouth County Correction Facility, a maximum-security facility that also houses juveniles convicted of adult crimes.

Released at age eighteen, over the next ten years, Nolan was charged five separate times with crimes ranging from assault to murder but never convicted. In fact, the cases never made it to court. In three instances, the victims recanted their testimony, and in two instances, the victims disappeared. He was suspected but never charged, in five murders. He has a scar from a bullet wound on his left shoulder, and he's allergic to shrimp. He drives a 2017 Mercedes-Benz S-Class, the price starts at ninety-six thousand dollars and goes up from there.

Interestingly enough, he is employed by an independently owned coffee shop in Boston. His job is listed as delivering coffee.

Dillon called Suel over to his desk. Suel gave him a nod, then pointed to the cellphone up against his ear. Five minutes later, he was at Dillon's desk.

"Something? Anything?" Suel asked.

"Nothing concrete, but the information I'm receiving makes this Richie Nolan individual a lot more interesting than just some wiseass at the airport." Dillon went on to give Suel the details. A criminal record stretching back thirty years, a hundred-thousand-dollar car, no apparent income, a million-dollar condo in a building owned by Joey Touhy—the same building where Gerri Greco, the other victim shot at the same time as Touhy lived.

"But nothing we can arrest him for," Suel said.

"Not yet," Dillon said. "I think it would be worth it to keep an eye on him. I think he's staying at This Little Piggy, that dive pub over in Finglas. Might be worth a trip over there to pay him a visit."

"That would also alert him to the fact that we're watching him." Suel's cellphone rang. He glanced at the number, frowned, then answered it. "Yeah, Jerry. Really? When? Christ on a cross, we're on our way," he said and hung up.

"You don't look pleased," Dillon said.

"Another shooting. This time outside the Botanic Road Post Office."

"What's that got to do—"

"An Ace of Spades playing card was shoved into your man's mouth."

"Damn it."

THIRTY-FIVE

Traffic appeared to be backed up for blocks as Suel inched the car along Botanic Road. For the past five minutes, they'd been making absolutely no progress, sitting in front of the Sunny Bank Hotel, a derelict structure. They could see flashing lights on squad cars up ahead and two Garda officers directing traffic. On a good day, the intersection was five lanes of traffic merging into three. Today it was five lanes attempting to merge into one lane. It didn't seem to be working.

"Oh, for God's sake," Suel said, then pulled up onto the sidewalk, drove another hundred feet, and parked. "This is as good as it's going to get."

They climbed out of the car and headed toward the flashing lights. They crossed the intersection, past a bus driver and a frustrated guy driving a lorry, both of whom were on their cellphones. Technically, using a cellphone while behind the wheel was against the law in Ireland, but since they hadn't moved in the last five minutes and probably wouldn't in the next five, it didn't really appear to be much of a violation.

"How's it going, Brian?" Suel called to one of the officers attempting to direct traffic.

"Just peachy, Detective. People just keep signaling I'm number one," he laughed, then flashed his middle finger at Suel.

"They obviously know all about you," Suel said.

They walked past the Botanic House, a charming two-story pub that Dillon had never been in, but only because it had been under reconstruction for the past two years.

The Botanic Road Post Office was at the opposite end of the short block from the pub. It was one of four storefronts set in a three-story brick building dating back to about 1915. The front of the post office, like all Irish post offices, was painted green. Two squad cars were parked behind a black SUV. Dillon guessed the victim was in the SUV. Two more squad cars were parked alongside the SUV, effectively blocking the lane and leaving only one lane open.

He found it interesting that the SUV had parked on the street, just stopped in a traffic lane. The normal Dublin action would have been to pull onto the sidewalk so that other vehicles could get around, but apparently, people getting around hadn't been a concern with this particular driver.

He recognized two of the uniformed officers standing in front of the post office and remembered one of their names, Mick something. The other man looked familiar, they'd probably been introduced, but he couldn't recall a name. Someone in a white hazmat suit was in the process of leaning into the vehicle and placing an item in an evidence bag.

"Help me with names, here. I'm blanking on the guy with the mustache," Dillon said as they approached.

"Mick, Andy, good to see you. Andy, the ladies haven't given up on the mustache yet?" Suel said.

Both of them laughed. They were in the standard blue Gardaí uniforms, wearing high visibility vests. Mick had sergeant stripes on his sleeve and a ruddy complexion. Andy, with the dark mustache, looked like something out of a Victorian photograph.

"Good to see you again, Jack Dillon," Dillon said, and extended his hand, nodding at them as they both shook it.

Ruddy-faced Mick looked at Dillon and said, "Sorry to disappoint, but your man's not American, he's a Russian."

"How do you know that?" Suel asked.

"Wallet is sitting in his lap, some sort of a Russian ID card, and then the tattoos on the back of his hand. Got an image of the devil and a number of crosses. I think each cross stands for a conviction. Pretty safe guess your man would not have made the best neighbor. I'm thinking if you look beneath that t-shirt, you'll find an awful lot of ink."

"What do you know about it, the shooting?" Suel asked, then turned and watched the man in the hazmat suit for a moment before he turned back to Mick.

Dillon looked over at the victim. He was sitting in the driver's seat with his body leaning toward the console. He wore a black t-shirt and appeared to be fairly muscular. He sported a large bicep on the one tattooed arm Dillon could see and had well defined pectoral muscles on his chest. He had a thick neck and muscular shoulders.

"No witnesses to the actual incident," Mick said. "Although there were five people waiting in line in the post office. Apparently, no sound of shots being fired even though they were, what? Maybe ten, fifteen feet away? And no one appears to have been with your man." Mick nodded toward the SUV. "So he either decided to simply stop and block traffic or if there was someone with him, they just calmly walked away. Find anything, Tony?" he called to the guy in the hazmat suit.

"Coming up empty, Mick."

"There you have it. No letter or package to be mailed. I don't know what he was doing here."

"Maybe just buying stamps. Is there a security camera in the post office?" Suel asked.

"There is, but it's pointed toward the counter, so you'll see people conducting their business and leaving, but no recording of someone getting out of that vehicle and going in."

There was a beauty parlor next door on the corner of the building, but it was closed. The metal grill covering the entrance and the window was pulled down and secured with a padlock. An insurance office was on the other side of the post office, and next to that, on the far corner, an empty space with "For Rent" signs in both windows.

"You talk to any of the tenants upstairs?"

"Tried," Mick said. "But no answer on any of the doors. There's four units up there. I'm guessing they're all at work."

Suel shot a look at Dillon and gave a slight shake of his head. "Not a hell of a lot to go on right out of the chute."

The guy in the hazmat suit walked around the SUV, gathered up four or five evidence bags, and walked over to one of the squad cars with the flashing lights. He opened the trunk, placed the bags inside, then closed the lid, and headed towards Suel and Dillon.

"Tony," Suel said. "DI Suel, we've met before. This is Jack Dillon," Suel said, as he shook hands.

Tony shook Dillon's hand, then looked at Suel. "Who'd you piss off to grab this one?"

"Questions?" Suel said.

"Nothing but. Two rounds, one to the chest, another to the head. Close range. There's stippling around the wounds, burns on your man's t-shirt. Smaller caliber, my educated guess would be a .32, but the exit wounds suggest hollow point rounds. It looks like he was on his cellphone. A round went through the cell and took out a chunk on the other side. Death pretty much instantaneous."

Suel nodded and said, "Can we take a look?"

"Give me a couple of minutes to take some more photos, and it's all yours."

"Thanks, Tony. In the meantime, maybe we'll check in with your man at the postal counter. I have to mail a letter anyway," Suel said.

THIRTY-SIX

The post office consisted of one small room with a counter and two pens chained to holders. A service counter with a thick pane of foggy glass was built into the wall directly ahead. A poster announcing the calendar year dates the post office would be closed covered almost half of the window. The room was empty, and no one was sitting behind the service counter. There was a small chrome bell with a button on the top and a sign that read "Ring for Service."

Suel rang the bell three or four times. A stooped, older gentleman shuffled out from behind a file cabinet a moment later.

"We're closed," he growled. "Not sure how you managed to get past the Gardaí out there, but we're closed for the rest of the day."

Suel flashed an insincere smile along with his badge.

"Ummm, figures," the man said, looking unimpressed.

"Your name, sir."

"Postmaster Thomas Fitzgerald," he answered, then took a seat behind the glass in a worn desk chair.

"What can you tell us about the incident this morning, Mr. Fitzgerald?"

"Your man being murdered? Not a bloody thing. I wasn't even aware of him parked out there. I don't know who informed the Gardaí. All I know is the call didn't come from here. No one said anything, nothing. I can't even tell you how long that car was sitting out there before you lot showed up."

"Did you see anything suspicious?" Suel said.

"Suspicious? Were you just listening to what I said? No, nothing of the sort, well, other than the stupid things people do on a regular basis whenever they come in here— looking in purses for exact change. asking for a length of tape to seal an envelope. You wouldn't believe the things I'm expected to do. As I told you before, I didn't see anything, which means I didn't see anything. Not sure how much more specific I can be."

Suel's face seemed to grow a bit more red. As he spoke, he used a much softer tone, which Dillon knew from past experience meant he was in the process of attempting to check his temper. "I'd like to look at your security tape, please."

"It won't show you a thing. It doesn't cover outside."

Suel flashed a quick smile. "Maybe let us take a look, and we'll be able to determine if it was worth the effort. "

"Suit yourself," Fitzgerald said, with an audible sigh, and shook his head. He seemed to ponder his next move, then slid out of the chair and groaned as he hobbled around the grey file cabinet. A moment later, a lock snapped and a door with a poster from the previous year reminding people to mail early during the Christmas holidays opened. "You can step back here and have a look for yourself," Fitzgerald said and muttered something unintelligible.

"Thank you," Suel said politely, although he wore a look on his face that suggested violent action. They stepped into a small anteroom where every flat surface was covered with files and what appeared to be unopened pieces of mail. The air was stuffy, and as Postmaster Fitzgerald passed by, it had clearly been a number of days since he'd showered.

"Mind the mess. You can have a seat there. I think the keyboard is underneath this pile of nonsense," Fitzgerald said, then lifted a stack of files and official-looking envelopes off the desk and set them on a chair next to the desk. A pile of what looked like grocery store receipts and adding machine tape remained on the desk, and he carefully picked them up, more or less arranged them in some sort of order, then laid them on top of the files he'd just moved.

A keyboard and a mouse remained on the desk. Fitzgerald reached around to the back of the computer screen and pressed a button. A moment later, an orchestral sort of tone rang out, and the computer sprang to life.

"You have a password?" Suel asked.

"I can't be bothered."

Suel shot Dillon a look but didn't say anything. Eventually, a single icon appeared in the center of the screen labeled "View." Suel clicked on the icon, and the screen showed an image of the front counter.

"I'll leave you to it," Fitzgerald said and shuffled out of the anteroom. A moment later, an image of the interior appeared on the screen. Suel clicked on a blue bar running along the base of the screen and began to reverse the tape back two hours. He stopped at the image of a line of four people waiting behind an elderly woman at the counter.

"That's not our man," he said, indicating the second person in line. "But I'll lay you odds he was with him. The t-shirt, the tattoos, I mean, look at him. Now, if only the plonker would turn around."

The individual was muscular, dressed in a black t-shirt and jeans. His head was shaved, and his arms, neck, and the back of his head were heavily tattooed. When he stepped up to the window, he placed two envelopes on the counter, along with a five-euro note, said something to Fitzgerald, and waited.

A moment later, Fitzgerald tossed two stamps on top of the envelope and then some change. Suel stopped the screen.

"Mr. Fitzgerald, a moment of your time, please," Suel said.

They heard a groan coming from the area where they'd originally spoken to Fitzgerald, and a moment later, he appeared. "Now what is it?"

Suel backed the tape up a few seconds. "What can you tell me about this man?"

"Damn foreigner," Fitzgerald groaned. Suel ran the tape, and Fitzgerald watched as the man attached a stamp to each envelope. He said something to Fitzgerald, who immediately shook his head with a disgusted look on his face, then handed the man a small piece of tape, no more than an inch long.

"There, see it? See? Completely unprepared. Can't seal the bloody envelope, and now I'm supposed to fix the problem for the likes of him."

Suel paused the tape.

"He asked for a piece of tape?" Dillon said, not quite comprehending what the problem was.

"Exactly. Meanwhile, all the customers have to wait because this knacker can't get his act together. I tell you, the things I have to deal with on any given day."

Suel started the tape up, and they watched as the man slid both envelopes under the glass.

"I don't know, Russian, maybe Polish," Fitzgerald said, just as the man turned to walk out the door.

"Mother of Jesus, will you look at that," Suel said, as he paused the tape, then zeroed in and enlarged the tattooed face until it filled the screen. Two squiggly designs, maybe an inch wide, ran from the top of his forehead down to his chin over both eyes, blue, red, and green. "Your man has to be insane. He looks like a bleeding clown," Suel said, then sat and stared for a long moment.

"You know his name?" Dillon asked.

Fitzgerald shook his head, then said, "He was a man of few words. Heavy accent. I believe there's a return address on the envelopes he posted."

"Can you get them for us, the envelopes," Suel said, studying the tattooed face.

"Afraid not, it's against the law. Post Department policy. Once we've taken possession—"

"Oh, is it? Ahh, sure now, that makes sense. I tell you what, Mr. Fitzgerald. Why don't you come with us then, we'll hold you for the day, maybe overnight, and then when we get a warrant we'll bring you back, and you can hand the envelopes over to us at that time."

"Hold me? Overnight?"

"I'm sure I don't have to tell the likes of you, the difficulties of getting paperwork through a government organization. The levels, the bureaucracy, it's enough to make a grown man cry. But best get a move on, sooner we get started, the sooner we can get back." Suel stood, took hold of Fitzgerald's arm and said, "I don't think we'll need to handcuff you, leastwise not until we're down at the station. All for your own protection, never know who you'll end up with in a holding cell. Why I remember one time this big lad. Size of a house, he was, and—"

"If I got those envelopes for you, could you maybe keep it under your hat? You know, not report me or anything."

Suel looked at Dillon and said, "What do you think, Marshal? Bit of a desperate time. I'm certainly willing to hold my tongue."

Dillon nodded, and said, "Mum's the word here Detective."

Fitzgerald seemed to breathe a sigh of relief. "I'll have those for you in just a moment," he said and hurried around the corner.

Suel shook his head, then saved the image of the tattooed face and sent himself an email.

Fitzgerald was back around the corner with the two envelopes a moment later, one pink and the other gold. He placed them on the desk next to the keyboard. The return address was legible, but the name on both envelopes was written in Cyrillic characters.

"Thank you, sir," Suel said and stood. He pulled on a pair of latex gloves and picked up the envelopes. "We'll get these back to you just as soon as possible.

"But . . . ." Fitzgerald started to say something, then apparently thought better of it and just nodded.

"It's been a pleasure," Suel said and headed for the door.

"Thanks," Dillon said and followed Suel out of the post office.

THIRTY-SEVEN

Once outside on the sidewalk, Suel shook his head. "There's your textbook example of why people refer to government jobs as being in a no-fire zone. No matter how awful you are, you've still got the job. It's been a long time since that bastard smiled or brought one to someone's face."

Tony, in the hazmat suit, climbed out of his car and walked toward Suel. "Just put the third call into the medical examiner. The knackers should have been here two hours ago. You're free to go ahead and have a look at your man. Might be best to do it now, soon as they get here with the body bag, they'll no doubt be in a bloody hurry."

"Thanks, Tony," Suel said. "You can start, Dillon. I'm just going to put these envelopes in an evidence bag, and then I'll join you."

Dillon stepped over to the SUV and casually glanced down the street. Cars were backed up along Botanic Road for as far as he could see. He noticed that the driver's side window on the SUV was down, although it was a nice sunny day, and so that didn't seem strange. He checked the dashboard, and the air settings were turned to the coldest possible. The SUV had no air conditioning, which wasn't unusual for Ireland.

The body was leaning across the driver's seat, over the console, held in place by the seatbelt. Another Ace of Spades playing card was stuffed in his mouth. Dillon pulled it out and examined the card. If memory served, it matched the cards left in Joey Touhy's mouth and at the Odessa Club, black spade in the middle of the card with a human skull. A small banner just below that read "Ace of Spades."

There was a small wound alongside and just above the right eye and another in the t-shirt on the left side of the chest. What looked like a bit of grey plastic was embedded in the head wound, which Dillon figured was from the cellphone. The stippling from the pistol fired at close range stopped in a straight line along the side of the head, suggesting the cellphone was up against the ear. The black t-shirt was soaked in blood.

The back of the driver's seat, the headrest as well as the side of the passenger seat, and the ceiling were sprayed with blood, bits of skull, and brain matter. A number of flies were buzzing around the interior of the car. The brown leather wallet lay open on the victim's lap and displayed a picture ID with Cyrillic writing. Dillon reached a gloved hand through the open window and picked up the wallet.

He counted the cash in the back of the wallet, three hundred and ten euros, along with a condom in a foil wrapper, an Ulster bank credit card, and a picture of a blonde girl, who looked to be maybe seventeen or eighteen.

"Anything?" Suel asked from behind.

Dillon turned and handed him the wallet. "Three hundred plus in cash so it doesn't appear robbery was a motive. If memory serves that's the same Ace of Spades in the mouth. " He walked around to the passenger door, made a mental note that the window was up, and the door was unlocked. He opened the door and then opened the glove compartment. He pulled out an owner's manual for the SUV, two more condoms, a plastic container of breath mints, and a pistol.

"Here we go," Dillon said, holding the small pistol between his thumb and index finger. "A Makarov." The pistol was black, with dark brown bakelite handgrips. He pressed a small button at the bottom of the handgrip. The magazine released and dropped onto the passenger seat.

"It was loaded," Dillon said, examining the rounds in the magazine. "This guy just never had the chance to get to it."

Suel opened the driver's door, reached across the body, and undid the seat belt. He tilted the body forward and looked at the lump beneath the t-shirt, just at the small of the victim's back, at the beltline. "Looks like your man was armed as well," he said and hiked up the back of the t-shirt.

A holstered pistol was wedged in the belt.

"Surprise, surprise," Dillon said. "What do you think the odds are this guy knew the two victims shot outside the Odessa Club last night?"

Suel shook his head and said, "About one hundred percent."

THIRTY-EIGHT

lexei Bazanov nodded at the puffy-eyed tattooed face sitting across from him on the couch and pulled the vodka bottle from the ice bucket. They were seated on the red velvet couch in his office. Alexei was wearing a dark-blue silk robe with a monogram over his left breast, the same monogram as on his dark-blue velvet slippers. He refilled the glass in Pyotr's outstretched hand.

"You were just mailing a letter, Pyotr?" he said in Russian as he refilled the glass, then placed the bottle back in the bucket.

"Yes, sir. Two cards, one to my mother and another to my sister. They share the same birthday."

"And Nikita Kirden, he remained in the car?"

"He didn't want to go in. He was talking to a woman on the phone."

"Do you know who the woman was?"

Pyotr shook his head no, then took a healthy sip of vodka. "He said he met her the other night. He had called her earlier, wanted to ask her out, but she didn't answer, and he had to leave a message. She phoned him just as he pulled in front of the post office, and he signaled me to go in. I had to wait for an old woman in front of me, mailing a package and another one wanting to check the balance in a pension account. They seemed to take forever. I was waiting in line for a good five minutes. I came back out of the post office and—" Pyotr's voice seemed to fade, and he quickly downed the remainder of the vodka.

"And he had been shot," Alexei said.

Pyotr nodded. "I didn't hear the shot. No one heard it. I looked around but didn't see anyone. It's a busy street, lots of traffic. There was no one on the sidewalk, no one sitting in a car, nothing."

"And you were armed?"

"Always. Sergei took the weapon from me before I entered your office."

Alexei glanced over at the large, bearded man leaning against the desk with his arms crossed. He looked to be close to fifty, but in reality, he was sixty-five. Solid, muscular, with cold blue eyes. He nodded solemnly at Alexei but didn't say anything.

"And Nikita was armed?"

"Yes," Pyotr said and looked longingly at his empty glass. "We always tease him. He takes his gun to bed with him, even when he's with a woman." He coughed and sniffled, then glanced at his glass again.

"Had you told anyone where you were going?" Alexei asked, then reached for the bottle and refilled the glass Pyotr held in his outstretched hand.

"No, sir. In fact, I'd meant to mail the cards for the last two days, but I forgot. It was only when we came around the corner that I saw the post office and told Nikita to stop. He pulled over, cut someone off who began to honk until they saw me get out of the car. They hurried off once they got a look at me."

Alexei nodded at the hideously tattooed face, thinking someone hurrying away made perfect sense.

"And so you took a taxi here?"

"No, sir, I had the taxi drop me off two blocks away, then walked here. I didn't want to bring attention to you."

"Smart. Very smart of you. Thank you for letting me know of this, this incident," Alexei said. He could feel his temper beginning to get the best of him, and he took a deep breath. "Go home and stay there. When we find out who is responsible, you will be given the opportunity to avenge Nikita. In the meantime, do not mention this to anyone. Is that clear?"

Pyotr nodded, downed his vodka, looked longingly at the bottle in the ice bucket for a brief moment, then set his empty glass on the end table and stood.

Alexei held up a finger and reminded, "You are not to tell a soul."

"I swear on my grave," Pyotr said and held up his right hand.

"Yes, you are," Alexei said.

Sergei stood from the desk and led the young man out of the office. Alexei rose and watched as they left the room, then walked behind his desk. He listened as their footsteps faded down the massive hallway. He heard the front door open and, after a few seconds, close. Sergei stepped back into the office a moment later and closed the door behind him.

"What do you think?"

Sergei shrugged. "Three of our men, in less than twelve hours. Who is doing this, and why?"

"And we have no knowledge of who killed this American guest of Boyle's?"

"No, but I wouldn't be surprised if he blamed us and was responsible for these murders. Maybe the time has come to offer him a flag of truce."

"A flag of . . . Sergei, we haven't done anything. We didn't kill the American."

"I know that Alexei, but does he know that? We can stop this with a phone call, maybe a short meeting, before it becomes really crazy. How soon will it be before they're hunting you?"

Alexei frowned, shook his head, and took a deep breath. "He will think I'm weak."

"No, he'll think you are trying to stop this foolishness before it gets out of hand. Can either one of you afford a bloodbath? There is too much money to be made to let something you weren't even involved in, in the first place, stand in the way. Call him, bring this to a close before it takes on a life of its own."

"You think I should call him?"

"I know you should. Let me make the call, and when he comes on the line, I will have you speak to him. Set up a meeting, or you can talk on the phone."

"I would prefer to speak with him on the phone. It is safer than meeting him."

"All right, but let me make the call now," Sergei said.

THIRTY-NINE

Dillon tossed the evidence bag with the Ace of Spades card on his desk and then picked up the phone and called Brian McFadden at the Dublin City mortuary.

"Dublin City—"

"Hi, Maura," Dillon said, cutting her off. "Jack Dillon, I need to talk to Brian if he's available."

"Just a moment and I'll connect you."

McFadden answered on the second ring. "Brian McFadden."

"Hi, Brian. Jack Dillon."

"Yeah, got your message on the paternity test. I should have something for you by the end of the day."

"Call me when you've got something," Dillon said. "You had two bodies transported to you this morning, gunshot victims."

"Yeah, you're referring to those two from outside the Odessa Club? I haven't had a chance to get to them yet, may not be until tomorrow."

"You'll have another one arriving shortly from the Phibsboro Post Office."

"Don't tell me someone finally had enough of that grouchy bastard sitting behind the counter there."

"Fitzgerald is his name," Dillon laughed.

"So, you know the bollocks. Miserable, unhappy, little—"

"Unfortunately, it wasn't him. This was someone else with an Ace of Spades playing card in their mouth, just like the card left with one of the Odessa victims and Touhy."

"Oh?"

"What I'd like you to do is check for similarities in the wounds. This one coming in looks like another smaller-caliber weapon. We're thinking hollow point rounds based on the damage in the exit wounds."

"You think the same shooter?"

"If not the same, certainly very similar."

"All right then, I'll get on that as soon as it arrives."

"Much appreciated, Brian. Call me as soon as you have something," Dillon said and hung up.

He pulled a magnifying glass out of his pocket and examined the bloodstained Ace of Spades in the plastic evidence bag. He felt it between his fingers, put some slight pressure, bending it against the edge of his desk. He turned the card over and looked at the back. It was blank.

Suel walked over and said, "Thinking of dealing?"

"This isn't a playing card," Dillon said.

"What?"

"The stock it's printed on is wrong, the finish well, actually there is no finish on the card and look at the back, it's blank. This thing has been run off on a copy machine or something?"

"You're kidding me. Let me see that," Suel said.

Dillon handed him the evidence bag and said, "We should look at the other cards. I'll lay you odds they're the same as this one."

"Meaning?"

"For one thing, meaning whoever the shooter is, he's too damn cheap to buy a deck of cards. The next question would be, how many of these damn things does he expect to use?" Dillon said.

Suel tossed the evidence bag back on Dillon's desk. Dillon picked it up and began to examine it again through the magnifying glass. "The skull and the little designs in the corners, the thing looks almost Victorian."

"I'm going for a tea. You want one?" Suel said.

"Tea? No, thanks." He caught some copy in the corner of the card. The letters looked like a part of the design until he examined them through the magnifying glass. "Globe Card Co." He clicked on his computer, brought up Google and typed in "Globe Card Co." He scrolled through seventeen pages and only came up with one listing of the company, and that was in a book index, next to the word "Boston" and a date, "1874."

Suel came back, munching a tea biscuit and slurping tea. "What'd you find out?"

"I found out that the Globe Playing Card Company was out of Boston, back in 1874."

"Boston? That brings to mind our friend, Richie Nolan."

"That's exactly what I'm thinking."

"I'm thinking we might pay a visit to your man who mailed the letters. We've got the return address."

"That fool with the tattooed face?" Dillon said.

"Unless you've got a better idea."

"Right now, I feel like we're grasping at straws."

"Then let's go. I'd like to view that face up close."

FORTY

The return address on the envelopes was in Tallaght, the largest town and the county seat of South Dublin. "Tallaght is said to derive from támh-leacht. It means 'plague pit' in Irish," Suel said, as he turned off the M50 expressway and onto Tallaght Road.

"Plague pit?" Dillon said, looking over at Suel. "Charming."

"Supposed to have been a plague a few thousand years ago. Population here was about six thousand people back in 1970. It grew by fifty thousand over the next ten years. No way an area can keep up with that sort of growth, and of course, with it came all sorts of problems. There's nice parts, a lot of cultural activity, parks, and then in the west some real shit holes with all sorts of knackers. You'll be happy to know that's where we're headed."

"To the west of Tallaght?"

"Council housing," Suel said, then accelerated when the traffic light turned yellow. They made it through the better part of the four-lane intersection before it turned red. Five minutes later, he turned onto a side street, and things immediately began to look dismal. The homes in the area, "an estate" was how Suel referred to it, were identical. Two-story stucco, six, eight, or ten attached to one another, all exactly the same layout. Most appeared run down, and quite a few were boarded up.

Each unit had a front door with a picture window next to the door on the first floor and two windows above on the second floor, a three-foot stucco wall across the front enclosed a tiny front yard, maybe just ten feet deep. Each place was painted a different color and looked to be no more than fifteen feet wide.

Suel slowed down in the middle of the block, searching for a house number. He pulled to a stop in front of a lime green structure. The unit to the left of it had been painted pink at some point. Now the door and window on the first floor were boarded up. The two second-floor windows were broken. Dingy, torn, lace curtains hung out of the broken glass and fluttered in the breeze. The unit to the right of it was painted a faded yellow. A brown, swaybacked horse stood in the front yard and didn't bother to look as Suel and Dillon climbed out of the car. Based on the deposits covering the yard and the smell, the horse had been there for a while.

"You can't make it up," Suel said, shaking his head. He grabbed the evidence bag with the two envelopes from the back seat and headed for the front door.

The doorbell was missing and in its place were two bare copper wires sticking out of a hole in the door frame. The front door had a scratched and foggy plastic panel originally meant to simulate beveled glass. Suel pounded loudly on the door. The horse next door snorted once or twice, just as Dillon thought he detected some shadow movement on the other side of the door.

A moment later, the door opened, and a tattooed face stared out at them, even more ridiculous looking in person than on the post office security tape. He took one look at Dillon and Suel and moved as if he was about to shut the door, but Suel slammed his foot against the door, shouldered the door back open, while at the same time slapping a pistol out of the man's hand.

"An Garda Síochána," Suel shouted and flashed his badge as he stepped into the house. Dillon followed with a hand on his pistol as the tattooed face backed up against a staircase leading to the second floor. The man glanced quickly at the pistol on the floor. Dillon kicked the pistol farther away, then picked it up off the floor and slipped it into his coat pocket.

They were standing in a small room with a couch, a chair, and a large flatscreen TV. A door on the far side of the room led to a small kitchen. The tattooed face stared wide-eyed at the evidence bag Suel held with the two pink and gold envelopes. He appeared to be wearing the same clothes, jeans and the black t-shirt he'd been wearing on the post office tape.

"Sorry to intrude." Suel smiled. "Wondering if we might have a word," he said, raising the evidence bag he held between his thumb and forefinger.

"Is only cards. To my mother and sister. Is their birthday."

"You Russian?" Suel asked

The man nodded.

"I like Russia," Suel said and smiled.

No response from the tattooed face.

"Your name?"

"Pyotr."

"Peter, you got a surname?"

"Blinov."

"Peter Blinov. Don't you think it would be polite to ask us to sit down?"

"I do nothing wrong. Only mail cards. I pay money for stamp."

"Yeah, you also left a car parked blocking traffic. Caused a real problem. Guess what we found in that car?"

He shrugged his shoulders and shook his head.

"Don't know? Interesting," Suel said, nodding with a look on his face that suggested he didn't believe a word. "You hear anything lately from your friend, Nikita Kirden?"

"I don't know this one, I think."

"Oh, really? Funny, because we have you on tape getting out of the car and leaving him in front of the post office," Suel lied. "We have you buying stamps for these envelopes. And let me refresh your memory, you asked for a piece of tape which the gentleman at the Post Office counter kindly gave to you. Now, I'm going to give you one more chance to tell me what you know, and if you do not, you will find yourself in jail tonight. But don't worry, we're not going to keep you long, just a night, maybe two. We'll only keep you however long it takes to let Alexei Bazanov know you're talking with us. Then we're going to let you go."

"But I not say anythings."

"I think you should ask us to sit down, Peter. What do you think? You talk to us, and we'll leave just as soon as you tell us what you know, and your friend Bazanov will never have to know we were here."

Blinov glanced nervously at the open door, then said, "I tell you what I know, but is not much. You maybe close door and sit."

An open suitcase sat on the couch, Blinov picked it up and set it on the floor.

"Planning on going somewhere?" Dillon asked.

"I just want to maybe see some sights. See famous castle," Pyotr said.

"Oh, a trip. Sounds fun," Suel said.

Blinov nodded and smiled.

"I didn't see a car out front. Someone driving you?"

The smile suddenly disappeared. "Yes. I mean, no. No one drive. I, umm, I take train. See Ireland."

Dillon nodded like this made sense, made note of the fact that things appeared to have been hurriedly dumped into the suitcase. "You know, Pyotr, if you lie to us, there are going to be serious problems."

Blinov seemed to swallow and then blinked a couple of times. "I tell truth to you, always."

"Okay, if you say so. If you're not, if you lie to us, we'll find out. We always do," Dillon said.

"I think it might be best if you sat down, Mr. Blinov. We're going to have a number of questions," Suel said.

FORTY-ONE

As Suel pulled back onto the M50 expressway, he said, "I'm not sure what we got out of that."

"You think he really didn't know about the Ace of Spades shoved in his pal's mouth?" Dillon said.

"He looked awful surprised. It makes sense, sort of. He heads out of the post office, sees him through the front window slumped over, steps outside, basically confirms his pal has been shot, and then takes off. Think about it. He can't move the body, at least not without attracting attention. He doesn't know if the shooter is still around, and he just wants to get the hell out of there."

"The fact that they just stopped there at the post office because they happened to be driving by and saw it. I mean, the trip wasn't planned."

"But he doesn't think they were being followed," Suel said.

"What he said was they always check, and no one was following. I'm thinking they maybe let their guard down. Someone was following, and the opportunity presented itself. Walk up to the vehicle, fire two rounds. What's that, a couple of seconds total?" Dillon said.

"Don't forget the card in the mouth."

"Okay, call it three seconds, and then the shooter climbs back in his car and drives off. He wouldn't have had to deal with the traffic jam we saw. Blinov told us he took a taxi home and locked the doors. I don't know."

"You've got that pistol?"

"Yeah. We'll run it through ballistics, but I don't think it's the murder weapon. It's a nine millimeter, heavier than whatever was used on the guy this morning and the two last night."

"And don't forget the suppressor, no one heard anything."

"Yeah," Dillon said. "The silencer. Same as the Odessa Club, no one heard anything. I initially had my doubts about that. Now I'm not so sure."

Once back in the office, Dillon ran the pistol he'd confiscated from Pyotr Blinov down to ballistics and requested a test. He was convinced the rounds in the magazine, although a heavier caliber, could not have done the sort of damage they'd seen on the three victims. On the way back up to the office, his phone rang.

"Dillon," was how he answered, then he leaned against the hallway wall.

"Marshal, Brian McFadden."

"Brian, what do you have for me?"

"Well, depending on your point of view, the good or bad news is, Joey Touhy is, or rather was, the father of that baby."

"Hmmm. I wonder if his wife knew?" Dillon said, half to himself.

"Maybe she's the one that had Touhy and the girl-friend killed. But I guess that's for you guys to figure out. No question on this end, Touhy was definitely the father. I'm going to be working late, this fellow from in front of the post office is on the table. I'll start in on him just as soon as we're off the phone. I'll compare the results with the findings on the other two bodies."

"The two from outside the Odessa Club?"

"Right."

"You'll be able to tell if it was the same weapon?"

"I'll be able to give you some probabilities. That's about all I can do unless we have the actual weapon, but it should be fairly conclusive. Maybe stop over a little after six tonight if you're desperate for an answer."

"I'll be there, Brian. Thanks for the update. Now, don't let me keep you from the task at hand," Dillon said, then chuckled and hung up. Once up in the office, he headed toward Suel's desk.

"You look like the cat that swallowed the canary," Suel said, then sat back in his desk chair and watched as Dillon approached.

"Just off the line with McFadden."

"He's already got results on the post office shooting?"

"No, in fact, he's just about to start in on that. But he did have results on the paternity test. Turns out Joey

Touhy was the father of the baby Gerri Greco was carrying."

Suel seemed to think for a long moment, then said, "He did the paternity test, and Touhy came up as the father?"

"Yeah."

"So what, exactly, does that mean?"

"Mean? Well, it would seem to suggest his wife may have been involved in the shooting of the couple, which possibly could implicate Eamon Boyle."

"I'd say that's a bit of a stretch," Suel said. "Eamon Boyle doesn't need any problems coming over from the States. Exhibit 'A' is this Richie Nolan character. Not the sort of attention Boyle wants or needs directed at him. But then having said that, I can't for the life of me see any sort of logic to anything that's happened in the past seventy-two hours."

"The only way it seems to be logical is if you have an unknown third party doing all this killing. Maybe someone like Richie Nolan," Dillon said.

"Yeah, great, except he was in the US when this whole thing started with Joey Touhy and the woman—"

"Gerri Greco," Dillon added.

"Yeah, so someone kills those two, and then Nolan comes to town to wage a one-man war against Alexei Bazanov? Doesn't make any sense," Suel said, shaking his head.

"Well, anyway you look at it, Nolan is a person of interest in at least three murders. I say we bring him in and have a chat."

"I can't disagree. But it's going to take more than the two of us to haul him out of his lair at This Little Piggy."

"What if we set it up for early morning, say five, maybe six in the morning. No customers to worry about. Everyone is asleep up on the second floor. If he's there, we nab him," Dillon said.

"You always make it sound so simple."

"What could go wrong? We just give him a gentle shake on the shoulder, ask him to kindly get up, maybe have a tea mug ready for him. Who wouldn't want to cooperate with us at that hour of the morning?"

"I'm sure that's exactly what he'd like to do, cooperate. Shall I set it up?" Suel said.

"Yeah." Dillon nodded. "Tomorrow morning. I think the sooner we bring Richie Nolan in, the better."

Suel nodded, then reached over and picked up his phone. "I'll put it together. Let's just hope it's worth our while."

"I'm all ears if you've got a better idea."

Suel seemed to think for a moment, then shook his head and punched in a three-digit extension on his phone.

FORTY-TWO

Dillon pulled up in front of his house and headed for the door. He gave a perfunctory nod to his next-door neighbor, Deitora, a permanently unhappy, humorless woman who seemed less than thrilled with Dillon and his dog Lucifer. She was wearing baggy jeans, a red-plaid, long-sleeved flannel shirt, and a straw hat with netting that covered her face and the back of her neck.

"Are you going to release that, that animal outside?" she said as she leaned over and smelled a bloom on the pink rose she'd just finished trimming, closing her eyes and apparently getting lost in the fragrance, no doubt in an effort to erase the thought of Dillon as her neighbor.

"Yeah. Just home for a moment. Not to worry, he'll stay over here," Dillon said as he increased his pace toward the front door.

"It would be nice for the rest of us on the road if you cleaned up after him." She nodded disgustedly at the four or five piles Lucifer had left over the last few days. "And that lawn, your grass gets much longer, I don't know if he'll be able to find his way back to the door."

"I'll keep that in mind. Appreciate the input. Enjoy the rest of your day," Dillon said, and meaning anything but. He unlocked the door and quickly stepped inside. Four pieces of mail were lying on the floor just inside the door. He picked them up and quickly flipped through them. A credit card offer, a car insurance advertisement, a request to subscribe to the Irish Times, and a circular from a grocery chain, all items that could go directly into recycling.

"Lucifer," he called up the stairs, then listened as he heard the dog jump off the bed, stretch, and shake. A moment later, Lucifer appeared at the top of the stairs. "Come on boy. Come on downstairs," Dillon called. The dog gave his usual blank stare.

Dillon walked into the kitchen, tossed the mail into the recycling bag, then shook the large glass jar containing dog biscuits, and unscrewed the lid. At the sound of the jar shaking, Lucifer bounded down the stairs. Dillon held the dog biscuit in his hand and walked back toward the front door. Lucifer followed, intently focused on the biscuit. Dillon opened the door, tossed the biscuit out the door, and Lucifer followed, leaping down the two steps and snapping up the biscuit on the first bounce.

"Oh, saints preserve us," Deitora half shrieked from her rose garden and hurried into her house.

Dillon filled Lucifer's food and water dish then grabbed another biscuit and opened the front door. There was a fresh deposit from Lucifer over toward the three-foot wall that separated his front yard from Deitora's.

"Lucifer, come on. Biscuit, boy. Come on, biscuit," Dillon called.

The dog ran into the house, leaping over the front steps and into the entryway. Dillon tossed the biscuit onto the kitchen floor, then closed and locked the door behind him. Mercifully, Deitora was apparently still in her house, and he hurried out to his car before she took the opportunity to return to her garden and offer up more free advice.

As he settled in behind the steering wheel, he thought he saw the curtains move in her front window. He turned the key in the ignition, prayed silently that the engine would start, then hurried down the street and around the corner before she opened the front door.

FORTY-THREE

He pulled alongside the Dublin City Morgue about five minutes later. He drove up over the curb, parked on the boulevard in front of the post office and turned off the engine, then sat behind the wheel for a long moment, thinking about the recent murders.

The first two, Joey Touhy and Gerri Greco were different from the standpoint of who the victims were. The weapon seemed similar, and Dillon hoped to get clarification on that fact in just a few moments. It struck him as a strange coincidence that all five murders had occurred with the victims sitting in cars. Were they being followed and then murdered at the earliest convenience? In all cases, the victims had been armed and yet apparently caught off guard. The Odessa Club was in a busy tourist area with lots of foot traffic, yet no one saw or heard anything. The Phibsboro Post Office was on a busy street, the victim's car partially blocking a busy intersection, four or five people waiting in line just inside the post office, but again, no one heard or saw anything. And then, of course, the common denominator, the Ace of Spades card.

Since it was after hours, Dillon took his phone out and called Brian McFadden.

"McFadden."

"Brian, Jack Dillon. I just pulled up, and I'll be at the door in a half minute."

"Perfect timing, I just finished up. On my way to let you in."

Dillon climbed out of his car, locked the doors, then walked up the short asphalt drive to the Morgue. He waited no more than a minute before McFadden pulled the door open, and stepped aside so Dillon could enter. He wore blue hospital scrubs, and he looked tired. Once he closed the door, he rubbed his face with both hands and yawned.

"Long day?" Dillon said.

"Actually, a number of them. Let's go on back to my office, and we can go over what I've come up with."

Dillon followed McFadden through the small lobby, then down the hallway with the framed watercolors of Dublin street scenes hanging on the wall. They passed the three viewing rooms, now empty with the exception of the third room, which had a man in dark blue trousers and a matching shirt vacuuming the carpet.

McFadden nodded at the man and said some sort of greeting Dillon didn't quite catch. They walked into the break room, and McFadden stopped at a machine.

"I'm going to grab a tea. You want one?"

Dillon shook his head and said, "No, thanks." He'd had tea from the Morgue's machine on more than one occasion and fortunately wasn't that desperate tonight.

Once the paper cup was filled, McFadden pulled it out of the machine. He took a slurpy sip and grimaced. "Oh, but that's desperate," he said and shook his head. "Come on back."

Dillon followed him through the autopsy room. Three metal tables were in the process of being hosed down, and the bodies were nowhere to be seen. "Thanks, Tim," McFadden called to the man in rubber boots hosing down the metal tables and the floor, then headed into his office. Dillon followed.

"Close the door, and have a seat," McFadden said, walking around to the back of his desk. He set his tea on top of some three-ringed binders sitting on a shelf, then moved a stack of files over to the edge of his desk, grabbed his tea, and sat down.

Dillon pulled out a chair in front of McFadden's desk and sat. McFadden leaned back, took another sip of tea and grimaced. "God, it doesn't get any better halfway through the cup."

"You're a braver man than I, Brian."

"So, your five victims. All shot with a .25-caliber weapon. I can't be positive without the weapon itself, but if I had to guess, I would say it was the same weapon. The rounds are all hollow points." He reached back to the credenza behind him and picked up five small plastic bags. Three had the remnants of two rounds, the other two each held one round.

He laid the bags down in front of Dillon. Dillon picked up one of the bags, noted it was labeled with the name Nikita Kirden, the victim from outside the post office. The round almost appeared to have been split down the middle and peeled back, making it maybe three times larger in the process.

"In all instances," McFadden said, "death had to be almost instantaneous. Each individual was shot twice, usually one round in the chest and another to the head. Both shots fired at extremely close range, an inch, maybe two. Stippling was present on all the head wounds and on the clothing around the chest wounds."

"Up close and personal," Dillon said, shaking his head. "It would appear we're dealing with a pro."

McFadden gave a tired sigh and rubbed a hand across his face. "I can't disagree. Given the victims, all armed, it seems more than a little surprising they were caught off guard."

"Drugs, copious quantities of alcohol, anything like that in the systems?" Dillon said.

"No, not really. The two at the Odessa Club registered zero point eight and nine, respectively, alcohol in the bloodstream. They could have had two beers over the course of an hour, maybe ninety minutes. They certainly weren't pounding drinks down if that's what you're thinking. Were they over the legal limit? Yeah, naturally.

But they weren't staggering and falling down. Theoretically, they would have been pretty alert. Your man outside the post office, nothing in his system. He may have been distracted talking on his phone, but he wasn't intoxicated, and I found no trace of drugs."

McFadden took a final sip of his tea, grimaced once again, and carefully set the half-empty cup in his wastebasket. "Any thoughts?"

"Yeah, we've got a real mess on our hands."

"I wish I could tell you more," McFadden said, then slowly rose out of his chair.

Dillon nodded, then stood. "You should go home and get some sleep, Brian. You look exhausted."

"I intend to do just that."

On the way home, Dillon phoned Suel.

"Please tell me one of the victims wrote the shooter's name on the back of their hand," was how he answered the phone.

"If only," Dillon said. "All the rounds appear to be from the same weapon, a .25-caliber. Hollow points. Similar pattern, shot in the head and the chest. Whoever is doing this is able to get up close and pull the trigger. The two at the Odessa Club had a beer, maybe two in their system, but they should have been on the ball. Apparently, our shooter is able to get up close and pull the damn trigger. I don't get it."

"By the way, we're on for tomorrow morning," Suel said. "We'll be waking Mr. Nolan at This Little Piggy nice and early around five. Maybe we can start getting some answers from the likes of him."

"Let's just hope he's in there."

"We've had someone in there undercover, and Nolan's been enjoying himself the last two nights. I should get a confirmation later this evening. It appears they've made the menu quite available to him."

"The food?"

"Dillon, you idjit, not the food. Lord, save me. The entertainment."

"Oh, yeah, sure, now I get it."

"Seems to be enjoying himself. Listen, we'll be meeting at the station at half-past three. Best to get some sleep while you can."

"I can't think of anything I'd rather do at that early morning hour than be with you," Dillon said and disconnected.

FORTY-FOUR

Dillon's alarm went off at two forty-five. Lucifer groaned and shoved his head under a pillow as Dillon crawled out of bed and headed toward the bathroom in the dark, feeling like he'd been asleep for only a minute or two. He grabbed a quick shower, quickly dressed, and was out the door twenty minutes later. It was raining lightly, just enough to have the wipers on intermittently. Other than a few taxis, the streets were empty, and he made it to the station in under fifteen minutes.

Suel and a team of eight individuals were already assembled. At this hour of the morning, everyone was relatively quiet. Protective vests were issued as Suel went over the interior layout of This Little Piggy while he handed out an 8x10 sheet of paper with Nolan's passport photo printed on it.

The man who'd been working undercover for the past few nights, an officer named Dabney, was alongside Suel, and he added some updated information as they went through the briefing. Basically, there was a set of double doors leading into the place, and next to the kitchen door, a metal door marked "Private" that led up-stairs. Four bedrooms overlooked the street, Richie Nolan had been in the second bedroom with a redheaded woman the past three nights.

"We're going in to grab Nolan and only Nolan. Consider him armed and dangerous, but let's try to get him with as little fanfare as possible. Just in and out, gentlemen, in and out."

"That's what this plonker Nolan has been doing the past three nights, in and out, in and out," Dabney joked.

On that note, the eight men climbed into a SWAT team vehicle. The flat black vehicle had bulletproof glass, bulletproof tires, and blast resistant double doors on the back and both sides. A set of iron bars was mounted across the front bumper to push through barricades.

The rain had picked up a bit, and Suel led the way in his car. At this dark hour of the morning, it was no more than a ten-minute drive. Two blocks from the This Little Piggy pub, Suel pulled alongside two Garda squad cars parked on the street. The officers climbed out and walked up to the driver's side as Suel lowered his window.

"Anything happening?" Suel asked.

They stood in the rain with their shoulders hunched and shook their heads. One of them, a fellow with a neatly trimmed mustache, said, "All very quiet. Closed early, little before half-past one. No customers in this weather. Never saw your man Nolan step out, so he should still be in there."

"You'll block off either end of the street?" Suel said.

"We will. It'll take just a moment."

"All right, we'll pull right in front of the entrance and go in. The two of us will follow," Suel said, indicating he and Dillon. "Hold your positions blocking the street until we leave. We're just going to grab your man and get out of there, no searches, no ID checks, nothing, so hoping it will be fast and without incident," Suel said.

"Good luck to you, sir," they said in unison and then hurried back to their cars. The officer with the mustache drove down the street past the pub, then pulled across the street, effectively blocking any traffic. The second vehicle waved the SWAT team and then Suel on down toward This Little Piggy before he pulled across the street, blocking it.

The SWAT team picked up speed then pulled to a stop in front of This Little Piggy. The building was dark, with the exception of a red neon CLOSED sign in an oval window next to the front door and what looked like a lamp in one of the upstairs windows. The second-floor windows all appeared to have lace curtains hanging from them.

Doors on both sides and the back of the SWAT vehicle suddenly burst open, and eight figures, all dressed in black, wearing helmets, protective vests, and carrying automatic weapons flew out of the doors. They quickly gathered at the front door of the pub, which burst open a second later, and everyone hurried inside. Suel and Dillon followed, half running to keep up.

The barroom consisted of two rooms. The first had a bar with stools and a half-dozen tables. The stools had been placed on top of the bar, and the tables had chairs resting upside down on top of them. An aluminum Christmas tree stood just a few feet from the front door. The second room was all tables with chairs resting upside down on top of the tables. The last two SWAT team members were going through the door and heading up the stairs. Thus far, no one had said a word.

Dillon and Suel hurried across the room toward the stairs. The stairway was steep, narrow, and lit by a single dim light at the top of the stairs. Dillon caught just the slightest hint of perfume as he entered the stairway. The scent seemed to grow stronger as they climbed up to the second floor. A long hallway ran off to the left with four doors, all on the left-hand side of the hall. The team spread out along the hall, with an individual standing guard next to each door. Five members huddled around the second door, looked at one another, and then one of them gave the nod. He quietly turned the doorknob, and everyone tiptoed into the room.

A moment later, there was a deep groan, a thump and a woman's scream that seemed to be cut short. Suel and Dillon stepped into the room a moment later.

A redheaded woman was standing in front of the window, clutching a pillow in front of her. She was naked with the corner of the pillow wedged beneath her breasts. The pillow hung down, not quite covering her. She had a tattoo just above her pubic area, a red letter "Q" and below that a red heart. Her breasts hung over the pillow, and she almost appeared posed. The left side of her face and her thighs were pinkish and chapped-looking. She stood staring at the armed intruders, but she didn't seem to be upset.

"What's your name?" Suel asked after a long moment.

"Morna," she said, smiling and raising her eyebrows, not bothering to adjust the pillow and making her name sound almost like an invitation.

Dillon glanced around the room. It had a double bed that looked about a hundred years old, and an old chest of drawers pushed up against the wall with an oval mirror on top of it. Two end tables stood on either side of the bed, with an empty martini glass on the table closest to the window. A pistol rested on the other end table.

Nolan was lying face down and naked on the floor. One of the SWAT team guys had his knee in the middle of Nolan's back and was in the process of handcuffing his hands behind his back. Another team member had his weapon pointed about an inch from Nolan's head.

His dark, curly hair was angled off to the side, a definite case of bed head. He still had what looked like a four-day growth of beard, just enough for a serious whisker burn, and Dillon put it together with the chapped appearance of the woman's face and thighs. He noted the tattoo on Nolan's left shoulder, the Ace of Spades with a human skull. The ink wasn't black, more of a brownish sort of color. But the tattoo design looked like it matched the cards that had been shoved in the victim's mouths. A puckered scar that looked like it might be from a bullet wound was next to the tattoo.

Once Nolan was cuffed, the two SWAT team members took hold of his arms and raised him to his feet. Nolan looked around the room and seemed to focus on Dillon for half a moment before he was pulled toward the door.

Suel gave a nod, and the rest of the team headed out the door.

"Oh, you gotta be kidding me. Can I at least put some pants on," Nolan said, as they led him down the hall. "Come on, you guys, have a heart. All the women will be trying to grab me, and you'll all feel jealous."

The rest of the team filed out. Suel picked up a pair of jeans and a shirt from the end of the bed, then nodded at the redhead and said, "Sweet dreams, darling."

Dillon pulled an evidence bag out of his coat pocket, placed the pistol inside, then quickly went through the four dresser drawers, and found them all empty. He turned and smiled at the redhead.

She smiled back as she climbed into bed, then said, "Close the door on your way out if you're not going to stay."

He nodded reflexively and walked out of the room, quietly closing the door behind him. The SWAT members stationed at the other doors walked backward down the hall, then went down the stairs, following everyone out onto the street.

Suel tossed Nolan's jeans and shirt into the back of the SWAT vehicle and said something to the team that brought a chuckle, although Dillon couldn't make out what he had said.

Dillon and Suel climbed in the car, waited for a minute before the SWAT vehicle made its way down the street. Dillon looked up at the windows on the second floor but couldn't detect anything that suggested they were being watched. As they pulled away from the pub and followed the SWAT vehicle, he watched the two squad cars that were blocking the street in the side mirror. They followed briefly, then turned off at the first intersection.

"Well, that went surprisingly well," Suel said.

"Maybe too well," Dillon said. "It bother you at all that no one looked out any of the other doors? No one asked what was going on?"

"I'd guess one of two things, either they're quite used to all sorts of noises coming from other rooms, or the rooms were empty. Maybe your man was the only customer up there tonight."

"That woman, the redhead, it seemed like she almost expected us," Dillon said.

"Nice looking slapper. Maybe she's just used to having a line at her door."

FORTY-FIVE

s they pulled into the station behind the SWAT vehicle, Suel Asked, "Fancy some breakfast? I'm thinking we'll let Mr. Nolan cool his heels in an interrogation room for an hour or two before we begin our chat." They sat in the car watching the SWAT team begin to exit out the side doors of the vehicle and hurry out of the rain.

"I could be up for that," Dillon said. "Did you happen to pick up on that tattoo Nolan has on his shoulder?"

"The Ace of Spades? You're damn right I did. Looked just like those cards. I'd say we've got our man. It's almost as good as a signature."

"I don't know. The color seemed wrong, it wasn't black, and—"

"The color? Dillon, it was the Ace of Spades, the same design as those cards. What was the date you found online? 1870 something? That's a hundred and fifty years ago, and you're thinking this is just a coincidence? This bastard has been wandering around Dublin blowing people's brains out, and you're worried about the color of a tattoo? Get a grip, man."

At that moment, the rear doors opened up on the SWAT vehicle, and the last two members of the team began to climb out. They helped Nolan step out of the back. He was still barefoot, but he was wearing the jeans and shirt, although the shirt was unbuttoned and just hanging over his shoulders. He said something to one of the Garda helping him out of the vehicle, and they both laughed. They seemed to exchange a joke back and forth for a moment, the officer finishing up with a funny face back to Nolan, saying something else that had them both laughing. Then the officer seemed to take his time leading Nolan into the building.

"Looks like he's already made friends," Dillon said.

Suel chuckled and said, "Maybe. Just making sure your man gets a good soaking in the rain. Now he can sit and be miserable in wet clothes for an hour or two before we get started."

They pulled into a parking place, climbed out of the car, and hurried through the rain into the building. Once upstairs in the office, things were still relatively quiet at this hour, and Suel said, "When you're done with the paperwork, put him in interview room two and let him sit. We'll get to him in a bit."

Nolan was sitting in a distant chair, just staring at the floor. He looked soaked. Water was dripping off his curly hair into a small puddle on the floor. He was wet, no doubt cold, and yet still appeared completely at ease.

Dillon carried the evidence bag down to ballistics and gave them the pistol from Nolan's room, then went back up and met Suel in the cafeteria on the first floor. Suel was in the process of directing a server who was loading up his plate with a full Irish breakfast.

"Maybe another black pudding, and if you could add a second scoop of baked beans, too." The woman gave him a quick look, but then dumped a second scoop of baked beans onto his plate.

"I'm not sure I want to be next to you later today," Dillon said.

"Part of the preparation for our closed room discussion with Mr. Nolan," Suel said, then took the plate, set it on the tray, and headed toward the cash register.

"Pancakes for me, and a yogurt," Dillon said and followed behind Suel. As the cashier rang up Suel's breakfast, Dillon came in behind him, grabbed a coffee, and said, "He's paying for mine, too."

The cashier looked at Suel, who said, "Oh, might as well, he probably doesn't have the three quid to cover his breakfast."

They made their way to a table in the far corner and sat down. Suel shoveled a large forkful of scrambled eggs into his mouth, then said, "You don't seem to be all that thrilled with this morning's adventure. We got your man, without incident. Everyone's back safe and sound. What's not to like?"

"I just can't shake the feeling that they were waiting for us. Did you notice they didn't seem to be all that surprised when we arrived?"

"Waiting for us? You mean they knew we were coming? Don't be ridiculous. We caught them unawares, they were sound asleep. For Christ sake, the two of them were naked in bed. God only knows what we might have interrupted."

"When we left, the redhead asked me to close the door on the way out, like our entry was no big thing, and then she just crawled back into bed. When was the last time you hauled some idiot out the door, and his wife or girlfriend simply asked you to close the door on the way out? In my experience, they're always screaming and crying. We'd a half dozen people in there, armed to the teeth, dressed in protective gear, and she carefully places a pillow, so she's still exposed? That doesn't make any sense to me. Not so much as a word from her except telling me to close the door so she can get back to sleep."

"Dillon, she's a bloody prostitute. All she was doing with that pillow was a bit of free advertising. She was probably in shock, that's why she didn't say anything. We're lucky she didn't hand us a card with her hourly rate, offer a discount if we formed a line."

"And Nolan," Dillon said. "He's laughing up a storm, making jokes on his way out the door. No argument, no struggle. I checked the dresser drawers. They were all empty, just his jeans and a shirt hanging on the bedpost."

"Like you said, we'd a half dozen armed men, one with the barrel up against your man's thick skull. Just what would you expect him to do?"

"I don't know, protest, say he's innocent, complain about us interrupting, something, anything. Instead, he just goes along and jokes about it."

"I'm telling you, we got our man. He was armed. You just brought his pistol down to ballistics. He's got that bloody tattoo, and he was at least a business acquaintance if not a friend with your man, Touhy. Now, if it's all right with the likes of you, I'd like to finish my breakfast, relax for a moment, then go up to that interview room and take your man's confession."

FORTY-SIX

Nolan had been seated at a metal-topped table in interview room two for the past couple of hours. Suel and Dillon were watching him through the one-way glass in the viewing room next door. He appeared to be asleep. The table and chair were both bolted into position. Nolan's handcuffs had been removed, and his head was resting on his arms folded on the table. It sounded like he was lightly snoring.

"Well, he certainly doesn't look concerned," Dillon said.

Suel gave a loud sigh, then said, "Well, he should be, he's about to be locked up for life. Let's see what we can find out." Dillon followed him out into the hall. Suel stopped outside the door to the interview room and seemed to think for a second, then said, "Hold on for just a moment." He hurried down the hall and was back a couple of minutes later with two cups of tea. "What do you think?" he asked.

"I think once he has a taste, he'll figure you're trying to poison him," Dillon said.

"Open the door, Mr. Positive."

They stepped into the room, and Suel half shouted, "Rise and shine, Richie, rise and shine. Ahh, there's a good lad. So sorry for the delay, but thanks for waiting for us. Brought you a bit of nice, hot tea, just the thing to start the day."

Suel took up a seat across from Nolan while Dillon leaned against the wall behind Suel. Nolan slowly sat up and stretched, then gave a long yawn, not bothering to cover his mouth. He blinked a couple of times, turned his head from side to side cracking his neck, and said, "Oh man, long night. I guess I was out cold."

"Help yourself to a drop of tea," Suel said and sipped from his cup.

"Tea? No thanks, I can't stand the stuff."

Dillon tried not to smile.

"So when'd you get to Ireland?" Suel asked.

"Couple of days ago."

"Visiting friends, are you?"

Nolan shook his head. "No. I don't really know anyone here. Just came over to see the sights. Always heard about it. I'm Irish, you know."

"Are you now? Do tell. Where were you born?"

"Boston."

"That makes you an American, Richie. You know what that means?"

"I can celebrate the fourth of July?"

"Yeah, I suppose. Course, it also means that since you aren't an Irish citizen, we really don't have to follow the normal protocol. We can ask you all sorts of questions, and if we think you're lying to us, well, we can just lock you up, let you sit for a week or two, maybe three, see if that doesn't jog the old memory."

"I've got nothing to hide. Go ahead and ask me anything you want. I'm more than happy to cooperate."

"What are you really doing over here, Richie? See, we've been watching you since you got off the plane coming in from Amsterdam. We know who met you at the airport, who you've talked to, been with, what you've been up to. Anything you tell us that doesn't fit, you know what it does, Richie? It builds a case for us, digs an even deeper hole for the likes of you."

"Like I said, I've got nothing to hide. I've just been doing tourist things. Taking in the sights, enjoying some of the locals."

"Mmm-mmm, like your woman, Morna?"

"Yeah, along with some others. I've always been lucky when it comes to the opposite sex. They just can't seem to get enough of me."

"How well did you know Joey Touhy?"

"Joey Touhy? I sort of know a guy with that name back in Boston."

"Yeah, that's your man. Sort of know him? Come on, Richie stop playing games. He owns the building you live in back in Boston."

"I don't really know him that well. I purchased a condo in the building. He used to own it, the building, but now we do, the condo association. Hell, I just got hit with an assessment last spring. We all had to pay fifteen hundred bucks for some kind of stupid flowers and a bunch of bushes they were putting around the place."

"You have a job, Richie?"

"Yes, I do."

"Care to share your career path?"

"I deliver coffee."

"Deliver coffee? And that pays well?"

"Not really, but I get small tips from people. It helps make ends meet."

Suel nodded like this seemed to make sense, then said, "Just so I understand, you're living in a million-dollar condo unit that you own. You drive a Mercedes that starts at ninety-six thousand dollars. That must be a lot of tip money coming your way. You see where I'm going here? It's not making a lot of sense."

"Well, once in a while, I've been given stock tips, and I've gotten lucky playing cards from time to time."

"You had a gun in your possession this morning, Richie. I'm afraid that's against the law."

"Yeah, funny thing. That came with the room. Part of the décor. They like to pretend it's sort of like the 1920s. Michael Collins, your civil war and all that history shit. That gun ain't mine. In fact, I was afraid to even touch it. Morna told me to just ignore it, so that's what I did. I don't like guns. I think they got one like that in every room."

"You've a bullet wound in your left shoulder."

"Hunting accident, from a lot of years back. It's the reason I don't like guns," he said and smiled.

"What were you doing yesterday morning, Richie?"

"Yesterday morning, let's see . . . I was up early and in the city center, caught a ride on the sightseeing bus called Hop On, Hop Off. I rode that around town for an hour or two then stayed on the bus and rode it back to the Guinness brewery. I toured the brewery, even signed their guestbook, bought a sweatshirt, then got back on the bus, took it out to Phoenix Park, and walked around there. Lovely place, the park. You ever been there? They got a bunch of deer just walking around the place."

Suel ignored his question and said, "What about the night before. Out late, were you?"

Nolan smiled. "Had a wonderful night down at the Brazen Head pub, had a late dinner then listened to a band there called the Brazen Hussies. A lot of fun. Closed the place at two, then took a taxi back to This Little Piggy."

"I don't suppose you can document any of this," Suel said, then visibly cringed as Nolan nodded.

"Oh yeah, sure. I've got all the receipts in my wallet. Saving 'em for a scrapbook of my trip over here. One of your fellas was kind enough to take my wallet from me. You can check it out. The receipts are right in the back of the wallet." He leaned forward and half-whispered, "Plan to use them for a tax deduction, make this into a business trip."

A knock on the door interrupted. Dillon opened the door and stepped out of the room. The officer said, "Sorry to disturb you, sir, but I'm afraid another incident."

"What sort of incident?" Dillon asked, then cringed fearing what the answer might be.

"I'm afraid there's been a shooting, sir. Glasnevin Cemetery."

"Another shooting?" Dillon said.

"Yes, sir, about thirty minutes ago. Another one of those playing cards in the victim's mouth, the Ace of Spades. Someone on the maintenance staff found the body. The ME has already been dispatched."

Dillon half-closed his eyes and shook his head. "Okay, better let them know we're on our way."

He stepped back into the interview room and, with a nod of his head, signaled Suel to step out into the hall.

"Excuse us for a moment, Richie," Suel said, and stormed from the room.

"Feck's sake, the bastard is laughing at us. What is it?" Suel said, clearly frustrated at how his conversation with Nolan was going.

"A shooting at Glasnevin Cemetery. Apparently, another Ace of Spades left in the victim's mouth."

"Jesus Christ," Suel growled.

FORTY-SEVEN

Suel had grabbed a squad car from the motor pool. He and Dillon raced through traffic with the siren going and the lights flashing. The rain had lightened up to little more than a mist, and the wipers moved slowly across the windshield every ten seconds or so.

"Wouldn't you think the bastards would pull over to the side?" Suel shouted as they shot past a car that had merely slowed, but not pulled over. He braked for a moment, quickly checked for cross traffic, then shot through the intersection.

Glasnevin Cemetery was up ahead a half-mile on the righthand side. As they rounded the curve, Dillon could see the high stone walls in the distance and beyond that the hundred-and-sixty-eight-foot O'Connell Tower just inside the main entrance to the cemetery. A minute later, Suel sped past the main entrance and continued on to an entrance further down the road. Two squad cars were just outside the entrance, with the lights flashing on their vehicles. A half dozen squad cars and two or three official-looking vehicles were scattered around just inside the entrance with maybe eight uniformed officers standing in a group.

What looked like the ME team in white hazmat suits were gathered around a red Mercedes. The area was taped off with white plastic tape with blue letters "GARDA NO ENTRY." Suel pulled over on a narrow lane leading further into the cemetery and slid to a stop on the wet pavement. As they climbed out of the car, the group of eight officers immediately began to scatter, leaving just two officers who turned and faced a red-faced Suel as he approached.

"What the hell happened, Kevin?" Suel growled.

"Good morning, DI Suel." The older of the two smiled. "Got the call just a little after nine this morning. One of the maintenance workers spotted the Mercedes." He nodded at the red Mercedes, and Dillon noted for the first time that the driver's door was open.

"He thought it didn't look quite right. Headed over, then saw the blood on your man behind the wheel, called to him a couple of times. Then, when he didn't respond, he hurried back to the office and phoned it in. We were first on the scene." He nodded towards the baby-faced officer staring at the ground next to him. "Got here at nine seventeen, reported what we'd found, and secured the area."

"Anyone else around? Another vehicle? Something? Anything?"

The officer shook his head. "No, sir, nothing. Although someone could have parked at the main entrance and we wouldn't have seen them leave. If they were on foot, they could have disappeared in about fifteen seconds and headed into the Botanic Garden or out the gate near the Gravediggers pub. They could still be here, and we wouldn't see them with all the gravestones and monuments. Or they could have just strolled out the entrance here."

"Christ on a cross," Suel groaned. "Where's your man who first called it in?"

"In the office. Guess he's pretty shook up. Funny, you'd think a dead body, you know, after you work in a cemetery that—"

A look from Suel halted the remainder of the remark.

"Maybe go up there, take his statement," Suel said.

One of the hazmat suits headed over as the two officers hurried away.

"Gentlemen," the hazmat suit said.

"Owen." Suel nodded. Dillon recognized the man but hadn't remembered his name. He recalled he was from the north, Omagh, if Dillon remembered correctly, and his accent had been difficult for Dillon to understand.

The man nodded at Suel, then looked at Dillon. "You're the American, right? We met a year ago— a Yank floating in the Royal Canal. Owen Robinson," he said, and extended his hand.

Dillon smiled, shook it, and said, "Yeah, I remember. Long time no see."

Robinson gave a funny look for a moment like he didn't quite get the phrase, then focused back on Suel. "More of the same you've been dealing with, from what I hear. Two shots, one to the head, another to the chest. Death would have been maybe two hours ago and pretty much instantaneous with your signature playing card stuck in the mouth."

"The Ace of Spades?" Dillon said.

"Right. Large black spade in the middle of the card with a skull. I'd say your shooter's seen too many movies," Robinson said, and half laughed.

"You're thinking this is funny?" Suel said. "This is the sixth victim we've had, and our only suspect was in custody when this happened."

"For Christ's sake, calm down, Suel. Some wigged-out bastard trying to make themselves famous is getting us some overtime."

Suel ignored the comment and said, "When can we get over there to take a look at him?"

Robinson turned around to look at a man in a hazmat suit crouching in front of the driver's door, taking photographs of the body. "Soon as Billy's finished photographing the scene, it's all yours. I'll have him let you know. Sorry, didn't mean to piss you off."

Suel gave a slight nod, then focused on the photographer. Robinson turned and quickly headed back over to the Mercedes.

"You might want to go a little easy," Dillon said.

"Fecking bastard. We're back to square one. Nolan was in custody when this happened. Damn it."

"He's still playing us. He's involved somehow, even if he's just a diversion."

"Bollocks," Suel said, and just shook his head.

They waited another ten minutes before the photographer walked over. "All yours, gentlemen. I'll be next to the van if you need me for anything," he said, then walked away. Clearly, Robinson had given him the word to be on guard around Suel.

FORTY-EIGHT

As they walked over to the Mercedes, Dillon and Suel pulled out blue latex gloves from their coat pockets. The car was an AMG-GT coupe. The license plate identified it as a 2018 model, purchased in Dublin. Suel shook his head in disgust as they slipped on the gloves. Three pockets attached to the lower-left corner of the windshield on the passenger side held tax, inspection, and insurance information. Dillon opened the passenger door, reached in, pulled out the insurance information, and frowned.

"Insured by some company named 'Gazorg.' That mean anything to you?"

"I'm guessing it's not an Irish company," Suel said, shaking his head. He was crouched down, studying the body. The car keys were in the victim's right hand. His seat belt was undone, but his left forearm was placed in such a way that the seat belt was still more or less pulled across his chest. His right leg hung out of the open door with the foot turned at a strange angle. His head leaned to the side and hung almost over the console.

From the passenger side, Dillon could only see the chest wound where it had bled through the victim's sweater. The sweater was a long-sleeved, crew neck with off white and black horizontal stripes about three inches wide. The grey trousers looked to be wool. The back seat was empty. Dillon opened the glove compartment and pulled out an owner's manual and a shot glass. There was a lipstick stain on the shot glass, and Dillon set it on the passenger seat, then quickly thumbed through the owner's manual. Satisfied there was nothing of note in the manual, he returned it to the glove compartment. He pulled an evidence bag from his pocket and placed the shot glass in the bag, then walked around to Suel on the driver's side.

There was a second wound, this one up against the temple on the right side of the victim's head. The entrance wound appeared puckered and small like it might have been made with a knitting needle. Dillon noted there was no exit wound.

"There's stippling," Suel said. "But it's different than the victim outside the Odessa Club and your man outside the post office. We'll see what they say at the autopsy, but I'm guessing the shooter wasn't quite as close. Maybe a foot away as opposed to an inch. Still, you have to wonder how in the hell they can get up so close. This dumb bastard was either just getting out or had just climbed into the driver's seat. It almost has to be someone they know doing this, someone they're not concerned about."

Dillon turned his head at an angle and studied the card shoved in the victim's mouth. It appeared to be like the others. It looked like a playing card, but on closer examination, it wasn't, just a computer generated print on stock, stock heavier than for a letter, or even a playing card for that matter. There was no finish on the stock, and the back of the card appeared blank.

"Mind if I bag the card?" Dillon said.

"Be my guest," Suel said, and took a step back and examined the car. "This thing costs more than most of us make in a year. This bollocks isn't some muscle-bound thug. You recognize him?"

Dillon looked at the face. A greying goatee, closely trimmed, grey eyes giving a glassy, blank stare. The salt and pepper hair was close-cropped on the sides and bald on top— no visible tattoos. A worn gold ring was on the ring finger of the left hand, gold and black onyx with a gold crest. Dillon reached in and moved the left hand, slightly.

"It looks like the Russian Imperial crest on this ring. Check it out. Another Russian?" Dillon said.

"God, it wouldn't surprise me. In fact, it would fit," Suel said.

A Garda van pulled into the cemetery and stopped at the white and blue Garda tape. Two men climbed out, walked to the back of the vehicle, and pulled out a gurney. One of them reached back inside the vehicle, then tossed a folded black body bag onto the gurney. They wheeled it beneath the Garda tape, then over next to the Mercedes.

"You guys going to be a bit?" one of them asked.

"Another thirty minutes at least," Dillon said.

Suel walked around to the passenger side of the vehicle and pulled out the insurance information Dillon had looked at a moment ago.

"We're going to head inside and grab a tea. Back in twenty minutes then."

"Enjoy," Dillon said.

Two Garda officers suddenly appeared out in the middle of the cemetery and began walking toward them. They looked left and right every couple of steps, apparently canvasing the area.

"Check your man's pockets, see if he's got some identification, and toss me those car keys," Suel said.

Dillon tossed the keys across to Suel. He caught them, then clicked the button that opened the trunk and walked to the rear of the vehicle.

Dillon checked the front pockets on the victim. They were empty. He pulled the seatbelt back and carefully leaned the body forward. There appeared to be a bulge in the left rear pocket— a wallet.

"When you're finished back there, I could use your help. Looks like a wallet in the back pocket here."

Suel closed the lid to the trunk.

"Anything back there?" Dillon asked.

"Not unless you're interested in a spare tire. Lean your man forward, and I'll get that wallet," Suel said.

Dillon took hold of the left shoulder, then carefully leaned the body forward and halfway out the door. He reached over and held the head by the chin, so it didn't drip blood on his coat, although at this stage it looked as though what little blood there was had dried.

"Yeah, that's good. Hold him for a moment, let me get this thing out," Suel said. A moment later, he stood up, smiled, and held out a thin, slate blue crocodile skin affair. He opened it up, raised his eyebrows, and looked at Dillon. "Gucci. Not bad." He moved his lips, counting the cards, then opened up the back. "Four hundred quid, a half dozen credit cards. I'm tempted to buy us lunch."

"Any ID?"

Suel pulled out a couple of credit cards. "Makar Yenin," Suel said and seemed to think for a moment.

"Ring a bell?"

"Yeah, but I'm not sure why."

"Well, given the car and clothes and now the wallet, whoever he is, it looks as though money wasn't much of a problem."

"I'm guessing the same weapon was used. They'll probably find small-caliber hollow points in there. One to the head and one to the chest," Suel said, shaking his head. "Then, just in case we didn't get the message, they left the calling card."

Suel's phone rang, and he glanced at the screen before he answered it.

"Suel," he answered. "Really? When? We'll be there shortly. Text me his name and room number. Okay. Thank you."

"Tell me Nolan confessed."

"No, but our taxi man from Joey Touhy's murder is out of intensive care. We can talk to him for a few minutes. God, I can only hope he saw something."

The two officers who'd been walking the cemetery grounds ducked under the Garda tape.

"We've got a potential witness to interview," Suel said. "The crew to haul the body is in grabbing a tea. They should be back in about ten minutes. You see anything out there?"

They both shook their heads. "Tourists, a couple of families. Even if he was out there, there's really no way to know who it was. You find anything?"

"More questions than answers," Suel said, then pulled an evidence bag from his pocket and dropped the wallet into it. "We're off to Saint Vincent's in Drumcondra."

Dillon nodded at the two officers, then followed Suel back to the car. Once in the car, Suel reversed back toward the Mercedes. He slowly straightened out and exited Glasnevin Cemetery, stopping at the sidewalk to check for pedestrians. Once on the road, he turned on the flashing lights and siren and made his way toward Saint Vincent's hospital. Fifteen minutes later, they pulled up in front and parked in the no parking zone.

FORTY-NINE

Saint Vincent's hospital consisted of a number of three and four-story attached structures. All built of red brick in the mid to late 1800s. Suel parked the squad car close to the front door in a no-parking zone marked by a red curb and the words "NO PARKING ZONE," painted on the curb.

"He's up on the third floor. Man's name is Abshir Jama," Suel said and made a face.

"Sounds Irish," Dillon said.

"Hopefully, he can tell us what he saw," Suel said, ignoring the comment.

He pretended he didn't see the look from the couple walking down the front steps of the building as he and Dillon bounded up the steps two at a time.

"Wankers. Probably going to look at a new baby," the man said after they'd passed, shaking his head, apparently commenting on Suel's choice of parking spots.

They walked past an information desk and down a long hall with handrails attached to the wall on both sides. They walked all the way to the back of the building, then stepped onto an elevator that was clearly built as a later addition, maybe seventy years ago. Suel pushed the button for the third floor. The doors closed and the elevator immediately dropped a good six inches, then slowly began to climb up to the third floor. They could hear a rhythmic squeak and grinding as they rose.

"Sounds like it could use some oil," Dillon said, then followed up with a nervous laugh.

"Jesus Christ, if we make it out of here, I think we'll take the stairs on the way down," Suel said.

Once the doors opened on the third floor, they couldn't get out fast enough. Suel led them through a maze of corridors to a nurse's station with no nurses. The door to the room was just off to the right, so they entered, took about three steps then scanned the length of the room, an old fashioned hospital ward.

Dillon had seen photos of similar hospital wards in a book about the American Civil war following the battle of Gettysburg in 1863. Ten beds were arranged against the outside wall with a tall window between every two beds. White plastic curtains, all but one pushed back against the wall, hung from a rail attached to the ceiling that surrounded each bed. A grey plastic visitor's chair was pushed against the wall between every bed. A small wooden table with a drawer that looked to be original to the room stood at the foot of each bed. A black rosary rested on every table. All appeared to be in their original, arranged position and untouched. A series of various monitors were lined up against the wall behind each bed. There appeared to be no televisions or even so much as a radio anywhere in the ward.

Seven of the ten beds were occupied. The only black man in the room lay in the bed at the far end of the room, with two empty beds between him and the next patient. He was flanked by two women in traditional dress, one in gold the other in a blue garment that went from their shoulders down to the floor. Each wore a red silk cloth completely covering their head, but leaving the face exposed. A much older, grey-haired man in a yellowed t-shirt and jeans sat in the visitor's chair. Dillon and Suel headed toward the group. From the looks on the faces of the other patients, they were the first bit of activity anyone had seen in a while.

"Looks like he's maybe an Arab," Suel said.

"I'm guessing Somali," Dillon half-whispered.

"Mr. Jama," Suel said, as they drew near.

The two women immediately glanced at the floor and stepped backward.

The older man in the chair slowly stood.

The man in the bed smiled and said, "Hi."

"Mr. Jama, we're with An Garda Síochána. Detective Inspector Suel and Marshal Dillon. How are you doing?" Suel said. As he spoke, he opened his coat to reveal the badge attached to his belt. Dillon simply nodded.

"I've been better, and I was much worse earlier this week. Please, tell me you have arrested the man who shot me?" His words were heavily accented, and as he spoke, the older man nodded.

Suel gave an audible sigh and said, "We're working on it, and we were hoping you might be able to help."

Jama frowned. "What can I do from here?" he said, indicating the hospital bed.

"Did you get a look at the shooter?"

Jama shook his head. "No. I'm sorry, but I didn't see anyone. My fare handed me two twenty-euro notes. I put the notes on the console," he said, mimicking that movement with his hands as if he was placing the cash next to him. "I'm reaching for change in my pocket. There is a loud noise, and I wake up here, in this hospital. I was shot. He shot me. Shot me in the back."

"Did he say anything?"

Jama shook his head no.

"Did either of your passengers say anything?" Dillon asked.

Jama focused on Dillon for a moment, and seemed to be thinking something, maybe related to Dillon, although Dillon couldn't be sure.

"The man, he say something, 'I got it,' and he hands me two twenty-euro notes. He said something to the woman, asked her if she was okay, but that wasn't it," he said, shaking his head. He closed his eyes for a moment, thinking, and the older man began to say something, not in English. Jama quickly put his hand up, silencing the man, then opened his eyes. "He ask her, 'Are you okay, Honey?' This is what he said, I'm sure."

"And did she say anything?"

"She open the car door, step out of my car, then she say, 'Joey to he.' I can't translate this, what she means."

"Joey Touhy," Suel said.

"It was the man's name," Dillon added.

"You're sure that's what she said?" Suel asked.

Jama nodded. "Yes, it is what she say, but then the noise from the shooting, and, well." He shrugged and looked around, indicating the hospital ward.

"Where did you pick them up?" Suel asked.

"On the south side, a large house. It has a wall with a fence on top of it. A large home, brick with fancy two doors—"

"Double doors?" Suel said.

"Yes, two doors, and fancy, carved all around the doors," Jama said, indicating the shape of a door with his hands. "The driveway went around. It was like the palace for a king. When I pull in front the door open, and a large man come out. Very big. He looks scary, and he brings my fare out, the man and a woman. He opens the car door for the man, then tells me the address to take them."

"Do you remember the address?" Suel said.

Jama shook his head, then said, "It is on my phone, the GP. But my phone was in the car."

"The GPS?" Dillon said, then mentally kicked himself for not looking at the phone earlier. It was basic. How the hell could they have missed it?

"Yes, this is it, this GPS."

"What did they talk about, your passengers?" Suel said.

Jama shook his head. "Nothing. They not say a word until I stop, and he tells me he has the money. They say nothing all the way I drive. Not one word."

Suel looked at Dillon, then said, "We appreciate your help, Mr. Jama. Is there anything else you would like to add?"

Jama seemed to think for a moment, then said, "Get this man, the one who shoots me, and put him to death."

"We'll see what we can do," Suel said.

"Speedy recovery," Dillon said, and they walked out of the hospital ward.

"What do you think about the house he described?" Dillon asked as they made their way down the stairs to the ground floor."

"We'll verify as soon as I get my hands on that damn cellphone. Christ, we were asleep at the switch on that. But I'm laying odds it's your close personal friend, Eamon Boyle," Suel said, then pushed the door open on the ground floor.

"As soon as he mentioned the circular drive and the thug opening the door for Touhy, I was thinking Mousey at Boyle's house, and the address he gave him would be Jimmy Ryan's. Why would the woman, Gerri Greco, why the hell would she say 'Joey Touhy?' Wouldn't she just say 'Joey?'"

"He said they didn't say anything. She was probably giving him the silent treatment. You know how they can be," Suel said and opened the door exiting the stairwell.

"One more thing not quite adding up," Dillon said.

"At least we'll have confirmation from the GPS on his phone if we can get the damn thing," Suel said. They walked through the ground floor, then out the door.

There was a piece of paper stuck beneath the windshield wiper on the squad car. Dillon pulled it out as Suel climbed in the driver's seat. It was actually a used envelope with a handwritten note, just two words.

"What the hell is that?" Suel said, then started the engine.

"Apparently, it's addressed to you. It says, 'Lazy Bollocks,'" Dillon said, then handed the envelope to Suel and climbed into the passenger seat.

FIFTY

Back at the office, Dillon took the three tea mugs, two plates, and the candy bar wrapper that had been discarded on his desk into the break room and left everything on the counter. As he walked back toward his desk, he noticed a woman entering the office. She stopped just inside the door and seemed to scan the room for a moment before she focused on Dillon and headed his way.

She had short hair, blonde with sort of auburn highlights. She couldn't have been any taller than five foot one. She passed a number of desks, nodded at a couple of people, stopped, and said a brief something to Suel, who was talking to a dark-haired female officer. They all laughed about something, and then the blonde woman walked over to Dillon's desk.

He didn't sit down but watched her approach. She wore blue jeans and a navy blue golf shirt beneath her white lab coat. The lab coat was unbuttoned. "You that Marshal Dillon bloke?" she said.

"Yeah," he said, hoping he didn't sound too surprised. He focused on the evidence bag in her right hand.

"You brought this down to ballistics?" She half tossed the evidence bag onto his desk, where it landed with a heavy thunk. The pistol from Richie Nolan's room at This Little Piggy was in the bag.

"Yeah?" he said, not sure what this was all about.

"I can give you some general information on your weapon." She glanced at the evidence bag as Dillon picked it up. "But we can't do a ballistics test, there's no firing pin."

"No firing pin?"

"Nope. And, from what I can determine, it was removed some time back, years ago, probably decades."

"Decades?"

"Yeah, a number of decades, I'm afraid. Now, you're that American, right? We haven't met. I'm Janie McGuire. I work down in ballistics," she said and held out her hand.

"Jack Dillon," he said, and thought she seemed to hold onto his hand just a moment longer than normal.

"Dillon. Humph, that was my mother's maiden name. She came from a big family. All culchies, country folk."

"Well then, could be we're cousins. I came from a family of five," Dillon said and smiled.

"Cousins? I don't think so," she said, sounding deadly serious.

"No firing pin?"

"I'm afraid not. I looked long and hard, but I couldn't find one," she joked. "I've put a list of specifics in there. That's about all I can give you. I'd guess that piece hasn't been fired for quite a few years. It's a 1909 model, unusual because the barrel has a unique marking that says 'Officers' Model .38.' See, right there," she said, then pointed along the side of the barrel as Dillon held the gun.

"Which means what?" Dillon said.

"I'm not sure it means anything, but if I had to hazard an educated guess, I'd say it could suggest this was one of the first of the line. That embossing would go a way in establishing an accurate age, but I couldn't find any mention of it in the Colt book. The weapon clearly shows a lot of wear, but then again, it's a hundred and ten years old. Given that, it's in pretty good shape. But like I said, the firing pin was removed quite some time ago."

Dillon shook his head. Richie Nolan telling them he had receipts in his wallet that placed him somewhere else when the post office shooting occurred, the fact that they'd completely missed the taxi driver's cellphone, Nolan being in their custody when the shooting at Glasnevin cemetery occurred, and now, the weapon they'd thought was Richie Nolan's turns out to be little more than a paperweight. Things seemed to be going to hell in a handbasket.

"You okay?" McGuire asked. "You don't look too happy."

"The hits just seem to keep on coming," Dillon said and smiled.

"You don't have to tell me. Been there, and will be again. Well, anyway, nice to finally meet you. I've heard nice things about you, so, umm, don't give up just yet," she said, then extended her hand again.

As Dillon took her right hand, she wrapped her left hand around his. He glanced down for a brief moment, noticed that the gold ring on her left hand was on the middle finger rather than her ring finger.

"Hope to see more of you," Dillon said.

"That would be nice," she said, raised her eyebrows, then smiled and headed back out of the office. Dillon watched her as she nodded at Suel and a couple of other guys, then disappeared out the door.

FIFTY-ONE

S uel stepped over a moment later. "Janie already finished with the ballistics test? You must have some very special pull to get results on the same day."

"Or just more bad luck. Turns out, she couldn't do a ballistics test because the firing pin was apparently removed. To quote her, 'years ago, probably decades.'"

"So that's not the weapon?"

"No, not even close. First of all, it's a .38. We're looking for something smaller caliber than that damn thing." Dillon nodded at the evidence bag holding the pistol sitting on his desk. "She said it's probably a hundred and ten years old. I don't know, you get the feeling everything in this case seems to be turning to absolute shit?"

"A hundred and ten years old?"

"I know, I know. I had my doubts, but I was just so anxious to get that son of a bitch Nolan out of that pub and then start tearing him apart in the interview room. I feel like an absolute idiot."

"Well, misery loves company, but let's not go there. I think it might be a good idea to turn Nolan loose. We can hold him for another twenty-four hours if you want, but it's not going to do any good. The Glasnevin shooting only served to point to his innocence, at least on that count. He's involved, I'm sure of it, but right now, we're looking like bigger fools for every minute we hold him."

"But his damn tattoo," Dillon said. "That particular Ace of Spades, there is no way iin hell that's a one-in-a-million coincidence that just happens to be an exact match to the cards stuffed in the victims' mouths."

"Yeah, about the tattoo."

"Now what?"

"Well, it turns out it's not really a tattoo, you know with ink?"

"What?"

"I just talked with one of the officers who escorted Nolan back to his cell. She told me—"

"The woman who was just at your desk?"

Suel nodded. "Officer Dermond. She got a look at the thing once Nolan was back in his cell. It's something that's big with kids right now."

"Big with kids?"

"It's henna. She said the damn stuff can be removed with a number of homemade remedies, everything from toothpaste to olive oil and salt. Hell, you can even scrub it off. Might take a while and a number of attempts, but you can get rid of the design. Or you can just leave it alone, and the thing will fade away over a couple of weeks. I guess one of the best ways is to make a paste from baking soda and lemon juice, let that dry and then wash it off."

"Are you kidding me?"

"No, and she'd know, she's a mom. My God, she and her husband have six kids. If anyone would knows about this shite it would be her. She—"

"I meant that even the tattoo isn't what it seems. You can't make it up. God, this thing is falling apart so fast I literally can't keep up." Dillon picked up the evidence bag with the hundred-and-ten-year-old pistol. "Let's hold onto Nolan for another hour or two. I want to go back to that pub and check the room he was in. We can tell them we're returning this and hopefully get upstairs again."

"I thought you said you went through all the dresser drawers, and they were all empty."

"Yeah, I did, but remember, he got off that airplane with carry-on luggage. Where did that go? Even if it was stuffed with gifts he brought for that redhead he was sleeping with, where did the damn suitcase go?"

"Sounds awful thin to me."

"And me. But you got a better idea?"

Suel shook his head and said, "I've got that squad car drawn for another couple of hours."

Dillon shook his head no. "That'll attract too much attention. It's liable to shut down whatever slim chance we have of getting someone to talk. How about we take my car, and I'll drive?"

"I got a better idea. Why don't you go to This Little Piggy, and I'll go to the impound lot, see if I can get hold of Jama's cellphone."

"Much better idea," Dillon said.

FIFTY-TWO

Dillon drove up to Finglas. About two blocks before the pub, he passed a squad car sitting at the curb and recognized the officer with the mustache from his last trip to This Little Piggy. He pulled in front of the car and climbed out. The officer lowered his window as Dillon approached. "Marshal Dillon, what brings you to sunny Finglas this afternoon?" The sky was threatening rain at any moment.

"I plan on returning an item we took from that room the other night, hope to maybe look around a bit."

"They know you're coming?"

Dillon shook his head.

"That your car?"

"Yeah."

"You'll be lucky if some knacker doesn't set it on fire. Maybe pull up there. I'll follow you and park just to keep an eye on it."

Dillon was about to protest, but the more he thought about it, the better it sounded. "Thanks, I'd appreciate that," he said and walked back to his car. He pulled to the curb across the street from This Little Piggy. Two guys were leaning against the building smoking ciga-rettes. One looked to be about fifty, with close-cropped grey hair and a large tattoo on his neck. The other couldn't have been more than mid-twenties, muscular, with tattooed arms and hands. Neither one looked like the sort of person who would warrant a positive experi-ence.

Dillon got out of his car just as the squad car pulled over, maybe fifty feet behind him. He crossed the street and gave a quick nod to the two smokers. As he opened the door to the pub the younger guy said, "Afternoon, Officer," and they both laughed.

Dillon shot a quick, reflexive look then stepped in-side. All the chairs and barstools were right side up, sit-ting on the floor. Two men sat at the bar, looking neither left nor right, just staring straight ahead. One had what looked like a whiskey in front of him, the other a pint of Guinness. A half dozen empty stools were between them. Green and red lights flashed on the aluminum Christmas tree next to the front door.

The bartender had his back to Dillon. He looked like he was drying glasses, but Dillon caught him carefully watching the reflection in the mirror behind the bar. Back in a far corner, four men sat around a table, appar-ently playing cards. Whatever conversation they were having immediately stopped as Dillon entered the pub.

He headed across the second barroom toward the door leading upstairs.

"Hey, you. That there's private. You're not allowed to be going up there, less you pay," the bartender shouted.

Dillon turned and looked at him, then pulled open his coat, revealing his badge and the grips on the nine-millimeter tucked into his waist.

The bartender shook his head, picked up another glass, and started to dry it. As Dillon opened the door to the staircase, he heard a couple of chairs push back from the table of card players. He hurried up the stairs, then turned around when he stood at the top of the stairs and looked down. He had his hand on the grip of his nine-millimeter, and his coat pulled back, exposing his badge. A moment later, the door opened, and two men started to climb the steps.

"Far enough," Dillon shouted.

"That's private up there," the first man on the stairs said, but he didn't take another step.

"Just returning an item," Dillon said. He reached into his pocket and pulled out the .38 without a firing pin. "I'll call you if I need any help."

The man on the stairs shook his head, flashed a quick smile, then seemed to catch himself and said, "Don't take too long. It already smells like spoiled ham around here." He whispered something to the other guy as they left, closing the door behind them.

Dillon waited for a long minute, but no one came back through the door. He walked down the hall, stopped at the second door, and listened. He heard something, or rather someone, groaning, rhythmically, and he opened the door.

The same redhead was half sitting up in bed, filing her nails. The bed cover was pulled up to just below her breasts, and her knees were raised. A second pair of feet hung out from the end of the bed. She gave Dillon a questioning look, then frowned. She tossed her emery board onto the end table next to what looked like a glass of whiskey and reached beneath the bed cover. A moment later, a bald head appeared and kissed her. She indicated Dillon with a wave of her chin.

The bald head half rolled over, then grew wide-eyed at the sight of Dillon standing and watching. He looked like he might have been in his sixties, and his red face grew scarlet as Dillon flashed his badge. "I think your time is up."

"Am I under arrest?" the man half cried.

"Not if you get dressed and get your ass out of here, fast."

The man jumped out of bed and pulled on a pair of boxers. He pulled on a shirt, trousers, stuffed a pair of socks in his pockets, slipped his shoes on, took his suit coat off the bedpost, and started to leave.

"Wait a minute. You forgot to leave a tip," Dillon said.

"But, but I paid downstairs," the man half-whispered.

"And left this woman… unsatisfied. Or I suppose we could add failure to fulfill the terms of your contract to the charges," Dillon said.

"But I—"

Dillon pulled the .38 in the evidence bag out of his coat pocket, and the man quickly pulled his wallet from a back pocket, opened it and pulled out a fifty euro note, and handed it to Dillon.

"I didn't do anything," Dillon said and nodded at the redhead sitting in bed. She was just in the process of taking a sip from the whiskey glass.

"Oh, yeah, yeah, here you go," the man said and tossed the bill on the end table. He flashed a nervous smile and quickly hurried out of the room.

The redhead looked at the fifty-euro note resting on the end table, smiled, then looked up at Dillon, took another sip, and said, "Next?"

FIFTY-THREE

Dillon placed the .38 on top of the fifty-euro note sitting on the end table.

"Returning that? Don't tell me you're actually an honest cop? You must be the only one in this town."

"Might be more of us than you know," Dillon said. "What about your bunkmate from last night, Mr. Nolan?"

"Ahhh, your man Richie, the king of whisker burn. I haven't seen hide nor hair of him since he left with you lot."

"Not what I asked," Dillon said. "What can you tell me about him?"

"Richie? What can I say? Typical American." She smiled. "He seems highly impressed with himself, and for the life of me, I can't figure out why. Certainly not what you'd call a *marathon* performer, if that's what you're asking about," she said, then picked up her emery board and went back to filing her nails.

Dillon knew next to nothing about manicures, but he recognized her French nails, a neutral base with white tips, although there was something about hers, not quite precise, and he guessed it was probably a home job. "What can you tell me about Mr. Nolan?"

"Nothing to tell. He came in last night sometime after two, three sheets to the wind. Rolled on top of me for all of about sixty seconds, couldn't get it up, and promptly fell asleep. You lot barged in a few hours later. There, end of story."

"Why was he here?"

She tossed the emery board back on the table and grabbed her whiskey glass. "Because right now, I'm the best he, or you, or any other bollocks in this fair city, will ever have. Besides, he's apparently got some connections, which means I've had to sleep with him the last few nights and pretend to enjoy it. Believe it or not, this job ain't all it's cracked up to be. Having to sleep with some knacker who seems to have a permanent case of brewer's droop can be rather disappointing," she said, then raised her eyebrows, smiled, and took a sip.

"Mmm-mmm, maybe more than I wanted to know. What was he doing during the day?"

"Doing? How in the bloody hell would I know? He played cards with those fools downstairs, lost more than a few bets on the football games."

"Football games?"

"Real Madrid and Chelsea for sure, lost both of those. You could hear him swearing all the way up here," she said and flashed another quick smile. "Hey, don't take this the wrong way, but are we just about finished with the twenty questions routine? I'm going to get my ass kicked if you're in here much longer."

"You want to get out of here. You can walk out with me, be nice and safe," Dillon said.

"Yeah, sure, great idea, then where in the hell would I go? Cops, you lot are so damn stupid, you haven't a clue. You just don't get it."

"You said he spent the last few nights in this room with you, right?"

The look on her face suggested Dillon was correct. "Yeah, you maybe could call it good customer service. Let's just say some eejit, snoring their ass off, woke me up the last three mornings, and every time I rolled over to see who in the hell it was, that plonker was next to me."

"Richie have a suitcase?"

"I wouldn't know."

Dillon crouched down and looked under the bed, which caused her to laugh. "Yeah, right, that's what he did, he left his suitcase under the bed," she said, took a small sip of whiskey then set her glass on the end table and picked up the emery board again.

"Tell me about Richie's connections," Dillon said.

She stopped filing her nails and looked at him. "Seriously? You gotta be kidding me. You'd find me floating in the Liffey before happy hour if they thought I told you anything about that bastard."

"I know all about Eamon Boyle," Dillon said, taking a stab in the dark.

"Then what else is there to know? Richie has the fecking carpet rolled out for him. Whatever he wants, he seems to get. God, I'm just lucky he didn't have anyone else's tight little bum in here with the both of us."

"Sounds like Richie's been enjoying himself?" Dillon said, trying to make it appear like he was making a joke.

"All I know, the money they're supposed to have paid him, I'd have to ride every wanker in Dublin, twice, to even come close."

"Guess he's just lucky."

"That's why he's got me for his little night time romps. No one better. But just between you and me, I'll be glad to see the backside of him. Little too impressed with himself for my tastes."

"Well, let me give you a heads-up, Richie Nolan's gonna be back on the street in the next hour or so. I'm thinking this is liable to be the first place he heads to, just so you're prepared."

She frowned and said, "Really? I was sort of looking forward to a couple of days off. I got family visiting."

Dillon raised his right hand and said, "Scout's honor. Probably be back on the street in the next ninety minutes."

"Oh shit, that plonker damn near rubbed my thighs raw over the last couple of nights with that wretched beard of his. I'm gonna have to get out of here for a bit," she said, then rolled over to the far side of the bed and stood with her back to Dillon. She picked up a black thong from off the floor, stepped into it, then turned to face him.

"Offer's still open," Dillon said. "I can get you out of here and drop you off somewhere."

She seemed to think for a moment, then shook her head. "No, they'd find me by midnight, and it'd just look like I'd run off. I'll just tell 'em I gotta go to the clinic again. That'll keep 'em away for a couple of days. Besides, I got a contact or two of my own that's gonna put me in a little better position."

She walked over to the door, pulled a short purple robe with white piping off a hook hanging on the back of the door, and slipped it on. The sleeves on the robe hung down to her elbows, and although it looked sort of silky, Dillon figured it was probably cheap nylon. She left the robe untied, but not so much on purpose as she was maybe just oblivious to being exposed in front of a complete stranger.

"Thanks for the tip, and the heads-up on Mister Whisker Burn. Now get out of here so I can go downstairs in a bit," she said, then stepped over to the end table, stuck the fifty euro note in the pocket of her robe, and drained her whiskey glass. "Go on, get your arse out of here," she said, not turning to look at Dillon.

Dillon opened the door, shot a final glance her way, and headed down the stairs. He pushed the door into the pub open, then made a show of slamming it closed behind him. Everyone except the guy drinking a whiskey at the bar looked over and stared at him.

Dillon stomped over to the table of card players and placed his hands on his hips, making sure his Marshal's badge and the handgrips on his pistol were exposed. The two thugs who'd been smoking out front when he arrived had joined the group at the table. He took a long moment going around the table, looking each of the six men in the eye.

"Whichever one of you is in charge around here, you better tell that redheaded bitch upstairs the next time I'm here I expect some answers or I'm going to lock her up and throw away the key," he said, then stormed out of the pub. His ears were perked for the sound of chairs being pushed away from the table, but he didn't hear anything.

As he pulled the front door open, one of the six said, "Fecking arsehole. That American slapper Gemma finds out about this, she'll be leaving her five-star palace and looking for the likes of him." Everyone laughed.

Dillon hurried across the street to his car, waved at the squad car still parked a short distance behind him, then climbed in and locked the door. He glanced up toward the second floor and just caught the lace curtains suddenly close in the room with the redhead. He started the car and drove off. Fortunately, no one stepped out of This Little Piggy with a gun.

FIFTY-FOUR

Dillon was back at work early the next morning. As he stepped into the office, he saw Suel already sitting at his desk, talking on the phone. A cellphone in an evidence bag sat on the corner of Suel's desk. Suel hung up the phone just as Dillon approached.

"Abshir Jama?" Dillon said and nodded at the evidence bag.

"Yeah. Fortunately, since six murders doesn't seem to rate any sort of priority down at the impound lot, they hadn't gotten around to examining the taxi Touhy and the woman were murdered in. I also found a shell underneath the front seat that was missed. It's bagged and down in ballistics now. How'd you get on at This Little Piggy?"

"Charming, as always. I got upstairs, told the two thugs about to follow me I'd call them if I needed anything. Your favorite redhead was servicing a customer, or was he servicing her? Kind of hard to remember."

"She was there? Working?"

"Actually filing her nails and sipping a whiskey while some bald fool old enough to be her father or grandfather, was going down on her."

Suel laughed and said, "I hope you washed your hands after you got out of there."

Dillon wiped his hand across Suel's shoulder and said, "No need to now. She seemed less than impressed with Richie Nolan. In fact," Dillon laughed, "I told her he was going to be out in a bit, and she said she was going to give the excuse she had to go back to the clinic for a treatment so he'd end up with someone else last night."

"You find anything?"

Dillon shook his head. "No, nothing. But on the way out I heard one of those thugs in there say if that American slapper Gemma ever found out I'd been there she'd check out of her five-star palace and come looking for me."

"What's that got to do with anything? She another working girl providing service at This Little Piggy?"

"It didn't sound like it."

"So what's that got to do with our particular headaches?" Suel said.

"I'm not sure, but I've been thinking, and—"

"Oh shit."

"Just suppose for a moment that Richie Nolan really doesn't know anything, or at least not much. What if he's over here as nothing more than a decoy. What if—"

"You're crazy. He's our man."

"But what if he isn't? What if he's just here to attract our attention? What if everything from hassling Jackie Greco on the flight over, to saying something in front of us at the airport, to that fake Ace of Spades tattoo, what if all that is just a diversion from what's really going on?"

"Meaning you've got someone else out there stacking up this body count? And you've the bright idea it's a bloody woman?"

"Anything's possible. We certainly know it's not this Richie Nolan."

"You're as daft as a brush, Dillon. I'm not sure what you've been slipping into your coffee, but you'd best knock it off. You're beginning to sound crazy."

"Paddy, bear with me and just think about it for a minute. What's the one thing the taxi man heard from Touhy and Gerri Greco?"

"He didn't hear anything. Remember? They didn't say a word the entire drive from the south side all the way up to Clontarf. I'm guessing she was giving your man the silent treatment the whole way, and he was probably wondering why in the hell he even bothered to bring her along. You know how women get, we've both been there."

"But then when they got to Clontarf, what'd he hear?"

"Touhy told your taxi man he had the fare, he tossed two twenty-euro notes onto the console, then told your man to keep the damn change," Suel said, clearly sounding frustrated.

"And then Touhy asked Geri Greco if she was okay. According to the driver he say's, 'You okay, honey?'"

"Yeah, so?" Suel said.

"And what did she say?" Dillon asked.

Suel frowned and thought for a moment. "She says his name, Joey Touhy. So?"

"Paddy, think about it. She's getting out of the car, and she says his first and last name, and then the shots are fired. It doesn't make sense. It's been bugging me, and I've been thinking about it ever since Abshir Jama told us about it. After the thug in the pub mentioned this Gemma woman, it suddenly dawned on me."

"Help me out, Dillon, I'm not exactly following your logic here. You're not really making any sense."

"They don't talk during the entire taxi ride. They stop, Touhy pays, and he asks the woman if she's okay."

"Yeah, and she gets out of the car. Sounds to me like she's been pissed off about something and—" Suel suddenly gave Dillon a look like he understood.

"Yeah, and some woman runs up as she opens the car door, says 'Joey Touhy?', shoots the Greco woman twice, shoots Touhy twice before he realizes what's happening and can get his gun out, then shoots Abshir Jama, thinking she killed him, too. Stuffs the Ace of Spades in Touhy's mouth, and disappears."

"But what about these other shootings? The Odessa Club, the post office, your man yesterday morning at the cemetery?"

"Look at it, it all fits. You've got these guys sitting in cars, and no one has been shot through the window. We can't figure out why they would ever lower their window to someone they don't know. But what if that someone was a woman? Maybe a nice looking woman? We've both lowered the window or chatted with a woman we didn't know, never thinking for a moment there might be a problem. These idiots should be on guard, but instead, they've all apparently been shot through an open window. Those two at the Odessa Club, it was raining that night, and one of them had his window down. Doesn't make sense, unless— what if she just walks up to the car? No one expects a woman. She's attractive, they lower the window, and they end up dead."

"Hell of a price to pay for just staring," Suel said.

FIFTY-FIVE

Dillon checked his calendar and wrote down the dates on a legal pad for the week before Joey Touhy was murdered. Then he phoned Pat Mathews, his New York contact with the Marshals Service.

"To what do I owe the pleasure?" was how Mathews answered.

"Hi, Pat. Hey, we might be on to something over here, maybe. But a big maybe. Would you be able to check female passengers on flights to Dublin for the seven days prior to Joey Touhy's murder?"

"You just want to see if an individual flew over?"

"Correct. I'm open to any suggestions, but right now, my thought is to check Boston and JFK departures, direct flights or flights into Amsterdam and Paris, and then a hop into Dublin. We're looking for a woman traveling on an American passport with the first name of Gemma, most likely spelled with two M's," Dillon said.

There was a pause on the other end for a moment before Mathews asked, "And what's the last name?"

"We don't have it yet."

"Oh," Matthews said, not hiding his disappointment. "Man, this might take a bit. Any chance you can come up with a surname?"

"I'm trying. Can you give me a contact in Boston?"

"With the Marshals Service?"

"Yeah. That's going to be my next call."

"I know a guy pretty well up there. We went through the basic training academy down in Georgia together. Let me give him a call and see if he can help."

"That would be great. Really appreciate it, Pat."

"Not a problem," Mathews said, then read off the dates just to double-check. When Dillon said they were correct, Matthews replied, "I suppose it could be worse, you could be looking for a Mary or a Cathy. Oh, and I appreciate the rare whiskey, both bottles, that you're going to be sending over to me."

"You find a flight this woman was on, and I'll send you four bottles, and a barmaid to pour for you."

"I'm on it," Mathews said and hung up.

Dillon phoned Poraig Sullivan in the Border Management office out at Dublin Airport, next.

"Sullivan," was how he answered, sounding busy.

"Hi, Poraig, Jack Dillon. Sorry to bother you."

"What do you need?" Sullivan said, not sounding all that thrilled to get Dillon's call.

"I'm wondering if you can look back through your files for an arriving American woman, first name Gemma. Flying out of either Boston, New York's JFK, Amsterdam or Paris, sometime between..." Dillon read off the dates for the week preceding Joey Touhy's murder from the legal pad.

"What's the last name? Wait, hang on, hold for just a minute, Marshal, " Sullivan said.

Dillon listened to bits of a back and forth conversation for a half minute, but couldn't make out what was actually being said. It sounded like Sullivan might have placed his hand over the receiver or pressed the phone against his leg, then he was back on the line.

"Sorry about that, Dillon. What did you say this woman's last name was?"

"I didn't. Unfortunately, we don't know."

"But she came in from the States?"

"Yeah, we're thinking either out of Boston or JFK, but to be honest, we're just guessing at this point. Paris or Amsterdam as a fallback."

"All right, I'll have someone look into it. We're short-handed today, so I can't promise anything. I'm sorry, but I'm afraid it might be a while."

"Anything you can do would help. Much appreciated, Poraig, and thanks."

"Like I said, I can't promise anything, but we'll get on it."

"Thanks," Dillon said, again, then hung up and called Pat Mathews back in New York.

"Mathews."

"Pat, Jack Dillon again. Just had a thought, on this Gemma name—"

"Yeah."

"You might want to check known acquaintances of Richie Nolan."

"You think a woman would be crazy enough to be associated with some low life like Richie Nolan?"

Dillon laughed, then said, "Well, they date you and me on rare occasions, so I think it's worth a try."

"That's going to make it four bottles of the best Irish whiskey."

"And the barmaid. Yeah, got it, not a problem," Dillon said.

Dillon hung up, then brought up the Richie Nolan file on his computer. It gave Nolan's address, his height, weight, eye color, date of birth, place of employment, a laundry list of past offenses, but no mention of known associates.

Next, Dillon clicked on Google and searched for a listing of five-star hotels in the Dublin city center. He came up with eight hotels, printed off the list with the names and addresses, and went over to Suel's desk. Suel finished his conversation and hung up the phone just as Dillon came over.

"You got a name?"

Dillon shook his head. "I've got people checking out at Dublin Airport as well as in Boston and New York. They're going back a week before Joey Touhy was murdered."

"How long do you think it will take?"

"Too long. I'm going to check five-star hotels in the city center, see if they have anyone by the name of

Gemma signed in. I'm pretty sure she's not staying with Eamon Boyle. She's most likely not at This Little Piggy. The redhead suggested she would have to work very hard to make the kind of money Richie Nolan was getting. So maybe this Gemma woman is making the big bucks and living high on the hog."

"What if the suite isn't registered in her name?"

"Then I'm thinking it might be in Eamon Boyle's name."

"Boyle? But isn't that who Touhy came over to meet with in the first place?"

"Yeah, but I'm starting to think there's something much bigger in play here. With the exception of Touhy, all the victims have been Russian. At first glance, it appears random, but all Russian? All associates of Alexei Bazanov?"

"I think you're grasping at straws, Dillon, making this up. And a woman no less? One we never heard of, and Eamon Boyle brings her all the way over to little old Ireland to shoot people, and stuff a playing card in their mouth. Meanwhile, just for fun, your man Richie Nolan, a convicted criminal, known hitman, is—"

"Suspected."

"Is strutting around as some sort of a diversion? You're mad."

"I know it sounds crazy, but—"

"Sounds crazy? No, Dillon, it is crazy. But then, since you got this information from a working prostitute, sipping whiskey in the middle of the day while servicing a paying customer, who's to say it isn't true? Saints preserve us."

"So you're not going to check out these hotels with me?"

"Oh, on the contrary, I wouldn't miss the opportunity. You know what hotels you're going to?"

"I've got the list," Dillon said and waved the paper he'd printed off.

"Well then, let's be off. Why pass on the opportunity for you to buy me dinner while at the same time I get to watch you make an absolute bloody fool of yourself?" Suel said and grabbed his coat off the chair.

FIFTY-SIX

Suel was behind the wheel of the squad car as he and Dillon headed into Dublin city center. They were waiting for the light to change alongside the Liffey River on Bachelors Walk.

"I've got eight possible hotels," Dillon said as he read down the list. The names were all familiar, and he'd actually been in a couple of them.

"Eight? And they're all five-star?"

"Actually, to tell you the truth, none of them are five-star, they're all four-and-a-half-star, I figured that's close enough. Besides, when I checked online, I couldn't find anything that rated an actual five."

"The Westin one of them?"

Dillon looked at his list. "Yeah, it is."

"That'll be the closest," Suel said and put his blinker on. Once the light changed, he took a right onto the O'Connell Street bridge and drove across the Liffey to D'Olier. He very slowly wound through the traffic nightmare on D'Olier and then College Street, swearing every five feet about the traffic mess now that the new Luas Line, the light rail tram system, was up and running. He finally pulled up onto the sidewalk in front of the Westin Hotel.

"God grant me the patience," Suel said and turned off the engine.

"That was fun," Dillon said, meaning anything but then climbed out of the car.

"Hang on a moment. I've got an idea." Suel opened the trunk of the squad car, hauled out a small black suitcase with wheels, extended the handle then pulled it behind him as they walked toward the door.

The doorman watched them as they climbed out of the squad car, then smiled, nodded, and held the door for them as they entered. "Good afternoon, gentlemen, and welcome to the Westin. Enjoy your stay."

"Thank you," Suel said and smiled as they entered the hotel lobby. The lobby was a long room with a number of thick granite pillars on either side. A polished wooden floor led to three desks at the far end of the lobby. A fireplace on the right-hand side of the lobby had a nice fire burning in it.

"Hmm-mmm, nice enough digs. Let's see if we can find someone who can help," Suel said.

"What are you doing with the case full of evidence bags and 'DO NOT CROSS' tape?" Dillon asked.

"Watch and learn, my lad, watch and learn."

Dillon followed Suel to the middle front desk. The female clerk behind the desk was dealing with a couple in the process of checking in. The clerk was dressed in a navy blue blazer with the hotel logo embroidered on the breast pocket. She wore a light blue blouse beneath the blazer and a grey skirt.

Dillon and Suel waited patiently for a few minutes until a man appeared behind the front desk just to the right. He was dressed in essentially the same uniform, only wearing trousers. He appeared to be busy at his computer, but after Suel cleared his throat a couple of times, the man nodded and said, "May I help you, gentlemen?"

"Yes, thank you," Suel said, stepping up to the desk and flashing his badge. "Sorry to be a bother. We've a bit of a problem."

The man glanced left and right, then leaned forward and almost whispered, "Problem?"

"Yes. We've got this case containing rather important files." He nodded down at the suitcase full of evidence bags. "Not even sure if the owner is staying here, to be honest, but we do know she was staying in a five-star hotel. Of course, the Westin was the first hotel to come to mind. We have to deliver this to her in person. Could you be so kind as to check your list of guests? I believe she's staying in one of your more luxurious suites."

"One moment, please," the man said with a smile. He clicked a number of keys on his keyboard. "Yes, all right then, and what is the name, please?"

"Gemma."

"And the surname?"

"I'm afraid that's part of the problem. We don't seem to have that. We do know she is American and that she checked in sometime within the past week."

The clerk looked up at Suel for a long moment, appeared about to say something, then apparently thought better of it and started clicking keys. After a few moments, he looked up again. "I'm very sorry, but I'm not finding anyone registered under that first name, let alone an American."

"Perhaps the name Eamon Boyle," Dillon said.

"The gangster?" the clerk said, almost too loud.

"Same name, different man altogether," Suel quickly added, then gave Dillon a look.

"Yeah, sorry, different person," Dillon said.

"Well, where do you suggest next?" Suel said a few minutes later as they climbed back into the car.

"The Merrion would be the closest," Dillon said, looking at his list. He took a pen from his inside coat pocket and drew a line through the word "Westin."

"The Merrion. Right. This time let me do *all* the talking," Suel said.

They came up empty-handed at the Merrion Hotel, as well as the Fitzwilliam Hotel.

"Well, so much for that great idea. Next?" Suel said. He had settled in behind the wheel, started the car, and was waiting for a bus to pass before he pulled off the sidewalk and back into traffic.

"Next one would be the Shelbourne," Dillon said. "And how 'bout a little more positive thought here? We've only been to three hotels."

"Yeah, and the Shelbourne will make four. That's halfway through your list, and we've got absolutely nothing."

"If you've got a better idea, I'm all ears."

"Unfortunately, I don't. I think— oh, for Christ sake, now what?" Suel said, then pulled his phone out and answered it. "Suel." He shot a quick look over at Dillon, then put the car in park and turned off the engine. "When? Really? Where? What! Yeah, I know exactly where it is. He one of the victims? We're on our way. Tell them fifteen minutes," he shouted, then disconnected.

He turned the car back on, then the flashing lights, and the siren, and pulled into traffic. A car suddenly skidded to a stop just an inch from Suel's door. The driver leaned on his horn, then gave them the middle finger.

"Come on, you buggers, would you ever move out of the way, ya damn bollocks? Move, damn it, move," Suel yelled.

"What is it?"

"Another shooting. While we've been wasting our time looking in five-star hotels, our mysterious shooter seems to have struck again."

"Oh shit."

"Curious as to where?" Suel asked, then whipped around a bus. He pulled into the oncoming traffic lane, no more than a half-inch away from the side of the bus, then raced past and zipped back in just ahead of the bus, narrowly missing an oncoming dump truck with a wide-eyed driver screeching to a stop. The bus driver flashed his lights and blasted his horn.

"Jesus, Paddy, you keep driving like this, we're never going to make it. Where'd it happen?"

"Another one of your close personal friends," Suel said, and glanced over at Dillon, wild-eyed and grinning. "Alexei Bazanov's home."

"God, how in the hell? Victims?"

"Two that we know of."

"Is Bazanov one of them?"

"They didn't say," Suel said as he blasted through a red light and skidded around the corner.

FIFTY-SEVEN

They made the fifteen-minute drive in under ten. Suel shot past the lone Garda standing at the entrance to Bazanov's estate and parked at the rear of nine or ten vehicles pulled around the circular drive. Two uniformed officers headed toward the squad car, then stopped as Suel stepped out.

"Oh, sorry, sir. We just weren't sure who it was."

Suel nodded as he and Dillon hurried past them and headed toward the massive front door. Dillon slipped on his latex gloves as they wound their way past the various vehicles. A Garda crime scene van was backed up to the front entrance. The van was white with the An Garda Síochána logo on the side. Next to the logo were the words, "CRIME SCENE INVESTIGATION UNIT," and above all of that, "TECHNICAL BUREAU."

A man in a white hazmat suit was on his knees in the front doorway dusting the brass doorknob on the front door. As they approached, he glanced up, then stood and said, "Please don't touch the door, sir."

Suel pulled on his latex gloves. "Is it okay if we go in, Timmy?"

"Yeah. Bit of a disaster. Most everyone is in the office at the back of the hall. Just a heads up, DCI McCabe is in there as well. Didn't appear to be all that happy."

"Thanks for the warning," Suel said, then he and Dillon stepped into the front hallway with the black and white marble tiled floor and headed toward the elaborate wooden stairwell at the far end.

A number of small plastic tents, white, maybe four inches high and numbered, were positioned along the marble tile floor on the left side of the hallway. Dillon counted eleven of them. He glanced at the one closest to him, labeled "7." His first thought was that they marked shell casings, then realized they were all aligned with splatters of blood on the floor.

There was a body lying on its back halfway down the hall. A man in a white hazmat suit was on his knees just a couple of feet from the body, rummaging through what looked like a toolbox.

A pool of dark blood, almost black, had puddled around the victim's head. The body was that of a think-necked muscular man with close-cropped dark hair, a widow's peak hairline, and an S-shaped nose that looked to have been broken more than once. His flat brown eyes gave a glassy stare. About an inch of the left side of his forehead was gone. A large blood splatter and bits of bone were sprayed across the wall above him.

He still held a black automatic pistol in his right hand. Dillon paused and bent over to look at the markings emblazoned along the pistol slide. STEYR M9-A1, the new Russian military pistol.

If Dillon remembered correctly, it had a magazine capacity of twelve rounds. There was what looked like a bullet hole in the lower portion of the wall, maybe three feet from the marble floor. A large chip was in one of the nearby black marble tiles with bits of marble flakes scattered across the floor. Dillon figured the weapon probably fired a couple of times as the man went down. A uniformed officer stepped out of the door on the left side of the hall next to the stairwell. He gave a perfunctory nod to Dillon and Suel, then hurried toward the front door.

A large dining room with an elaborately carved table was on the right side of the hall. The table sat on a plush-looking red and blue oriental rug. A long, marble-topped buffet stood against one of the paneled walls with a number of crystal decanters and glasses arranged along the top. Dillon counted a total of sixteen chairs around the table, all heavily carved with red and cream-colored velvet seats. A large fireplace with a beveled glass mirror above the marble mantel was centered on the far wall. An older, heavyset woman, with her grey hair arranged in a braid that was then wrapped in a tight bun, sat at the dining room table. She was sniffling and brushing tears from her cheeks. She nodded slightly as an interpreter translated whatever a uniformed Garda officer had just said.

Dillon followed Suel into the room across the hall. Clearly an office. A tall man, solid-looking, with dark hair and a full beard, lay facedown on the floor. A small, round, end table with a shattered marble top lay on the floor next to him. What looked like a silver ice bucket and a broken vodka bottle lay in a puddle on the floor. Blood from a wound along the side of the man's neck had turned the puddle pink. The bullet appeared to have exited out the back of his neck, shattering his cervical spine. His icy blue eyes looked flat and seemed to stare into distant space.

Dillon nodded at DCI McCabe, standing next to a red velvet couch. McCabe looked from Suel to Dillon, then back to Suel. "Here he is, Alexei Bazanov," McCabe said and tilted his head in the direction of a massive, heavily carved desk. The black leather desk chair lay on its back behind the desk. One foot, the left, dangled over the edge of the chair. The foot was clad in what looked like a navy-blue velvet slipper with some sort of crest embroidered on the velvet upper.

Dillon leaned over the desk and looked at Alexei Bazanov. He was a short man, small actually. He wore a navy-blue velvet robe with silk lapels and what appeared to be light blue silk pajamas. The remnants of a small, shattered crystal glass were scattered across the floor next to Bazanov's body. A small hole, no more than a quarter of an inch diameter, was above the eyes, roughly in the middle of his forehead. Another entrance wound was on the right side of his nose, just below the bridge. An Ace of Spades playing card hung out of his mouth.

McCabe glanced around the room, shook his head, and smiled. "It seems the logical conclusion to a misspent life. I'm tempted to simply look up and down the road, and if we don't see anyone offering to surrender themselves, we simply declare the case closed and move on."

"How? How in God's name could anyone even get inside here? Let alone with a weapon. It had to be someone they knew," Suel said.

"One would think so," McCabe said and shook his head again.

"Or someone they thought would not be a problem. Someone they were interested in for another reason," Dillon said.

"Dillon?" McCabe said.

"We picked up a rumor from a working girl at This Little Piggy."

"This Little Piggy? That nefarious pub in Finglas?"

"Yes, sir."

"And what? This woman was a waitress? A bartender?"

"Not exactly, sir," Suel said.

"She's a prostitute," Dillon said. "The American, Richie Nolan, has been spending his late nights with her."

"He's in custody, correct?"

"No, sir, he was released earlier."

"Released?" McCabe half-shouted. "Why in God's name was he released?"

"He was in custody when the last shooting occurred, sir, the murder in Glasnevin cemetery. And, truth be told, we didn't have any reason to hold him, sir." Suel glanced at his watch. "He's been released for no more than ninety minutes. The chance that he somehow was in here and is responsible for this is just about zero."

"But what about the murder of that American gangster?"

"Joey Touhy," Dillon said. "When he and his girlfriend were murdered, Richie Nolan was still back in Boston. He didn't arrive in Dublin for another thirty-six hours. We actually saw him in the baggage area at the airport. In fact, he was met by some associates of Eamon Boyle's."

McCabe stared at the two bodies, Alexei Bazanov, with the Ace of Spades in his mouth and his right hand man, Sergei, both lying in Bazanov's office and shook his head. "Like I said, I'm tempted to just look up and down the road, and if I don't see anyone waving their hands and admitting to the crime, I'll simply declare the case closed and move on."

FIFTY-EIGHT

Suel licked his finger tips and asked, "Umm-mmm, you going to eat that?"

"Nah, go ahead and help yourself," Dillon said, and handed the paper tray with his remaining kabob over to Suel.

They were sitting in the squad car, parked on the sidewalk next to the bus stop in front of Mother's Kabobs. Mother's was a somewhat greasy takeout place on Phibsboro Road, and Dillon had never, ever seen a woman working behind the counter in there, let alone someone's mother.

"Nice of you to share," Suel said and took a large bite from Dillon's kabob. "Mmm-mmm, you know, I have to almost agree with McCabe. Whoever got in there and shot Bazanov did us a hell of a favor."

"Yeah, until someone steps into the position Bazanov unintentionally vacated, maybe with the idea of revenge in his mind, and starts going after Eamon Boyle and his crew. They'll be shooting one another all over the city."

"In which case, we should just let them all have at it, and when they're finished, we can sweep up the pieces."

"Yeah, maybe."

"Anyway, nice of you to pop for dinner," Suel said, and took another bite.

"Remember? You were the one who told me I had to buy."

"Well, good thing I like kabobs." Suel smiled and stuffed the last of Dillon's leftover one into his mouth. "Mmm-mmm, here, hold this," he said and handed both empty food trays to Dillon.

"You sure you don't want to lick them clean? There might be a little left."

Suel leaned over and studied the trays in Dillon's lap. "Nah, I'm good. I was thinking you were going to take me into Goodley's, but they only take reservations. Guess it's *the* place to be seen," he said and nodded at the restaurant four doors down.

Goodley's was a trendy place with white table-cloths, cloth napkins, and candles. The nightly menu was posted in the front window. Just now, two women stood out in front, reading the menu, nodding to one another, and looking excited.

The door suddenly opened, and a couple stepped out of Goodley's. The man put his left arm around the woman and kissed her on the forehead. Her dark hair was done in a pageboy cut. When he kissed her, she grinned, then reached down, gave his crotch a quick rub, and nodded excitedly, which earned her his smile along with another kiss on the forehead.

"Will you look at that. Gorgeous face, check that wonderfully hot body out, and she can't wait to get him home and have him all to herself. And here I am, eating kabobs behind the wheel and sitting next to the likes of you."

Suel turned the key in the ignition, and the car started just as the couple strolled past. Dillon stared through the window at the woman's pearl necklace. "Hang on just a second," he said and opened the car door.

"Dillon? What? What the hell do you think you're doing?"

Dillon stepped onto the sidewalk. He left the car door open, took a couple of steps, and said, "Brianna?"

The couple stopped and turned. The man kept his arm around the woman's shoulder but pulled her closer. It was her. Brianna. As she focused on Dillon, her eyes grew wide, and she seemed to tuck herself in even closer to her partner.

"Oh, umm, Jack. Surprise, surprise. What, what are you doing here?" she said, then looked at the empty kabob trays Dillon was still holding.

"Working." He shrugged. "Late night."

He remembered giving her the pearl necklace. She'd unwrapped it last year in front of her Christmas tree, immediately put it on, then made love on the floor with him. The last time he saw it, the necklace, she was asleep in her bed with the black silk sheets, and he was heading out the door to respond to Joey Touhy's murder in Clontarf. He was thinking he should ask for the necklace back, maybe suggest it apparently didn't take her all that long to replace him.

"Yeah, well, thanks for saying hi. Umm, nice to see you again," she said, breaking the uncomfortable silence.

"Jack Dillon," Dillon said and held his hand out to her partner.

The man kept his arm around Brianna, but extended his hand and squeezed Dillon's in a death-defying grip. "Oh yeah, you're the Yank. Right? Yeah, Brianna's told me a bit about you. What you do and all." He made it sound like whatever he'd heard hadn't been all that complimentary.

"Well, we need to get going. A real surprise seeing you, Jack. Ahh, stay safe," she said, then they quickly turned and hurried away about three times faster than their previous pace.

The guy's arm was no longer around her shoulder.

Brianna's arms were now crossed over her chest, her head was bowed, and she was shaking it back and forth. The guy glanced back at Dillon with a look that suggested all his plans for later that night had just been ruined.

"What the hell was that?" Suel said, as Dillon climbed back in the car and buckled up.

"Just someone I used to know."

"Wasn't that Brianna? The woman you were mad about, right? What the hell is she doing with that wanker?"

Dillon's phone rang, saving him from having to answer. "Dillon."

"Hey, Jack. Pat Mathews in New York. I may have something for you."

Dillon looked over at Suel and nodded, then pulled a pen from the inside pocket of his coat as he said, "Go ahead, Pat."

"My contact in Boston, Tony Russo, came across a woman who traveled from Boston to Amsterdam and then Dublin five days prior to the Touhy murder. Her name is Gemma O'Carroll." Mathews spelled the last name out. "Two back-to-back tours in Afghanistan, special ops."

"Special ops? A woman?"

"Yeah. She was there in 2010 and 2011. She was one of a number of women who'd go out on patrols. They could talk to women in the villages. I guess Afghan soldiers couldn't even look at other women, let alone talk to them. Ahhh, let's see. She's got a bronze star for valor, combat infantry badge, Purple Heart, jump wings, a bunch of commendations," he said, sounding like he was reading off the information.

"So far, other than the first name, it doesn't seem to jive," Dillon said, then looked over at Suel and shook his head

"Okay, Mister Negative, but she is from Boston, and with her service experience, she would have the capabilities to pull off something like Touhy's murder. She's also the only Gemma we found, well, other than a woman who was seventy-eight, and we actually went back two weeks."

Dillon thought about that for a moment, still figured it was pretty lean, but better than the nothing at all they'd been dealing with up to this point. "Email the file to me, Pat. You got an image?"

"Couple of passport photos and military IDs."

"Okay. Thanks Pat. We'll check it out. Not like we're drowning in leads over here right now. Hey, any relationship with Richie Nolan? Or, for that matter, Touhy?"

"Nothing I came across. I'll double-check, but it's probably slim to none. I'll send them your way," Mathews said, and then hung up.

"A break?" Suel said.

"I doubt it. A woman named Gemma, who was an Army veteran, flew out of Boston five days before Touhy was shot. It sounds pretty damn lean."

"Sounds better than the leads we don't have."

"True."

"So," Suel said. "Where's our next stop?"

"The Shelbourne. Ever been there?"

"Only in the bar a few times. Never enjoyed a room," Suel said.

FIFTY-NINE

The Shelbourne Hotel was just a ten-minute drive from Mother Kabobs, three minutes as the crow flies. Suel parked on Kildare Street, and they walked around the corner to the front door.

The hotel had been established in 1824 and was a Dublin landmark. Among other events, in 1922, the Irish Constitution was drafted there in room 112 under the leadership of Michael Collins. It was just across the street from Stephens Green, and as they came around the corner of the building, a horse pulling a white carriage trotted past. A glass-roofed canopy supported by wrought iron covered the entryway. As Suel dragged the suitcase holding the evidence bags into the entrance, a doorman in a dark coat with tails and a grey top hat held the door open for them.

"Good evening, gentlemen, and welcome to the Shelbourne. Luggage?"

"Thanks, but just this, and I've got it," Suel said and followed Dillon in the door.

Inside, the elegant lobby featured a marble floor. Classic plaster trim decorated the walls and ran along the ceiling. A red carpet led the way up to the front desk, where a man in a grey suit smiled at them as they walked the roughly one hundred feet toward the desk.

"Good evening, gentlemen. A reservation?" He wore a dark coat and a red name tag that said, "Stefan." Dillon guessed from the slight accent he might be German.

"Not quite," Suel said, then flashed his badge and made a show of wheeling the small suitcase up against the marble counter. "We're to deliver these files to one of your guests. That is, we hope she's your guest, there seems to be some confusion on that point. Imagine, the government gets the information wrong," he said.

Stefan flashed a smile and said, "Yes, imagine."

"Would you be so kind as to check for us? Her name is Gemma." Suel shot Dillon a sideways glance as he mentioned the name.

"The last name may be O'Carroll, but there seems to be some confusion on that point," Dillon said.

"Be happy to check. Just a moment please, and we'll see what we have… ahhh, yes, in the Princess Grace suite?"

"That sounds right," Dillon said, unable to hide the wide-eyed look he gave Suel.

"If you'd like to leave that here, I'll see that someone brings it up to her suite immediately—"

"I'm sorry, but we're not to let this out of our sight except to surrender it to Miss O'Carroll."

Stefan seemed to process that for half a second, then said, "Very well. Let me just call up there and alert her to—"

"Best not to call, she's been working long hours, and we'd hate to wake her with a phone call. Really, if you could just direct us, we—"

"I'm sorry, but policy is that we can't let you go up there unaccompanied."

"Even though we're the bloody coppers," Suel growled.

Stefan physically backed up a step or two and said, "Sorry. Please, just a moment, and let me check with my supervisor."

"You didn't have to take his head off," Dillon said as Stefan hurried around the corner.

"Jesus Christ, let's go find our way. Enough with this plonker wasting our time," Suel said.

Before they could take a step, a woman came out of the office with the clerk behind her. She was short and stocky, with unattractive brown hair and a large dark mole about the size of a dime on the left side of her cheek. A number of hairs were growing out of the mole. Her name tag read "Mafalda."

"What seems to be the problem?" she asked, then briefly flashed an insincere smile. Her English was just slightly accented, maybe Spanish or Portuguese.

"Not really a problem," Suel said. "We just need to deliver these files up to Miss O'Carroll in the Princess Grace Suite. They're of a rather confidential nature, and

I'm sure you can understand we, unfortunately, can't release them to anyone except Miss O'Carroll." Suel followed up with a big smile.

"Yes, I see," she said, then seemed to think for a moment. "I'm sorry, but may I see some identification?"

Suel slowly closed his eyes for a moment, but fortunately didn't say anything. He produced his badge, placing it on the granite-topped counter.

Mafalda flashed another insincere smile and said, "And perhaps something with your picture?"

This time Suel didn't smile, but he did take out his wallet, pulled out his ID card, and placed it on the counter.

She looked over at Dillon as he set his badge on the counter, then pulled his US Marshal's ID from his wallet.

She carefully studied both cards, pausing for a long moment on Dillon's before she shot a quick look at him and said, "American?"

"Yes."

She seemed to consider that for a bit, then said, "How about if I escort you up to the Princess Grace Suite?"

"As long as we can determine that Miss O'Carroll will be in receipt of what we're here to deliver, that will work," Suel said.

<h1 align="center">SIXTY</h1>

Mafalda pulled what looked like a white credit card with a red stripe from her coat pocket as she stepped out from behind the front desk. "If you'll follow me, please."

Suel looked at Dillon, gave a wink, and they followed her across the lobby to a bank of elevators. There were four elevators, and she stepped in front of the furthest one. It was set slightly off to the side from the other three. There wasn't a button to push. Mafalda inserted her white card into a slot, the elevator doors opened, and she stepped to the side so Suel and Dillon could enter.

"Thank you," they said, almost in unison.

Inside the elevator, she inserted the card in another slot. The doors closed a moment later, and the elevator began to rise. The inside was paneled with what looked like burled mahogany. The floor was carpeted and felt thick and plush beneath their shoes. Dillon glanced up in the corner and noticed a security camera. He smiled for the camera, then said, "We really appreciate you making the time. Sorry to interrupt your evening."

Mafalda flashed that nanosecond of a smile again, continued to look straight ahead then said, "It's all part of a day's work." Which, from the sound of it, translated into something along the lines of, "Just one more pain in the ass thing I have to do."

The doors opened, and she indicated they should step out with an overly gracious wave of her arm. The hotel hall, walls, and ceiling, were decorated in a sort of lime green color. A creamy-white chair rail ran along the wall on both sides of the hall about three feet off the floor. They made a right hand turn out of the elevator, then after ten or fifteen feet turned left into a short hallway, more of an alcove actually.

There was only one door in the alcove, and it was directly in front of them. The door was wide and painted a lemony sort of yellow color with two panels trimmed in more creamy-white molding. A large brass door handle was on the right side of the door. Centered about eye level was a shiny metal plaque, about a foot square, that had the room number; 331, and then the words, "'PRINCESS GRACE." Just beneath the plaque was a small peephole so one could look out and see who was at the door.

Dillon glanced at the bottom of the door to see if light might be coming from inside the suite. A shadow would have indicated that someone was there, just on the other side, but the door appeared to be tight against the frame, and so he couldn't tell.

Mafalda looked at Suel and Dillon for a half-second, grimaced, then knocked softly. When there was no answer, she gave a small sigh, knocked once more, and cleared her throat. They waited for a long minute before she looked at Dillon and Suel, nodded, and said, "It would appear she is not here."

Suel took a quick step toward her, extended his arm over her head, and pounded on the door loud enough that the noise echoed down the hall.

"Please, please, sir, that sort of response is not necessary. It would appear Miss O'Carroll is not here. Now, if the two of you would kindly return to the lobby, we can leave a message on—"

"Open the bloody door," Suel said, in a tone that caused even Dillon to jump.

"I'm afraid that is out of the—"

"I said, open the bloody door. Didn't you hear it? Someone is inside calling for help."

"I, I didn't hear anything," Mafalda said, not sounding all that sure. She stepped toward the door and placed her ear against it. "No, I don't—"

"There, did you hear it again? Someone is hurt. Open the door, or I'm going to kick the damn thing in."

"No, wait. Please, let me phone the suite," she said and pulled out a cellphone. She quickly pressed a couple of numbers on the screen using her thumbs, then put the phone up to her ear, shooting a worried look at both Dillon and Suel in the process. A moment later they heard a phone ringing on the other side of the door.

"There, I heard her again," Suel said, this time giving Dillon a wink.

"I can't hear anything," Mafalda said.

"Wait, listen," Dillon said. "There it is, a woman's voice. I heard her."

"Step aside," Suel said, taking a step back and looking as if he was getting in position to kick the door open.

"No, no, wait. I have a passkey. Here, see?" Mafalda said as she inserted the card into the slot. A moment later, a small green light flashed, and she opened the door. Suel half pushed her aside and charged into the suite with Dillon right behind him. The phone continued to ring from somewhere in the suite.

"Hang up the bloody phone," Suel said, and a moment later, the ringing stopped.

They were standing in a long hallway with ten-foot ceilings and elaborate plaster trim where the ceiling and wall met. Four doorways, two on either side, were further down the hall. A mahogany table, maybe five feet long, was centered on the far wall. Above the table in an elaborate gilt frame was an oil painting that looked as if it could have come from the sixteenth century, two women sitting at a table with a bowl of red grapes between them and a small child looking across the table.

"Miss O'Carroll? Miss O'Carroll, are you all right?" Mafalda called.

Dillon indicated they should move forward with a nod of his head. He took hold of the pistol in his belt and cautiously entered the room on the right while Suel entered the room on the left.

"No, wait, you can't do that. Detective, you've no right to be going in there. Please, stop. Detective," Mafalda shouted and stomped her foot.

Dillon walked into a dining room with a polished oak floor and a solid antique table and chairs. The eight chairs around the table had red velvet cushions. The room had wainscoting about four feet high running around all four walls and a window that looked out onto the street. Two antique chests of drawers rested on either side of a large archway leading into an even larger living room. Two more large oil paintings surrounded by a gilt frame hung above both chests of drawers.

The living room had a dark beige upholstered couch facing the black marble fireplace on the far wall. A marble-topped table was positioned behind the couch, and two matching stuffed chairs sat on either side of the fireplace. Two windows on the right side of the room overlooked the street. The room was empty, and just as Dillon turned to exit Suel called from the master bedroom, "Dillon, in here."

Dillon hurried down the hall and through the bedroom door, just as Suel called again, "Dillon." Suel was in the bathroom, and his voice echoed.

"What'd you find?" Dillon said, then stopped in his tracks.

The bathroom had a white marble floor and white cabinets. The bathtub was at the far end of the room, surrounded at the head and foot by white and pink marble walls. The back wall, running the length of the tub, was one huge mirror. Another mirror ran along the length of the front of the tub. The tub was large enough that both Dillon and Suel could have comfortably fit into it. Not that they would have wanted to. The tub and the marble around it were covered in blood.

A pile of clothes lay on the floor, black stretch pants, and a pair of running shoes. An empty box of gauze pads, another larger box of gauze rolls, and an empty tube of wound care ointment sat on the towel shelf. A bloody handprint was smeared down the marble wall, and two towels lying on the floor were soaked in blood.

Dillon pulled a pen out of his pocket and moved the stretch pants slightly to the side, revealing a matching black top, soaked in blood. He moved the top over with his pen and spotted a baseball cap beneath.

The cap was black with a gold Russian imperial crest on the crown and a half-circle on the front of the bill with white, blue, and red horizontal stripes maybe an inch wide all edged in gold— the Russian flag.

SIXTY-ONE

They were sitting in the living room of the Princess Grace Suite, keeping out of the way of another crime scene investigation unit. Suel was on the couch.

Dillon was in one of the matching chairs with his legs stretched out in front of the empty fireplace. He was in the process of leaving a long voice message for Pat Mathews back in New York, asking him to find out any and everything on Gemma O'Carroll.

Suel, afraid the official notification might not get out until tomorrow sometime, had sent a text to the Border Management office at Dublin Airport, telling them to be on the lookout for one Gemma O'Carroll, traveling on an American passport. He had included her passport number and photo and was following up with a phone call to make sure they opened his text message.

They disconnected their phones at roughly the same time. Suel tossed his cellphone on the coffee table just as Dillon said, "So what have we been missing?"

Suel shook his head. "Well, for starters, where in the hell did she go?"

"Hospital?" Dillon said, and shrugged.

"I doubt it. They'd have to report the wound, and no report has come across. Garda would welcome her into their open arms in about fifteen minutes, so, if she's smart, she'll stay clear."

"She's all bandaged up, and she's lost blood, a pretty fair amount," Dillon said. "She'd want to get the bleeding stopped first and foremost, then, depending on the wound, have the bullet removed, certainly clean the wound, get some rest, lay low. She'd have to change that bandage three or four times a day to start, hopefully, take antibiotics and probably pain killers. I just don't see her hopping on a plane."

"She'll have to avoid the Gardaí," Suel said.

"Maybe Eamon Boyle's place?"

"And we've a car there, waiting out in front of his place. Get this, that plonker Boyle has already sent out mugs of tea and chocolate biscuits to the lads in the car. Apparently, whoever brought the tea out told them thanks for keeping an eye on the place."

"Unbelievable," Dillon said and shook his head. "I'm thinking of the blood along the hallway floor at Bazanov's place. I thought it belonged to that body lying on the floor. Now I'm thinking it was the always beautiful, ever-elusive Gemma O'Carroll, making her way back out the front door after she'd been shot," Dillon said.

"Think that's why they let her in, in the first place? She's attractive, and she was wearing a Russian hat?"

"It's maybe just stupid enough to work."

"What do you say we pay a visit to Richie Nolan and your redheaded girlfriend at This Little Piggy?" Suel said.

Dillon seemed to think about that for a moment, then slowly nodded. "Not the worst idea, and we're just wasting time here. Let's go."

They walked out to the hallway, but couldn't access the elevator because they didn't have a room key. So they headed down the stairs.

Once on the ground floor, Dillon said, "Let me check on something before we leave. It'll only take a minute," and headed toward the front desk.

Stefan, the desk clerk they'd originally dealt with, was standing there with his hands clasped behind his back. He pasted a fake smile across his face as they approached and seemed to grow more nervous with every step they took.

"Good evening, Stefan. We need some information," Dillon said.

"Information?" Stefan said, then glanced around nervously.

"Yes, regarding Miss O'Carroll. She was your guest in the Princess Grace suite."

Stefan licked his lips back and forth and swallowed. "I, I never spoke with her, never even saw her, ever."

Dillon nodded, then said, "Could you tell me when she was scheduled to check out of the Shelbourne?"

"When she was scheduled to check out? Why yes, yes, I can do that," he said, sounding relieved. He quickly clicked a number of keys on the keyboard. "Yes, sir, here we have it. She is scheduled to check out tomorrow morning by noon. That is unless she informs us of a late checkout, in which case we'll allow her to remain until two o'clock. Hotel policy," he said, then looked up and smiled.

"Thank you, Stefan."

SIXTY-TWO

Dillon asked, "You think we should call for some backup?"

Suel had just turned onto Glasnevin Road, heading toward Finglas and This Little Piggy. "I suppose we could if you want to, but we'll be waiting another hour for someone to show up. It's still all hands on deck at Bazanov's place. I'm sure they've got everyone searching under every damn bush on the estate for the shooter. Did you get a look at all the news vehicles and cameras when we left there? How in the hell did they even hear about the shooting that fast? They must have gotten the word almost sooner than we did."

"Yeah, and then we had to threaten to kick the damn door in at the Shelbourne."

A few minutes later, Suel pulled to the curb and turned off the engine. They both looked across the street at This Little Piggy. Two guys had been leaning against the front wall of the pub, smoking cigarettes. One of them had a Mohawk haircut, shaved on the sides, and spiked down the middle of his head. As Suel pulled to the curb in the squad car, the guy with the Mohawk tossed his cigarette on the sidewalk and hurried back into the pub. The neon sign in the oval window next to the front door read "OPEN," and behind it, red and green lights flashed on and off.

"Well, no doubt he's about to tell them we're out here. It would be a shame to disappoint," Suel said and opened the door.

Dillon climbed out and hurried around the front of the car. The lone man still leaning against the front of the building watched as they waited for a car to pass and then crossed the street. He loudly cleared his throat and spit a large glob on the sidewalk just as they stepped up on the curb.

"Evening, Officers, and a very Happy Christmas to you," he said, then took a long, final drag from his cigarette and tossed the butt onto the sidewalk.

"Oh, oh, littering. That's a fifty-euro offense," Suel said. "We'll let it go this time, but mind yourself, not everyone is as generous as we are. Happy Christmas, mate."

They stepped inside the pub. The place wasn't just crowded, it was jammed. The cheap tin Christmas tree next to the door had bent branches and just three ornaments. A single, sparse string of lights along one side of the tree flashed red and green.

The guy with the Mohawk was leaning over talking to a muscular looking bartender. He just happened to glance toward the door at that moment and pointed at Dillon and Suel as they stood next to the tree, looking around.

Music was blaring loudly from a DJ set up at the far end of the bar. He was playing a song Dillon recognized, drunken Shane McGowan and Kirsty MacColl singing the Irish Christmas song *Fairytale of New York* with the Pogues. When he'd first heard the tune, Dillon had thought it was dreadful. Nothing had changed in two years. He also knew he was in the minority. It was one of, if not *the* most popular Christmas song in Ireland, evidenced by the fact, in case he had any doubts, that the vast majority of people in the pub were swaying back and forth in their chairs, singing along while sloshing their drinks from side to side.

As they began to make their way through the crowd, the singing and laughter immediately stopped at each table they passed. Occasionally Dillon could read the lips on people grumbling at their presence, none of it pleasant. By the time they reached the metal door leading to the second floor, everyone had stopped singing, and the music blaring over the speakers seemed to take on a hollow sound.

Suel turned and looked around at the two rooms full of glaring eyes for a long moment, then shouted, "Happy Christmas, you bunch of bollocks." A cheer suddenly erupted from the crowd. More than one hand flashed them the finger. Suel took a slight bow, then opened the door, and they headed up the stairs.

Suel stopped at the top of the stairs and said, "Let me stay here and keep anyone from coming up. You hurry and check that room."

Dillon quickly walked down the hall toward the second room and opened the door without bothering to knock. The room looked empty, although the lamp sitting on the bedside table was turned on. The sheets and duvet were rumpled and hanging over the far side of the empty bed. He made note of the fact that the antique .38 without the firing pin was nowhere to be seen. He walked back to the first room, opened the door, and looked in. The room was empty. The lamp was turned off, and the bed appeared to have been made. Two empty drink glasses, one with a lipstick-stained cigarette floating in the contents, rested on a bedside table.

Suel gave him a questioning look.

"Nothing. I don't know, maybe everyone is downstairs. Let me check the other two rooms," Dillon said, then hurried back down the hall. The third and fourth rooms were the same, empty, and dark, with the beds made. Apparently, the "working girls" were all downstairs, singing along with drunken Shane McGowan on the CD. He left the doors open and headed back down the hall to Suel.

As he passed the second room, he glanced in, took a step or two, then stopped and backed up. Was that a foot just barely hanging out on the far side of the bed? Dillon pulled the pistol from his belt and stepped into the room.

"Stay where you are, and let me see your hands," he shouted. "I said, let me see your hands," he shouted again and moved forward a couple more steps. "I need to see your hands now." He took the next three steps with his pistol extended and cautiously peeked around the edge of the bed.

"Find something?" Suel said, standing at the door.

"Something? No, just someone."

SIXTY-THREE

Richie Nolan was lying on the floor alongside the bed. He appeared to be staring at the wall and apparently wouldn't be going anywhere in the immediate future. He was naked, with the sheet and duvet twisted around his raised right leg. His head was turned toward the wall, and there was a very small puncture wound in his right temple. It looked like he may have tried to hurry out of bed, probably making an effort to escape, and got shot in the process. Dillon stepped forward and crouched down to check for a pulse on his neck, more of a mechanical reaction rather than thinking he might actually find one.

What looked like Nolan's clothes appeared to be crumpled on the floor beneath his body. Legs from a pair of blue jeans and the corner of a black t-shirt were peeking out from under his arm. Two comfortable looking brown shoes with spongy rubber soles and a pair of black socks were neatly arranged just beyond Nolan's head.

Dillon studied the body for a long moment. Glassy eyes stared off into space. He remembered reading somewhere that the human eye could take a photo of the very last thing it saw, and he stared at Nolan's eyes for a long moment, but couldn't detect any sort of image.

Suel walked over to the edge of the bed and looked down. "Oh for feck's sake. This plonker? I don't believe it."

Dillon rose to his feet. "He's cold, been here a lot longer than just a couple of minutes," he said, and reflexively looked out the window.

"What? Expecting to see someone fleeing the scene?"

"No, just wondering who in the hell did this," Dillon said and shook his head.

"Well, we know it wasn't Bazanov or his skinny bodyguard, that bastard Sergei, they were killed this morning. Christ on a cross. Who did it? Maybe some Russian? Eamon Boyle? Your American girlfriend, Gemma O'Carroll? God only knows."

Dillon could feel the vibration of the DJ's music coming up through the floor. "We got no one to talk to, and our shooter, whoever the hell it was, is in the wind."

"There's no exit wound. Could be the same small caliber as the other shootings. Your woman Gemma O'Carroll is starting to look pretty good for this," Suel said. He took a step next to Dillon and crouched down. "When I lift him, pull those clothes out from underneath."

"Paddy, it's a crime scene, we can't go—"

Suel shot a look, then took hold of Nolan's shoulders and raised his body. Once Suel lifted, Dillon took his pen out and slid the jeans and t-shirt across the floor using the pen. They made a heavy sort of scratching sound. Suel set the body down, then reached in his coat pocket and pulled out a latex glove. He slipped the glove on his hand before he carefully lifted the clothes. A nine-millimeter pistol lay on the floor beneath a pair of plaid boxer shorts.

"I'm thinking that's what your man was going for. Someone came in here, and he went for the pistol, or maybe your woman threatened him?" Suel said.

"What the hell would Gemma O'Carroll be doing here?"

"Maybe a safe house and Nolan was supposed to protect her. But if she's the shooter, she must have felt threatened in some way. Who knows? Maybe it was that redhead, and she'd finally had enough of your man."

"You think Gemma O'Carroll shot him?" Dillon said.

"Maybe he was supposed to tie up any loose ends, and if she's wounded—"

"But then why would she even come here?"

"Yeah. Not to mention, this happens when you've a pub about to be full of bloody eejit's sitting downstairs singing half-arsed Christmas carols? You can't make it up." Suel glanced down at Nolan's body and shook his head. "At least there's no Ace of Spades in his mouth, and look, the one on his shoulder is gone, too."

Dillon looked at Nolan's shoulder. The henna tattoo had been removed. "Oh, Jesus. We better call this in," Dillon said.

"Let me do it. We're going to need a lot of bodies. They'll want us to interview everyone downstairs," Suel said, just as the DJ started playing "Santa Baby," and it suddenly sounded like every woman in the place began to scream along.

* * *

Dillon had been sitting at one of the tables in the pub with Suel and a half-dozen other Gardaí. They'd been attempting to interview people for the past three hours. Things had gotten ugly the moment they locked the door and closed down the bar, then quickly gone downhill from there. Dillon had lost count of the people he'd attempted to interview only to determine they were too intoxicated to provide any intelligible information. He wrote down their names, not that it would do any good, they were intoxicated. No point in making a call tomorrow.

"So you're telling me you have no knowledge of anyone named Richie Nolan, is that correct?"

"Is he the lead singer in Poo?" his current interviewee asked.

"No, ma'am."

She was maybe fifty, with white-blonde hair piled on top of her head and eyeglasses in retro sky-blue frames that came to a rhinestone-jeweled point at the corners of the frame. Dillon pegged her at about seventy-five pounds overweight. She wore a sleeveless, low-cut, pink velvet dress and exuded a cloud of cheap perfume. Her death-defying cleavage began at the base of her triple chin.

"So, can I have a glass of wine now?"

"I'm sorry, ma'am, but the bar is closed for the evening. We've a lot of people we're attempting to talk to. There was a shooting upstairs."

"I know that, and I just got through telling the likes of you that I don't know the bastard. Never heard of him. Couldn't pick him out of a crowd of two. So what's it gonna hurt if I have another glass of wine?"

"I'm sorry, ma'am. I don't make the rules. I—"

"You lot just piss good folks like me off by making us follow your stupid rules. I suppose the loo is closed too, wouldn't want people to be able to take a pee, would ya's?"

"The bathrooms are open, ma'am."

"Oh, they are? Well then, if there's nothing else you need, I'll just be off to the loo."

"Thank you for your patience," Dillon said and smiled.

"Ahh, feck off, all of yas," she said, then pushed her chair back, groaned to her feet and waddled off toward the ladies' room.

Dillon nodded at the next person, and she quickly walked over and sat down.

"Hi. Crazy night, isn't it?" Dillon said.

She didn't respond and didn't look directly at him. She simply nodded, then shoved her hands beneath her thighs and focused on the tabletop.

"What's your name?"

"Caitlin Leary."

"You work here, Caitlin?" Dillon asked as he wrote down her name on a sheet of paper.

She nodded and said, "Yes."

She was dressed in a long-sleeve black shirt and black jeans. Her brown hair was pulled back and wrapped in a tight bun. She had small post earrings that sparkled, maybe diamonds but probably fakes, and another small sparkly stone piercing her left nostril.

"How long have you been employed here?"

"Off and on since I was sixteen, so about ten years."

"You're twenty-six?"

She nodded.

"You know what happened upstairs today?"

"No," she said and shook her head. "I don't know about anything that goes on up there. I wait tables, and that's all I do. Look," she said and leaned forward. "I'd like to help you, but I'm going to be late getting home to the babysitter, and when I'm late, she's gonna nick me for another ten or fifteen quid that I don't have. You lot shut down the bar, so no way in hell is this bunch gonna pay their tabs. I'm not getting any tips for waiting around or talking to the likes of you. And if they did see me talking to you's, giving you any information, the best thing that'd happen is I'd be out of a job. But more than likely, I'd probably end up like your American upstairs, so how 'bout you just finish up and let me go home."

"Nothing to add?"

"Not a thing."

"Just need your name and address in case of a follow-up," Dillon said.

"I already told you, my name's Caitlin Leary."

"And your address, Caitlin?"

"Forty-three Liscannor Road, Cabra."

"You own that?"

"You're kidding, right? God, no. Working here and for the county council? I'm lucky if I can make the rent in any given month."

"Okay. Thanks, Caitlin. Sorry to keep you," Dillon said, then watched as she stood and walked away. He talked to nine more people after Caitlin, and suddenly, he looked around, and they were finished. Other than three or four staff and the half-dozen Gardaí who'd been interviewing people, the place was empty.

Suel threw his pen onto the table in front of him, shook his head, and looked over at Dillon. "Nothing like chatting up pissed off people for three hours as a way to end one's very long day."

"You get anything?" Dillon said.

"Yeah, we're a bunch of plonkers, and one woman offered me some very personal service if I could find a way to get her driver's license reinstated."

"Better than I got. What'd you tell her?"

"Told her I'd check into it and get back to her," Suel said and laughed.

They waited around for another hour, then once Nolan's body was transported, and the crime scene team had finished up, Suel drove them back to the station. He pulled into the parking place and yawned.

"You heading inside?"

"Tell you the truth, unless you got something I'm just going to head home," Dillon said. "It's been a long, very unproductive day."

SIXTY-FOUR

Dillon pulled into the parking area in his front yard and turned off the car. He closed the small wrought iron gates behind the vehicle, then wound his way through the half-dozen deposits Lucifer had left between the car and the front door. He thanked his lucky stars, Deitora, his next-door neighbor, wasn't out front as he unlocked the door. Lucifer bounded down the stairs at the sound of the door being unlocked and ran outside before Dillon had a chance to say anything.

He stepped inside, picked the mail up off the floor, then headed into the kitchen. He tossed the mail on the counter, grabbed a dog biscuit, and waited a couple of minutes before he coaxed Lucifer back into the house.

He glanced quickly at his mail, tossed the entire stack into recycling, and headed upstairs to bed. He grabbed a hot shower, shaved, then fell into bed and was asleep thirty seconds later.

He woke just a little after six the following morning. The sky was cloudless, and at least for the moment, the day looked to be pleasant. He dressed, coaxed Lucifer off the pillow and out the front door with the aid of a dog biscuit, then inhaled a breakfast of three cups of coffee and two toasted English muffins. He placed his dishes in the sink, coaxed Lucifer back inside with another dog biscuit, and headed for the office.

He cleared his desk of debris, two tea mugs, a bowl with some sort of leftover cereal and a spoon. At eight-thirty, he left a note on Suel's desk, then headed out to his car and drove to Cabra.

He drove past Caitlin Leary's rental unit on Liscannor Road twenty minutes later, parked up the street, and walked back to her place. It was a two-story, grey stucco structure, in the middle of a long row of ten units, all attached to one another. There was a white front door with a picture window just to the left. The entire unit appeared to be about fifteen feet wide with what looked like a bedsheet hanging over the picture window as a curtain. There were two windows on the second floor. One with frosted glass, apparently the bathroom, had a light on.

Dillon grabbed the paper bag from the passenger seat, climbed out of his car, and walked to the front door. The doorbell had a strip of grey duct tape over it with the word "NO" written in indelible marker. Dillon knocked loudly on the door. A moment later, he could see the semblance of a figure through the thick leaded glass in the front door.

"What do you want?" a woman's voice called from inside.

"US Marshal Jack Dillon with a question for Caitlin Leary," Dillon said. He waited a long moment, then said, "Miss Leary? This will only take a second."

The door opened partway a moment later, and Caitlin peeked out. "I told you last night. I could get in a lot of trouble if someone saw me talking to you."

"Then don't you think you better let me in? Shouldn't take but a minute. Besides," Dillon said, and held out the paper bag, "I brought you something."

"What's that?"

"Blueberry muffins. You like blueberry muffins, don't you?"

"I think I might be allergic."

"To blueberry muffins?" he said, opening the bag then holding it at an angle so she could look in.

She glanced inside the bag, hesitated for a brief moment, then looked at Dillon and said, "Okay, I guess you can come in, but you have to make this quick."

She quickly closed the door behind him, then walked through a small sitting room with a couch and a bookshelf that had a flatscreen sitting on it. She picked up a remote, turned off the flatscreen, and walked into a tiny kitchen. Dillon followed.

"Tea?" she said, then pressed the button on the electronic kettle without waiting for an answer. She took a second mug from the drying rack in the sink and tossed a teabag into it. Once the kettle came to a boil, she filled both mugs, then took the blueberry muffins, placed them on a plate in the microwave and turned it on.

"Milk or sugar in your tea?"

"No, black is perfect," Dillon said.

"So, what do you want?"

"I had the distinct feeling last night that there was something else you might know, but you didn't want to be seen talking to me."

"That group at This Little Piggy, they know people. I talk to you, I'm through, and I'm not talking about just losing me job. They're good people, but they don't like snitches."

"I get that, believe me. I deal with a lot of people who want to do the right thing, but first, they have to consider their own safety."

She nodded and passed him his tea mug. The microwave suddenly chirped, and she pulled out the plate with the muffins and set it on a small counter against the opposite wall. She pulled out the only stool from beneath the counter and sat. Dillon took a sip from his tea and waited for her to pass one of the blueberry muffins his way. It never happened.

After a couple of sips, he said, "So what can you tell me?"

She swallowed a mouthful of muffin and said, "You're not going to tell anyone what I say? Not going to tell them we talked, are you?"

"No, I'm just trying to find out what happened. I've got my suspicions, but that's all they are at this point, suspicions."

"There are girls that *work* upstairs," she said, putting an emphasis on the word 'work' and raising her eyebrows.

"I'm aware of that," Dillon said.

"I'm not sure how many. Maybe six or seven."

"Yeah, I spoke with one of them, a redhead. She was with the guy we questioned, the same American who was killed last night, Richie Nolan."

"Yeah, we all know about that. You came in the middle of the night and took him away. Not that anyone was sorry to see him leave. You's should have kept him longer. He was in the pub, drunk just about every night. Prick drank all day for free and couldn't be bothered to leave a tip. Tell you the truth, far as I'm concerned, he got what he deserved. A real bastard. Very impressed with himself. Liked to grab," she said and raised her eyebrows again.

"And the redhead?"

"That's just it. She didn't work there."

"Didn't work there? I saw her in bed with him. I saw her in bed with another guy, too. She looked like she was pretty used to being there and—"

"She was brought in for the American. Not 'cause she was special, but because she was s'posed to keep an eye on him."

"Keep an eye on him?"

"Yeah. I guess he got like a week-long stay or something at This Little Piggy. All he did was drink, party and ride your woman. They called her the Queen, but for the life of me, I don't know why. From what I hear, she wasn't all that nice."

"You know what her name was?"

She shook her head, stuffed the last of the blueberry muffin into her mouth, then peeled off the paper from the second muffin. "Just called her the Queen, that's all I know."

Dillon thought of her tattoo, that red-letter "Q" with the red heart just below it. Queen of Hearts.

"And she was there to be with the American?"

"Yeah. She left with another woman yesterday afternoon. I saw her wheeling her suitcase out."

"When was this?"

"Yesterday. Maybe four, four-thirty. We were getting ready for the party you lot shut down. It's always one of the busiest nights of the year, or at least it was in the past," she said, then pulled a large piece from the second muffin and placed it in her mouth.

Dillon was thinking none of this seemed to make any sense. He reached into his pocket, pulled out the copy of Gemma O'Carroll's passport photo, and set it on the small counter next to what remained of the second blueberry muffin. "You ever see this woman in This Little Piggy?"

Caitlin glanced at the image, swallowed, and said, "Yeah, that's the woman the Queen left with yesterday. Far as I know, they didn't talk to anyone. They just came down from upstairs and hurried out the door."

"Hurried? Like they were running?"

"No. The redhead, the Queen, was hurrying, almost running, but this woman here." She struck the image with her index finger and left a blueberry stain on Gemma O'Carroll's face. "She was taking her time. Looked kind of like she was in pain, or maybe not feeling all that good. I only saw the two of them for a couple of seconds before they were out the door."

"Anyone else see them leave?"

"Not that I know of. I was the only one out there setting tables for the party. We were closed yesterday until after five, getting ready for the Christmas party. It sells out every year, reservations only."

"You see the American guy at all yesterday?"

"No, thank God. I don't need that bollocks grabbing my bum again. Anyway, that's all I know, so you better leave now before someone cops on that we talked."

"And you don't know the Queen's name?"

"I already told you. I don't know her name and don't want to. If I ever saw her again, it'd be too soon."

Dillon headed back up the street to his car, watching for anyone looking out their window as he passed. He didn't see anyone, not that it mattered at this point. He climbed in his car, debated about calling Suel, and decided it might be better if he drove a few blocks over. He headed down the block, drove past two younger looking guys sipping beer from a can while sitting on a front wall.

They seemed to study him for a second or two as he drove past. He watched them in the rearview mirror once he passed, but they had already returned to whatever important conversation they'd been involved in, so he figured they didn't pay him any heed. He drove a good mile down the road before he pulled over.

SIXTY-FIVE

Dillon checked the rearview mirror once again, a force of habit, making sure he wasn't being followed, then phoned Suel.

"Where the hell are you?" was the way Suel answered.

"Cabra, working. I have it on good authority that Gemma O'Carroll was at This Little Piggy yesterday afternoon around four or four-thirty. She left with that redhead who was in bed with Nolan the morning we grabbed him. Apparently, at least according to my source, the redhead wasn't a regular working This Little Piggy. She was brought in special, to keep an eye on Nolan. He basically partied all day, every day, grabbed the waitresses, and went to bed with the redhead every night. They called her the Queen, I'm guessing because of that tattoo she has. She and Gemma were seen leaving the pub together, and the person I talked to said she thought Gemma looked hurt or maybe sick."

"She knew who Gemma O'Carroll was?"

"No, but she ID'd her from the passport image I had. Said she only saw her once, and that was yesterday afternoon, leaving the pub with the redhead."

"Now what?"

"See if we can find the redhead. Like I said, she's got that tattoo, and there can't be too many like that. If she's in the database, hopefully, it'll come up."

"I'll start checking that now. What are you doing?"

"I'm heading back, so I'll see you in about twenty minutes."

It was a little after ten when Dillon made it back to the office. Amazingly, there weren't any dirty mugs or candy bar wrappers piled up on his desk. Suel was on the phone, so Dillon went online. He had an email from Pat Mathews back in New York that had come in just after midnight, seven in the evening New York time. Dillon clicked on the email and started reading. He caught Suel out of the corner of his eye hanging up the phone, and yelled across the office to him.

"Suel, we might have something here. Take a look," he yelled. He was loud enough that a number of heads turned and stared as Suel hurried over. He didn't look happy.

"Tell me someone got your woman," Suel said.

"No, but some interesting information. Gemma O'Carroll is American, and she's traveling on an American passport. But her parents were Irish, immigrated to the States in the early eighties."

"And?"

"So maybe she's got family here, aunts, uncles, cousins."

"Any idea where the bloody hell they were from?"

Dillon sat back and smiled. "Dublin."

"There could be a couple hundred of them just in Dublin County."

"See if any of them are redheaded females in their mid-twenties, with a Queen of Hearts tattoo."

Suel seemed to think for a long moment, then slowly nodded.

"You were looking all pissed off a moment ago. Problem?" Dillon asked.

"Only that the search for the redhead was coming up empty, but a possible last name changes everything. I'm back on it," Suel said and hurried over to his desk. He called Dillon over fifteen minutes later.

"We got something," Suel yelled, and again heads turned throughout the office.

This time Dillon hurried over to Suel's desk.

Before he could ask a question, Suel said, "Look familiar?"

There, staring back at Dillon on Suel's computer, was the face of the redhead he'd talked to at This Little Piggy. The same woman who'd been in bed with Richie Nolan. The same woman with the Queen of Hearts tattoo.

Suel smiled up at Dillon and said, "Meet Miss Morna O'Carroll, aged twenty-six, born and raised in Dublin."

"That's her. That's the woman who was with Richie Nolan."

"Too bloody right." Suel pointed with a pencil at the Dublin address listed next to the booking image of Morna O'Carroll. "Interested in taking a little ride?"

SIXTY-SIX

Morna O'Carroll's home was in Meath Square in the Liberties section of Dublin. It was a corner, one-story, red brick structure with a slate roof and a grey paneled front door. A single window stood next to the front door, and if Dillon had to guess, he would have put the age of the place at maybe a hundred and fifty years. It was one of a long string of identical, attached units, that stretched down the street for as far as they could see. Still, although small and old, it looked to be in reasonably good shape.

A black Chrysler 300 with a Hertz rental sticker in the corner of the windshield was backed up in front of a brick wall along the side of the unit. Suel pulled their car over in front of the Chrysler, effectively blocking it in. Two squad cars were following Suel and Dillon. One drove past, and the other pulled in behind them.

"How do you want to play this?" Dillon asked, and pulled the side strap on his protective vest a notch tighter.

"I think we'll pretend we're perfect gentlemen and knock politely, just before we kick the fecking door down. We go in right behind the assault team. You ready?"

Dillon nodded and opened the car door. Because Suel had parked so close to the Chrysler, Dillon's door only opened partway, and with the protective vest on, he had to squirm and wiggle his way out of the car.

"Come on, Dildo, would you ever hurry up," Suel laughed, then nodded at the three officers behind them and the three on the far side of the front door.

The officers on the far side of the door carried the battering ram and waited a few feet away from the door. Suel, Dillon and the other three officers were crouched down alongside the cars twenty feet from the door, and away from any prying eyes at the front window.

Suel gave a wave at the three on the far side of the door, and they quickly approached with the battering ram. But just as they were ready to knock the door in, the officer with the battering ram got a funny look on his face and waved Suel over.

Suel and Dillon hurried over to the door. Suel swearing under his breath, "We're bloody exposed out here, you bleeding muppet."

The officer pointed at the large bootprint on the door next to the brass doorknob. The wood frame around the door was shattered, and one of the panels on the door was clearly cracked.

"What the hell," Suel said, then pushed the door partially open with his index finger. He looked at the officer holding the battering ram, then pushed the door wide open. The door squeaked on its hinge as it swung open, then bounced off the inside wall with a loud thud.

Dillon waved the three officers waiting next to the cars forward, and they all went in with automatic weapons at the ready. "Body," someone shouted as Dillon and Suel followed them inside with pistols drawn. The officers quickly moved through the small sitting room into a smaller kitchen, then on through a door into a small back room.

"Body," another voice called from the back of the house.

Someone yelled, "All clear," a moment later, and it was suddenly over in less than ten seconds.

Suel and Dillon stood looking at the body on the sitting room floor. A redheaded woman in a light-blue terrycloth robe was curled almost in the fetal position, lying on her side in front of a cheap-looking black leather couch. The robe was pulled back over her hip, and her tattoo, the red letter "Q" and the heart were clearly visible. Blood was splattered across the wall and the back of the couch. A flatscreen TV was facedown on the pine floor, lying partially in the dark blood that had puddled around her head.

"Morna O'Carroll," Dillon said, halfway to himself.

"DI Suel," a voice called from the small room off the kitchen, and Dillon and Suel hurried back through the kitchen.

The back room was actually a small bedroom. A bare lightbulb hung in the middle of the ceiling, and a cheap white laminate dresser leaned slightly to the right against the far wall. The top of the dresser was covered with boxes of gauze, and a half dozen tubes of wound care ointment. On the bedside table, an empty glass rested on its side on top of a half-dozen Ace of Spades cards. There was lipstick along the side of the glass and a small puddle of water on the floor.

A mound of round, little white pills were piled in a small bowl. Dillon picked up one of the pills and looked at it. The letters "OC" were on one side and the number "80" was on the other. "OxyContin, an eighty-milligram dose. Must be close to a hundred tablets here," he said.

"She best watch it, those things can be habit forming," Suel said, and half-chuckled.

Two, hundred-euro bills lay on the floor just under the bed. The three officers stood on the far side of the full-size bed, staring at what was left of a woman's body.

She was naked, lying crossways across the bed with the toes of her left foot just touching the worn wood floor. She still held a small pistol in her right hand. The pistol was black with what Dillon initially thought was a long barrel until he realized there was a silencer attached. Her midsection was wrapped in blood-soaked gauze, and Dillon gave up trying to count the number of bullet wounds in her upper torso and head. Her breasts were large, and what was left of her face still appeared smooth and soft.

She was barely recognizable, but there was no doubt who it was— Gemma O'Carroll, or at least what was left of her.

"Like McCabe said about Bazanov. I'm tempted to just look up the street, and if no one's waving their arms in surrender, we'll just declare the case closed," Dillon said.

"She has to have been shot at least a couple of dozen times," one of the officers said, then sort of grimaced and shook his head. "Pity, you can tell she was a hot number up until this."

"Someone obviously didn't want her going any-where," another said.

"This closes it up nice and tight for your man Eamon Boyle," Suel said.

"First, he eliminated his competition, and now it looks like he may have eliminated the eliminator," Dillon said. "I would guess her reactions were slowed down by the meds. Pity in a way, I suspect she would have had a lot of information to impart."

"It would have been interesting to hear what both of them had to say," Dillon said.

Suel pulled the cellphone out of his pocket and pushed a speed dial number. A moment later, he gave his name and badge number, then reported two bodies.

"They're sending the team out. Best we all step out of here," Suel said.

Dillon looked at the half-dozen Ace of Spades cards sitting on the bedside table. They appeared to be exact

matches to the ones they'd recovered from Joey Touhy
and the other bodies.

SIXTY-SEVEN

Dillon and Suel stood in the small kitchen, watching as the medical examiner finished up, and the crime scene team entered. "We've got to stop meeting like this," one of the crime scene guys said, then laughed and headed into the small bedroom where Gemma O'Carroll's body waited.

"What do you think the chances are they find something?" Suel half-whispered.

Dillon shook his head. "Another in and out in a few seconds. I'm guessing whoever did this just gave Miss O'Carroll a taste of her own medicine. Those two hundred-euro notes beneath the bed, are probably all that remains of whatever she was paid for her service. Whoever did this came in, shot the two of them, then recovered the cash she'd been paid and left."

"Well, we've got her weapon. Hopefully, we'll be able to tie it to all the murders and Joey Touhy."

"God, Joey Touhy," Dillon said and shook his head. "It seems like years ago, and it was just last week. We do a ballistics test, and it compares with the weapon she had, I can at least send Jackie Greco a message that her sister's killer has been caught."

Suel forced a smile. "I can see why all those Russians were caught off guard. Very pretty looking woman at one time just wants to talk for a minute, maybe ask directions, or looks like she needs help. Maybe she smiles or winks, puts her chest out. They lower the window and bang."

Dillon's phone rang at that moment. He pulled it out of his pocket and looked at the screen for a long moment. The phone ringtone continued to play. A breathless woman's voice moaned, "Oh, yes, yes, baby. Oh, yes, yes, baby."

"Who in the hell is that? Answer that damn thing," Suel said.

Dillon stared at the phone number on his screen with Brianna's name displayed above it. "Nah, just a wrong number," he said and disconnected.

EPILOGUE

Eamon Boyle raised his crystal glass toward Mousey and took a sip of whiskey. "To success," Boyle said. Mousey grinned, thought of the girl waiting for him upstairs, and drained his glass. Boyle looked at the Ace of Spades card Mousey had placed on his desk and marveled at how easy it had all been. He picked the card up by a corner and held it in the candle flame. He watched it ignite until the flames were close to his finger, then dropped it into the metal wastebasket.

Both the Americans and the Russians were out of the picture, at least for the time being, and the market was screaming for product. Now, he thought, the real fun begins.

THE END

Thanks for taking the time to read **Spade Work**, the sixth book in the Jack Dillon Dublin Tales series.If you enjoyed the read please consider leaving a review. I'm indie published and your review really, really helps, even if it's just a sentence or two.

Don't miss the following sample of, **Madeline Missing** the seventh book in the Jack Dillon Dublin Tales series on the next page. Thank You!

ONE

He watched her as he stood in the dark, looking out the sitting room window. She climbed out of the back seat and staggered for a couple of steps attempting to regain her balance. The three women in the car laughed, screamed good night, then drove off and disappeared around the corner. He took a final drag off his cigarette and stubbed it out on the white windowsill.

Aideen Suel waved goodbye as the car disappeared. She took a deep breath and attempted to make her way toward the front door, staggering along the sidewalk. She pulled out her keys, took a long moment to focus on the proper one, then struggled to insert it and unlock the door. It had been a fun night out with the girls, trading stories with way too much to drink. She unlocked the door, stepped inside, dropped her purse on the floor, and kicked off her heels, nearly falling in the process. She giggled, decided one more glass of wine couldn't hurt, and just might help her get to sleep. She staggered into the kitchen and made her way to the cupboard where she kept the wine glasses.

The bottle was on the granite counter next to the tea kettle. She emptied it, filling her glass almost to the rim, took a large sip, and headed for the staircase. As she stumbled out of the kitchen, she put the glass to her lips.

"Aideen, my love, imagine my surprise, you're jarred."

Her scream was cut off by the mouthful of red wine she spit onto the carpet leading upstairs. "What are you doing here? How in the feck did you get—. Get out of me house. You're not supposed to be here."

"Well, aren't you just the cute hoor. In case you hadn't noticed, I am here. Come on, I heard you've been out on the prowl again after your man left for greener pastures. It may have been a couple of years, but I'm guessing an old slapper like you still loves a good ride after a night out. I think—"

"Did you not hear what I said? Get the hell out of this house."

"Oh, I heard you all right."

"I'm gonna call the Garda, you limp—"

His fist caught her on the chin, spun her around, and slammed her against the wall.

Her wine glass shattered, spraying red wine down the wall, across the carpet, and over her blouse. He grabbed a fistful of her blonde hair, yanked hard, and spun her around. As she turned, she brought the broken stem of the wine glass up and slashed him across his nose and cheek.

"Go on. Get your worthless arse out of me house, you no good bastard. Do you—"

The uppercut to her chin caused her eyes to disappear into the top of her skull. He grabbed hold of her arms as she began to fall, pulled her back up, and gave her a solid head butt between the eyes. He let go, hit her with a right cross, and she bounced across the stairway landing. He took hold of her ankles and pulled her from the landing. Her head bounced off the step and then again as it hit the floor. He took hold of her dress, ripped it open, and unbuckled his belt.

TWO

addy Suel held up the Styrofoam cup of tea and said, "You sure you don't want this?"

Dillon shook his head. "No, you go ahead and help yourself. It wasn't that good when it was hot. I don't think the past forty minutes has done anything to improve it."

They'd been in the same spot for over four hours. Parked on Faussagh Avenue in Cabra, just across the street and down a few doors from the Cabra Club, waiting for Riley Dempsey to emerge so they could make an arrest. The club, a two-story brick structure painted black, officially closed at 1:30 am. That had been well over an hour ago, but there were still signs of activity inside.

"I suppose we could make a call, have the local Garda show up, tell the plonkers to shut it down, and grab this wanker on his way home," Suel said. He sipped the tea, grimaced, opened the passenger door, and dumped the tea onto the curb. "Ugh, for once in your life, you were right, more like drinking the piss."

"You'd know more about that than me," Dillon said.

"Wait now, what have we got here?" Suel said as the door to the club opened, and two men staggered out. They took a couple of steps, turned to face one another and chatted for a brief moment before heading off in opposite directions.

"If it's Dempsey, he lost his leather jacket, shaved his head, and put on an eye patch," Dillon said as the two climbed into cars at opposite ends of the block and drove off.

"Oughta phone in the license numbers and get the bastards on a drink-drive. Now what the hell?" Suel said as his cellphone rang. He pulled the phone from his pocket, glanced at the screen, then answered.

"Megan? Everything okay? What's wrong? What? How in the bloody hell? What hospital? No, no, on my way. Well, they'll by god not be stopping the likes of me. Yeah. Yes, soon as I know something. No darling, you'll just be in the way. Get some rest. I know. I know. But try. No, I'm on my way. Yeah. Appreciate the call."

"What's up?" Dillon said.

"My sister, Megan. Some fecker broke into Aideen's house, attacked her, she's in hospital. I'm going to call a squad, have them take me there. You okay to nail Dempsey on your own?"

Dillon turned the key in the ignition and started the engine. "Who the hell knows when a squad can get here. What hospital?"

"You don't—"

As Dillon pulled away from the curb, he turned on the flashing lights. "What hospital?"

"She's in James's."

He took a right and picked up speed heading for Old Cabra Road. Fortunately, at this time of night, there was virtually no traffic. He raced through Stoneybatter and Smithfield, crossed the Liffey, and tore up the hill into the Liberties then sped down James Street to Saint James Hospital.

"You know which building she's in?"

"Megan said she was in surgery, take a left just after the train tracks up here."

The traffic light turned yellow when they were two blocks away, turned red for a brief moment, and back to green as Dillon approached and sailed through, swerving around the corner past a stone building at least a hundred and fifty years old.

"You're going to get us both fecking killed, you crazy bastard," Suel shouted as he grabbed onto the dash with both fists. They sailed around another building, this one only a hundred and twenty years old. "That building on the left, with your man smoking in front of it. That's the ER let me off there."

Dillon screeched to a stop in front of the ER entrance and turned off the car.

"Thanks, Dillon, but you don't have to come in. This could be a long wait."

"I'm coming in just to keep you in line. Otherwise, you're bound to cause problems, so don't even think of trying to stop me," Dillon said.

"I take back some of the things the rest of the section has been saying about you," Suel half-joked, and hurried out of the car.

THREE

It was after five in the morning when they got the word Suel's younger sister, Aideen had been wheeled out of surgical recovery and brought into a room. She'd be one of four women in the room, each separated by a privacy curtain around the bed. Suel asked for her room number and explained he was family. When that didn't seem to work, both he and Dillon flashed their badges.

She was sedated now. Suel was sitting on an orange plastic chair next to her bed. His massive right hand rested on her shoulder as he fingered rosary beads with his left.

Dillon had taken up space out on the bench in the hallway and had just finished leaving a message on DCI McCabe's phone, giving a brief explanation of the situation when Suel stepped out of the room.

"Dillon, she's going to be out for a bit, but I want to be here when she wakes. You should go home and get some sleep."

"You sure? It's no problem for me to stay and—"

"No, now not another word. You've done more than enough. She's liable to be out for hours, and there's no point in the two of us becoming worthless. I'll phone McCabe after nine this morning," Suel said and followed up with a yawn.

"I already left McCabe a message so he'll have that initial information whenever he gets in. Tell me her address. I'll go over there and check some things out, secure the place until we can get a team over to process the site."

"I don't know if they'll send a team over, she wasn't murdered, thank God, and we—"

"You let me worry about getting a team over there. Right now, your top priority, in fact, your only priority, is to be here when she wakes up. Call me if you need anything, anything at all. I'll keep you posted if I learn something."

Suel nodded, wrote down her address in a small notebook he always carried then tore the page out and handed it to Dillon. "Thanks, much appreciated."

They shook hands, Dillon leaned in and gave Suel a hug, and headed down the hall and out to his car. On his drive home, he thought about the attack. Was it a relationship gone bad? A random burglar or rapist? Or was some fool trying to send a message to Paddy Suel? One thing he knew for sure, none of the options would end up positive for whoever was responsible.

He pulled in front of his house, rode up over the curb and parked on the sidewalk. All was quiet as he unlocked the door and stepped inside. Lucifer, his dog, was no-where to be seen, which meant he was probably upstairs asleep on Dillon's bed.

The wastebasket tipped over with contents scattered across the kitchen floor, suggested Lucifer had been busy. Dillon quietly climbed the stairs to the second floor. He was in the bathroom for a few minutes then tiptoed into the bedroom. Lucifer was asleep on the bed, snuggled onto one of the pillows. Remnants of two bones from the ribs Dillon had eaten for dinner rested on the pillow next to him.

He set his alarm clock for three hours, enough time for a decent catnap. He kicked off his shoes, dropped his coat over the chair, and crawled into bed. After a moment, he reached down by his lower back and pulled out another rib bone. Apparently, Lucifer had stored that one for future reference.

It seemed like only a minute or two later when the alarm woke him. He slowly opened his eyes and looked over to where Lucifer had been ensconced on the pillow, only now he was nowhere to be seen. Never a good sign. He went downstairs and found Lucifer waiting patiently at the front door. He opened the door, and Lucifer hur-ried outside. Dillon left the door open. He went into the kitchen, filled the food and water dish, and set the coffee maker to start brewing.

Lucifer entered the kitchen, walked around the counter, sat at Dillon's feet, and looked up expectantly.

"Oh, and I suppose you're looking for a biscuit. There's healthy food and fresh water in the bowls."

Lucifer blinked a couple of times and stared up with a mournful look.

"Good Lord, who the hell taught you how to do that?" He pulled the lid off the biscuit jar, reached in, and tossed a biscuit to Lucifer.

The dog caught it in midair and hurried back around the kitchen counter and into the front hallway where he wouldn't have to share. Dillon could hear the sound of the biscuit crunching back in the kitchen.

He walked out of the kitchen with a mug of coffee, stepped over Lucifer finishing the last of the biscuit, and closed the front door. He went upstairs, undressed, and headed into the shower.

FOUR

There was a text message on his cellphone from DCI McCabe when he climbed out of the shower.

'See me when you get in.'

It was after eleven by the time he made it into the office. He went through the security gate, parked in the lot, and took the elevator up to Special Branch. His desk had been the collection point for dirty plates, mugs, and trash in general before his arrival in Dublin. Over the past couple of years, nothing had really changed. Along with two dirty tea mugs, a plate with crumbs and the wrapper from a Yorkie candy bar there was a note on his desk from McCabe,

'See me!'

Dillon did his daily routine of dumping the mugs and the plate into the break room sink before he headed for McCabe's office. The door was open, and he gave a perfunctory knock on the door frame then took a couple of steps into the office.

"You wanted to see me, sir?"

McCabe's head was down, focused on the open file on his desk. His bald head reflected the fluorescent light in the ceiling, giving the appearance of a halo. He looked up at Dillon, closed the file, and said, "Come in, come in. I wanted to get an update on DI Suel. I understand you were with him this morning at the hospital. What's the status of his sister?"

"Couple hours in surgery. She was still sedated when I left around six this morning. Status? Based on what I saw pretty beat up— black eyes, broken nose, swollen jaw. We didn't get a report from anyone in the surgical team, but Suel may have received that by now. She was on an IV when I left, not sure what it was. I'm guessing a sedative. I don't know that she's been raped, but if she has, it wouldn't surprise me."

"And where was Dempsey during all this?"

"We watched him enter the Cabra Club a little after eleven. We waited until almost three for him to leave. It appeared they were still serving after closing. The occasional person stumbled out, none of whom were Dempsey. Suel got the call from his sister right around three, and we raced over to James's. If I might suggest, sir?"

McCabe nodded.

"If you could send a team over to Aideen Suel's home. That's apparently where the assault took place. There's at least the possibility someone is sending a message to DI Suel. No idea at this point who that would be. It may be nothing related to him, but it was a brutal attack, and it would be nice to have the scene processed before someone with the best of intentions stops in to help clean or cook or do a load of laundry."

McCabe flashed a smile. "Already done, forensics arrived around nine this morning. I want you to head over there as well. You need an address?"

"I've got one."

McCabe nodded, and half said to himself, "Of course you do."

"Anything else, sir?"

"Only that you remind DI Suel that he's not to be involved in any way, shape, or form in this investigation. We find out who's responsible, and we damn well will, I don't want any involvement from Suel that might suggest our work was tainted. Clear?"

"Yes, sir, couldn't agree more."

McCabe flashed another quick smile, suggesting he didn't quite believe Dillon. "Very well, dismissed, off with you now, and I'll want a report at days end."

Dillon left, headed back into the break room, where he grabbed four chocolate covered tea biscuits before he made his way out the door.

TO BE CONTINUED....

Thank you for taking the time to check out the sample of <u>Madeline Missing</u>, the seventh book in the Jack Dillon Dublin Tales series. Better grab a copy to see how Dillon, Suel, and Aideen are going to come out of this mess. Thanks and enjoy the read.

Don't miss the list of Mike Faricy books on the next page!

BOOKS BY MIKE FARICY
CRIME FICTION FIRSTS

A boxset of the first four books in four crime fiction series:

Russian Roulette; Dev Haskell series
Welcome; Jack Dillon Dublin Tales series
Corridor Man; Corridor Man series
Reduced Ransom! Hot Shot series

The following titles comprise the Dev Haskell series:

Russian Roulette: Case 1
Mr. Swirlee: Case 2
Bite Me: Case 3
Bombshell: Case 4
Tutti Frutti: Case 5
Last Shot: Case 6
Ting-A-Ling: Case 7
Crickett: Case 8
Bulldog: Case 9
Double Trouble: Case 10
Yellow Ribbon: Case 11
Dog Gone: Case 12
Scam Man: Case 13
Foiled: Case 14
What Happens in Vegas… Case 15
Art Hound: Case 16

The Office: Case 17
Star Struck: Case 18
International Incident: Case 19
Guest From Hell: Case 20
Art Attack: Case 21
Mystery Man: Case 22
Bow-Wow Rescue: Case 23
Cold Case: Case 24
Cash Up Front: Case 25
Dream House: Case 26
Alley Katz: Case 27
The Big Gamble: Case 28
Bad to the Bone: Case 29
Silencio!: Case 30
Surprise, Surprise: Case 31
Hit & Run: Case 32
Suspect Santa: Case 33
P.I. Apprentice: Case 34
Rebel Without a Clue: Case 35
Puppy Love: Case 36

The following titles are Dev Haskell novellas:
Dollhouse
The Dance
Pixie
Fore!
Twinkle Toes
(*a Dev Haskell short story*)

The following are Dev Haskell Boxsets:
Dev Haskell Boxset 1-3
Dev Haskell Boxset 4-6
Dev Haskell Boxset 7-9
Dev Haskell Boxset 10-12
Dev Haskell Boxset 13-15
Dev Haskell Boxset 16-18
Dev Haskell Boxset 19-21
Dev Haskell Boxset 22-24
Dev Haskell Boxset 25-27
Dev Haskell Boxset 28-30
Dev Haskell Boxset 1-7
Dev Haskell Boxset 8-14
Dev Haskell Boxset 15-19
Dev Haskell Boxset 20-24
Dev Haskell Boxset 25-29

The following titles comprise the Jack Dillon Dublin Tales series:
Welcome
Jack Dillon Dublin Tale 1
Sweet Dreams
Jack Dillon Dublin Tale 2
Mirror Mirror
Jack Dillon Dublin Tale 3
Silver Bullet
Jack Dillon Dublin Tale 4

Fair City Blues
Jack Dillon Dublin Tale 5
Spade Work
Jack Dillon Dublin Tale 6
Madeline Missing
Jack Dillon Dublin Tale 7
Mistaken Identity
Jack Dillon Dublin Tale 8
Picture Perfect
Jack Dillon Dublin Tale 9
Dublin Moon
Jack Dillon Dublin Tale 10
Mystery Woman
Jack Dillon Dublin Tale 11
Second Chance
Jack Dillon Dublin Tale 12
Payback Brother
Jack Dillon Dublin Tale 13
The Heist
Jack Dillon Dublin Tale 14
Jewels To Kill For
Jack Dillon Dublin Tale 15
Retirement Scheme
Jack Dillon Dublin Tale 16
The Collector
Jack Dillon Dublin Tale 17

Jack Dillon Dublin Tales Boxsets:
Jack Dillon Dublin Tales 1-3

Jack Dillon Dublin Tales 4-6
Jack Dillon Dublin Tales 1-5
Jack Dillon Dublin Tales 1-7
Jack Dillon Dublin Tales 6-10

The following titles comprise the Hotshot series;
Reduced Ransom! Second Edition
Finders Keepers! Second Edition
Bankers Hours Second Edition
Chow Down Second Edition
Moonlight Dance Academy Second Edition
Irish Dukes (Fight Card Series)
written under the pseudonym Jack Tunney

The following titles comprise the Corridor Man series:
Corridor Man
Corridor Man 2: Opportunity knocks
Corridor Man 3: The Dungeon
Corridor Man 4: Dead End
Corridor Man 5: Finger
Corridor Man 6: Exit Strategy
Corridor Man 7: Trunk Music
Corridor Man 8: Birthday Boy
Corridor Man 9: Boss Man
Corridor Man 10: Bye Bye Bobby

Corridor Man novellas:
Corridor Man: Valentine

Corridor Man: Auditor
Corridor Man: Howling
Corridor Man: Spa Day

The following are Corridor Man Boxsets:
Corridor Man Boxset 1-3
Corridor Man Boxset 1-5
Corridor Man Boxset 6-9

THANK YOU!

Contact the author:
- Email: mikefaricyauthor@gmail.com
- Twitter: @Mikefaricybooks
- Facebook: Mike Faricy Author
- Website: http://www.mikefaricybooks.com

Published by

MJF Publishing

www.ingramcontent.com/pod-product-compliance
Lightning Source LLC
Chambersburg PA
CBHW070339010826
48976CB00017B/308